# A Season for Smugglers

## GOLDEN ANGEL

Copyright © 2022 by Golden Angel

All rights reserved.

No part of this book may be reproduced in any form or by any electronic or mechanical means, including information storage and retrieval systems, without written permission from the author, except for the use of brief quotations in a book review.

Cover art by Eris Adderly
Edited by Personal Touch Editing and Jennifer Bene

**Thank you so much for picking up my book!**

Would you like to receive a free story from me as well? Join the Angel Legion and sign up for my newsletter! You'll immediately receive a free story from the Stronghold series in a welcome message, and as part of the Angel Legion you'll also receive one newsletter a month with teasers, sneak peeks, and news about upcoming releases, as well as what I'm reading now!

# Acknowledgments

I am so lucky to have wonderful beta readers, and I know it. Katherine, Candida, Marie, Annie, Karen, and Marta: thank you all so much for your continued support and help with these books! They are always made better for your contributions.

And, as always, a shoutout to my ever patient and supportive husband, who makes it possible for me to keep on writing.

Take care and stay sassy,

Angel

# Chapter One

## Nathan

The Season was nearly over, thank God. Captain Nathan Jones felt nothing but relief at the thought as he rode through the quiet streets of Mayfair.

Already, Mayfair was much quieter, the streets clearer, and he could go for a gallop through Hyde Park without having to arrive before dawn, which was what he was doing this morning. Not long after dawn, the sun barely over the horizon, the park was deserted.

Not that Nathan would return home once the Season proper had ended. He was serving as his brother's proxy in London. Now the Earl of Talbot, Sebastian was overwhelmed at home, trying to undo the harm their father had done to the estates.

Sebastian had sent Nathan to London to handle everything he could in the capital, which was fortuitous since Oliver Stuart, the Marquess of Camden and Spymaster to the Crown, had also requested Nathan's presence in London. Nathan had worked as an unofficial agent to the crown for quite a few years now, including when he'd been in the army. He was happy to serve his country. A hunt for a traitor who had attempted to assassinate the Duke of York had certainly spiced up the Season.

Though he wouldn't be returning to Brentwood Manor and the

family estates, the end of the Season would be a huge relief since it meant his social duties would be finished for now. Until the next Season, most of the *ton* were returning to the countryside, where they would host house parties, tend to their home duties, and otherwise occupy themselves.

Truth be told, Nathan preferred country life, so if he had to be in the city, he preferred it when everyone else... wasn't.

Nathan wasn't often an early riser, even when in the country, but this past week he had been plagued by anxiety. Every morning, he'd risen early and gone riding, trying to shake the elusive feeling *something* was going to happen. That sense of premonition had served him well as a captain in the army, but now it was far more ominous because he was in the middle of London, not a battleground.

The Season had ended without catching the traitor. He believed they had come close and were getting closer, but somehow, the traitor had eluded them.

None of his friends wanted to believe Miss Lillian Davies had anything to do with it. They did not believe it. However, Nathan knew from personal experience, women could be treacherous, pretending to be one thing when actually they were waiting for an opportunity to stab you in the back.

She was an unlikely suspect at first glance—a debutante, a good friend to the Marquess of Camden's family, a neighbor, in fact. Her father had once saved the Duke of Frederick's life.

Yet would that not be the perfect cover?

She was smart. Too smart for her own good. Nathan had heard the mutterings of gossip that swirled around her. Despite her quiet beauty, she did not have a quiet tongue, which she'd sharpened on several members of the *ton*. She certainly had made no new friends during the Season, but then, she did not need them. Before she had arrived in London, she had already collected an array of correspondents from across Europe, including powerful and influential figures, especially in the French government.

They had been unable to prove that the French were backing the traitor, but the French were who Nathan would put his money on. The other most likely option was the Russians, and while some evidence had recently come to the surface to suggest they were the true culprits, Nathan thought it best not to trust either until they knew for sure.

Miss Lillian Davies had contacts in Russia as well.

Unfortunately, neither the Marquess of Camden nor his son, Elijah, considered her a suspect. They still saw her as the little girl who had grown up next to them and eventually became a good friend of the Marquess' niece. To Nathan, that only meant she would be the perfect person to turn.

Elijah had already told him to drop the subject, and he had but still kept an eye out. He was sure the tingle on the back of his neck and his inability to sleep had to do with her. Not because of her wide, dark eyes, lithe figure, or beautiful face, though she had all of those attributes as well. If he was completely honest, the fact he remained attracted to her, despite his suspicions, stirred his resentment.

"Bloody women," he muttered under his breath, reining in Merlin abruptly. The stallion obediently came to a halt. Riding was not giving him the peace of mind he desired. He might as well return home rather than complete his circuit.

That sudden stop saved his life when the crack of a gunshot rang out, and a bullet whizzed by right in front of him.

Nathan did not stop to think. Reacting on pure instinct, he yanked Merlin's head around—much harder than he normally would have—and kicked him into a gallop. Despite being fairly even-tempered, Merlin loved to run and had likely been startled by the sound of the gun as well, though he could not have seen the bullet that flew in front of Nathan's chest. Later, Nathan would reflect on how lucky he'd been that the bullet's passage had gone betwixt him and Merlin's head rather than hitting either of them.

For now, he crouched low over Merlin's back, his gaze moving along the trees where the shot must have come from. There was no movement there, and he could not tell if his attacker had fled or—

*Crack!*

Another shot, this one aimed at Merlin, and Nathan cursed, turning his horse away from the trees. Without knowing how well-armed the shooter was, much less where he or she was hiding in the trees, and with no back-up, lingering was ill-advised. A tactical retreat was the only sane option, no matter how much it stung.

Giving Merlin his head, Nathan flew through the park, headed for the exit closest to the Marquess of Camden's London home. He had no doubt this attack was related to the hunt for the traitor—there was no other reason he could think of for someone to be shooting at him—so he wanted to not only report it but acquire assistance in investigating.

The shooter would likely be long gone before he returned, but perhaps they would leave some evidence behind.

The blood in his veins went ice cold when he rode Merlin up to the front of Camden House and saw the front door swinging open.

\* \* \*

*Lily*

Staring out the window at the rolling greenery of the countryside, which finally greeted her eyes rather than the rows of houses, Lily heaved a sigh of relief. Inside the barouche-landau, on the opposite bench, her maid looked up at her with an inquisitive brow before deciding Lily had not actually been trying to catch her attention and looked away again. Thankfully, Chastity was used to Lily's preference for quiet reflection over constant chattering.

The lady's maid had been a gift from the Duchess of Frederick, Lily's godmother, during the Season, but they had rubbed along well, so Lily had asked if Chastity would extend her employment and accompany her to the country. It was a special boon because Lily had left for Derbyshire several days before her parents, permissible only because she had her lady's maid to travel with her as an erstwhile chaperone. As there was no need to spend the night at an inn, she did not need a more formidable one.

Sighing happily again, Lily leaned back against her bench seat, inwardly smiling when Chastity ignored her this time. Several years older, Chastity's sober demeanor was a good match for Lily's quiet, bookish ways.

If she never had to go to London for the Season again, she would be perfectly happy. The only reason she had done so was her friend Evie had asked her and her other two best friends. Josie had thrived on her first foray into Society, and Mary had deftly dealt with her second Season, but Lily had hated every moment.

Gentlemen, she had discovered, did not like a woman with a mind of their own. At least, not the nincompoops she was introduced to. Several had been drawn in by her relationship with the Duke and Duchess of Frederick, but they had not stayed after realizing Lily was the type to speak her mind. Which was a relief, even if it was lowering. She had always imagined marrying and having children, but if that was what London had to offer...

Unfortunately, the options in Derbyshire were not much better. Perhaps she would become an aged bluestocking spinster, firmly on the shelf, playing doting auntie to her friends' children. After her first Season, Lily found the prospect far more appealing than she would have countenanced.

Granted, she had not gone into the Season with high hopes, knowing she was not what many considered 'sociable,' but whatever hopes she had were quickly crushed underfoot by the general attitudes of the *ton*. Her very first week out in Society, she'd heard the incredibly handsome Lord Broderick—with whom she'd thought she had a very interesting conversation—remark to one of his friends that the only way she would find a husband would be to sew her mouth shut.

After that, to gauge the gentlemen's reactions, Lily became even more outspoken about her views and opinions. Like Lord Broderick, they were polite enough to her face, but she saw through their facades and overheard enough of their comments to know those gentlemen were assuredly *not* for her.

The carriage came to a sudden, jerking stop, tumbling the occupants about. Chastity cried out, flinging her arms wide as she was thrown forward, and Lily opened hers to catch her. They fell back against Lily's bench, shocked by the abrupt halt.

"Stand and deliver!"

What? A highwayman? Lily and Chastity exchanged disbelieving looks before Lily quickly released her maid. Knowing she was being a perfect twit, Lily leaned out the window to see a man on horseback, wearing a long black cape and mask, pointing a gun at the carriage.

Botheration. This was the last thing she needed today.

"I said, stand and deliver!"

"We've already stopped," Lily called back waspishly. "What do you want delivered? And how?"

"Miss, get back in the coach," the driver ordered. Lily scowled. She was not *out* of the coach. Not truly. "I will deal with this blaggard."

"No—" Her protest was cut off as she watched in horror when her driver lifted his own arm, gun in hand, only to jerk back against the seat. The sound of the highwayman's gunshot seemed to echo across the fields, and her entire body went numb with shock. The driver slumped and fell to the ground, startling the horses. Lily was flung back painfully against the window's edge, causing her to drop back into the carriage as the horses lurched forward.

Chastity screamed, but the movement was over almost as soon as it began, and through the ringing in her ears, she could hear the highwayman shouting something.

*He stopped the horses from running away with us.*

*Is that good or bad?*

They were not in a runaway carriage, but that meant they were now at the mercy of the highwayman.

*He killed the driver.*

Lily did not even know the man's name, had not asked. A fact which she now felt wildly guilty about. The man had meant to defend her, and perhaps he had gone about it foolishly, but to pay with his life when she had not even known his name...

*This is not a constructive line of thought, and you do not have time to dwell. You can find out his name later. Right now, you need to get yourself and Chastity out of this alive.*

The door to the carriage was yanked open, and Chastity screamed again, quickly covering her mouth with her hands as a gun was leveled at them. The highwayman was dressed completely in black, his face mostly hidden by a black scarf wound around the lower half and the hat pulled down atop his head, but she could still see his cold, dark eyes as his gaze flickered back and forth between her and Chastity.

Fear for her life, the first time she had ever felt such a thing, paralyzed her.

## Chapter Two

*Nathan*

Tying Merlin to the inside of the gate, Nathan dashed up the stairs, though he slowed when he got to the door, listening carefully. The quiet was far more unnerving than anything he might have heard.

*Bloody hell.*

He slowly crept inside, moving as stealthily as he could. Pausing for a moment just inside the door, he moved to the right where the drawing-room was. It only took a moment to discover that the room was empty. Grabbing a poker from the fireplace, he returned to the hall.

*"Josie!"* Elijah's voice echoed through the house.

Dashing forward, Nathan ran up the stairs where Elijah's cry had come from. He paused only for a moment when he saw a body at the top of the stairs, invisible from the first floor, before jumping over it and continuing on his way. He was fairly certain it belonged to the Camden's butler, but he could not stop.

Not when others might need his help.

The Marquess' study was ahead, the door ajar, and he could hear a woman sobbing from within.

Nathan burst through the door, only realizing his mistake when

Elijah smoothly jumped to his feet from where he'd been kneeling, pointing a gun at Nathan.

"Bloody hell, Nathan! I could have shot you!"

"Your front door was ajar, and I heard a scream," Nathan got out, panting for breath. His heart felt as if it was going to pound out of his chest as he took in the scene before him.

The Marquess' office was familiar grounds to him, full of heavy furniture and decorated with a dark red Oriental carpet and burgundy drapes. The paintings on the walls were of the family, the Marquess and his late wife, and individual portraits of his sons and niece. Now, they seemed to stare down at the Marquess' body, where it lay behind his desk, with the blonde kneeling next to him, her hands bloody as they pressed against his chest.

*Not his body. He's still alive.*

"What happened?" His eyes darted around. There was another body, blood soaking the red carpet, off to the side, near the bookshelves.

"Assassin," Elijah said succinctly, already kneeling again and undoing his cravat. He handed the fabric to Josie, who lifted her hands long enough to take it and wad it against the wound in the Marquess' chest. Tears streamed down her face, but she didn't hesitate, just pressed her blood-covered hands, ignoring the red smears across her mint green dress. "Just breathe, Father. Try to relax."

More noise in the doorway made them turn. A footman was there, his face pale.

"Cooper, he... he..." the footman stuttered, his gaze affixed on the injured Marquess. *Cooper.* That was the name of the Camden's butler. From the expression on the footman's face, before he'd even seen the Marquess, the news was not good.

"Run for a doctor," Elijah ordered. "As fast as you can. My father's life depends on it."

The footman dashed off.

"I cannot believe someone tried to kill him... if we had not been here... if we had left yesterday as we were supposed to..." Josie's voice trailed off.

*Bloody hell.*

Clues began aligning themselves in Nathan's brain, puzzle pieces coming together to create a clear picture.

*A shooter in Hyde Park, exactly where Nathan usually rode his horse, at the exact time he had been riding for the past week.*

*An assassin in Camden House the morning after Elijah and Josie were supposed to have left. The morning after the Marquess' other sons had left.*

How coordinated were these attacks?

"Nathan?" Elijah's confusion was clear as his voice followed Nathan out of the room.

"I need to check on Anthony," Nathan tossed back over his shoulder, barely pausing. There was nothing he could do for the Marquess, Elijah could not, but if they were under attack...

He needed to find Anthony, who lived alone.

\* \* \*

<u>Lily</u>

"There's no need for further violence. Tell us what you want, and we'll give it to you." Though she wanted to sound strong, she knew her voice was shaking. How could it not? Her entire *body* was shaking. Chastity was beside her, hands pressed over her mouth, sobs wracking her body. It was so hard not to join her.

Though she could not see most of his face, something about the way his features changed at her words, around his eyes, made her think he was smiling.

"Very good, Miss. I want you." The words knocked the breath from her lungs again, and Lily stared at him. His eyes narrowed, and he swung the gun to point at Chastity. "However, she is unnecessary."

"Stop!" Lily threw herself across the carriage in front of her maid, whose sobs had abruptly stopped in sheer terror. The driver's death weighed heavily enough on her conscience. If he killed Chastity... Fear for the other woman gave her an inward strength she might not have been able to find for herself.

Gulping as she stared at the gun, she did not know which was more frightening—the weapon or the cold gaze of the man holding it.

"Leave my maid unharmed, and I will go with you willingly," she said, doing her best to cover her fear. "If you harm her in any manner, I will fight you 'til my last breath. And I can make myself into a veritable nuisance if I wish. It will be much easier for you if I cooperate."

The highwayman considered her words for a long moment before finally nodding.

"No, miss, you cannot!" Chastity's hands clutched at Lily's shoulders as she moved away. "Who knows what he will do to you?"

"Hush. I am sure it will be fine." Lily was hardly sure, but she needed to reassure her maid. She did not want the highwayman to become impatient and decide killing Chastity was worth Lily's ire. "You know my family will pay whatever it is he requires."

Another flicker in the man's expression and she wished so much of his face was not covered. On the other hand, it was likely good because if she could see his whole face, she would be able to recognize him. Clearly, he wanted her alive, at least for now, which was more than could be said for Chastity. A ransom effort was the only thing that made sense. Truthfully, she would not have thought herself a likely candidate for such a thing, but her godparents were a duke and a duchess. Somehow, this man must have discovered that fact.

Lily knew she was far more able to defend herself than her maid was. Becoming friends with Evie had made sure of that. Each one of their little group of friends could defend themselves somewhat, and Lily had been the best at boxing. If she could get within hands' reach of the highwayman... but she would not risk it with Chastity there.

She looked over her shoulder at her maid.

"Stay here, wait for help," she said softly, but not soft enough.

The highwayman snorted his derision at her statement but said nothing as Lily turned and moved toward him. He backed up, keeping the gun trained on her until Chastity was in view, then lifted it. Lily's heart stuttered.

"Keep moving," he ordered, pointing to his horse with his free hand.

Biting her lip, Lily did as he said and nearly cried out with relief when he finally stepped away from the carriage without harming Chastity.

As he approached, she wondered if this might be her chance, but he stayed well back, pointing his gun at her. His eyes darted this way and that, and she realized he must be worried about passersby. It was fairly early in the morning, but eventually, this would be a busy road.

"Up on the horse," he ordered.

Another young lady might protest at being forced to mount without a block, but Lily did not dare, not with Chastity's life still in danger. If she could not, that would be one thing, but she knew very well that she would have no difficulty, especially in the traveling gown she was wearing, with its orderly skirts. Pressing her lips together, she got herself up in the saddle, though it was hardly comfortable since it was not a side-saddle.

If not for Chastity, she would have taken off on the horse, but she could not leave her maid to such a fate. She would bide her time and wait for her chance.

The highwayman sprung up behind her, wrapped one arm around her waist, and grabbed the reins. She stiffened, her back arching away from him, his touch repulsing her, and realized too late he'd put the gun away. With the horse lurching forward into motion, she did not dare try to knock him off—her position was far more precarious than his, and they were still too close to the carriage and Chastity.

*Patience. Be patient. Be brave. You can do this.*

Her friend Evie, who had taught her how to box, had been through far worse. Lily lifted her chin as the horse thundered along the road, taking her farther and farther away from the carriage and Chastity. When the chance came, she would not hesitate.

*\* \* \**

*Nathan*

As he exited Camden House, Nathan hurried to Merlin's side. Damn. The stallion was fretting, dancing slightly, and very unhappy to have been hitched to the fence instead of properly stabled, but he did not have time.

"Jones!" The familiar sound of Anthony Browne's voice calling out his name allowed Nathan to relax. His friend was on the other side of the fence, seated on his own horse. Nathan's relief was short-lived as he caught the expression on his friend and fellow spy's face. "What is going on?"

"Assassination attempts this morning on myself and Camden. He's still alive." Nathan's jaw clenched. He could not even bring himself to say the words because the scene in the study had been dire.

"Blast."

Coming in through the gate, Anthony put his horse far enough from Merlin so the two stallions would not bother each other, and they went back into the house. This time, Nathan took the time to pause and check on Cooper. The man was dead, shot through the chest. Closing his eyes for a moment, Nathan said a short prayer. The man had been the Camden's butler for years and was a force in his own right. He would be missed. There was nothing they could do for him, though, so they moved on to the study.

There was a new arrival, another young woman, though this one dressed in servant garb. Her black hair was pulled back and mostly hidden away by a brown scarf tied around her head. Josie was holding her, the two of them crying soundlessly as they watched Elijah check the padded fabric against his father's wound. The clammy color of the Marquess' skin promised little hope, but he was still breathing. The other body had already been removed, and Nathan winced inwardly. Whoever it was must be dead.

"Bloody hell," Anthony said in a tone Nathan had never heard him use before, but when Nathan turned to look at him, his attention was directed at the servant, not at the Marquess. "You! What are you doing here?"

The servant straightened, glaring at him. Her eyes were a brilliant green, and her expression was not at all subservient.

"Leave my cousin alone, Anthony," Elijah said sharply, causing Anthony to stagger back. Nathan glanced at his friend. Elijah's focus was on his father, so Nathan did not know if Elijah knew how pale Anthony's face had just become. That servant was Evie Stuart? Somehow, Anthony clearly recognized her, and not just from her portrait on the wall, which showed a much younger girl. "What do you two need?"

"I came here because someone tried to shoot me in Hyde Park,"

Nathan said immediately. "I was hoping one of you could return there with me to look for anything the shooter might have left behind."

"I came because someone tried to sneak into my house and stab me," Anthony replied grimly. He was still looking at Elijah's cousin, clearly distracted by her mere presence, even though she was not looking at him. Neither was she disturbed by the bloodstains from Josie's hands, which had transferred onto her dress.

"All of you..." Evie murmured, then tightened her grip on Josie. "Someone needs to check on Mary and Lily. Now!" Her voice snapped out like a whip, distress and fear dripping from every word. She looked down at her uncle, clearly torn.

"Why—" Before Anthony could argue with her, Elijah cut him off.

"She's right... Go! Anthony, you run to Hartford House. Nathan—"

Now it was Josie's turn to interrupt.

"Lily left this morning, back to Derbyshire."

"I know the way," Nathan said, nodding in understanding, and turned on his heel. Though he had a myriad of questions about and for Evie Stuart, those could wait. Mary, Josie, and Lily had been up to their delicate necks, trying to hunt down the traitor, thanks to Evie, as had Anthony and Nathan.

The real question was whether Lily had left town when she had to throw off suspicion while her friends were attacked or if it was mere coincidence. Nathan hurried, not acknowledging the doctor as the man rushed by with the footman who had gone to fetch him. Behind him, Anthony was hot on his heels.

How far did the danger reach?

## Chapter Three

## *Lily*

Pressed far too close to the man behind her for comfort, Lily gritted her teeth. The horse was running at a full-out gallop. Her mind was racing ahead of them, going along the route, trying to guess where they would stop. Unfortunately, they did not pass anyone, though surely that would change soon as the day went on. Someone had to come from the other direction, even if most would travel away from London.

Unfortunately, almost as soon as she had that thought, the highwayman slowed the horse. Should she try to shove him off? As if he sensed her thoughts, his arm clamped more tightly around her, and Lily tensed.

"Don't even think about it." Menace threaded his words.

Lily pushed down the panic that welled beneath her breast. As a young lady, a debutante, in particular, she was used to being underestimated. Of course, the only man she'd met that did not do so this Season was a blasted highwayman.

They turned off the road on a path into the woods she probably would have missed if she'd been in the carriage. She had never noticed it before. It certainly was not large enough for a carriage, though it was clear horses traveled it occasionally.

*But how often?*

*It was a defined path but not well-worn.*

*Most likely to some kind of shelter... somewhere he can keep me. Unless he means to kill me in the woods, but then why would he not have done so already?*

Killing her back in the carriage would have been far easier. He *must* be doing this for a ransom. The thought was soothing in that it did not put her in any immediate danger, yet Lily had no intention of sitting around waiting for a ransom to be paid. Especially since her reputation would be thoroughly ruined by the time it was.

She did not know if she wanted to be married, but if she decided to marry, she did not want any hindrance to the process. Ruination would shrink the pool of suitors she had to choose from—and going by her Season in London, that pool was already depressing enough.

The best thing for her would be to escape as quickly as possible.

Through the trees, she saw the outline of a small cottage. Moving closer, it was rather ramshackle, though sturdy-looking. The highwayman slowed the horse, and Lily's heart raced, pounding so hard, she was sure he must feel it.

They drew to a halt in front of the cottage, and she finally made her move, jerking her head back the way Evie had taught her. The highwayman cried out in pain and outrage as the back of her head banged against his chin. Sadly, she was too short to hit his nose, which would have been far more effective. Lily did it again, ignoring the pain in her head, but this time it didn't work as well.

Rather than loosening his hold, he tightened it while trying to dodge, and the movements knocked both of them off balance. Lily cried out, and the horse neighed loudly, unhappy with their antics, and reared up. Both she and the highwayman fell from the horse.

Half tangled in his body, she was unable to hold out her hands to soften her fall, and her head glanced off a stone as she hit the ground, knocking her unconscious. The last thing she heard as she fell into darkness was the highwayman's curses, accompanied by the horse's unhappy whinnies.

\* \* \*

*Nathan*

Traffic was halted on the road, and Nathan felt an unhappy clench in his chest as he rode closer. The prickle on the back of his neck was growing stronger with every passing minute.

"Please, you cannot just stand around. You have to *help!*" The anguished plea rose high and shrill, causing an unhappy mutter to stir from the people around the distraught woman, a maid by the looks of her.

Frowning, Nathan drew to a halt, gathering the attention of the small crowd. There were three carriages, all in a row, and his frown deepened when he saw the body lying next to the first one. A well-dressed couple and their servants were standing well back from the body and from the ladies' maid, who had planted herself in the center of the road.

"Please, help!" The maid turned to him, wide-eyed, her expression going from anguished to hopeful as she took in his appearance. "My mistress had been kidnapped by a highwayman!"

The prickle on the back of his neck was so strong, Nathan had to reach back to scratch it. Behind the young woman, he could see the couple rolling their eyes. It took him a moment to place them—Lord and Lady Hatchet. Two denizens of the *haut ton*, who he'd had very little reason, much less desire, to interact with. Intrepid and vicious gossips who were convinced of their own self-worth and no one else's. They had been introduced, however, and they recognized him as well.

"Captain Jones, the gel is hysterical, talking nonsense." Lord Hatchet waved his hand. "There are no highwaymen along this road. We're far too close to London for such nonsense. It's perfectly safe."

"All evidence to the contrary," Nathan said dryly, arching an eyebrow and nodding his head at the body in the road. The maid was now at his side, reaching out to grab his ankle as if he were her last hope. Considering her other option was the selfish Hatchets, he could hardly blame her.

"Yes, well, obviously none of our business, is it? He's just a driver." Lady Hatchet sniffed. "He probably owed someone money, and they came to collect. We need to be moving on. We have urgent business waiting for us at home."

The callousness of people like the Hatchets sometimes made Nathan wonder what the point of fighting for his country had been. So vain, selfish people who thought everyone else was lower than them could continue in their delusions?

There were others, though—innocents who deserved protection, the ones he had fought for—and he could not pick and choose among them who would prosper., He made a mental note to keep Talbot affairs well away from anything the Hatchets had a part of. They were the worst of people.

The maid's face went red with fury, but she knew better than to turn and snap at the selfish creatures behind her, no matter how well-deserved.

"Please, sir, my mistress is Miss Lillian Davies, goddaughter to the Duke and Duchess of Frederick—"

Behind her, Lady Hatchet scoffed. "Not this again. As if someone so important would travel with no one but a maid and driver."

Nathan caught some of Lady Hatchet's servants exchanging glances. Clearly, they all believed the maid but were too afraid to speak up against their employers. Unfortunately, he could not take the time to give them the tongue lashing they deserved.

"What did he look like?" he asked, focusing on the maid. She swiped strands of auburn hair furiously back from her face, her hazel eyes widening and filling with hope someone would finally believe her and help. Nathan was busy trying to decide whether this was another ploy by Miss Davies or if she was in true danger.

After multiple assassination attempts this morning... was she kidnapped? It did not make sense. If she was connected to the traitor, a kidnapping might be insurance against suspicion when everyone else involved in the hunt was murdered—or if one of the attempts did not work. So far, they had been lucky. Whether or not that luck would hold... He forced his mind away from the memory of the Marquess lying on the floor and back to the matter at hand.

"He covered his face. He wore a scarf and a hat... his eyes were dark... murderous." The maid's eyes filled with tears. "*Please*, help her! She gave herself up willingly so he would not harm me."

"Which way did they go?"

She pointed down the road, letting his leg go and stepping back. The hope in her expression was nearly more than he could bear.

Was Miss Davies truly in danger? Or had she had an accomplice kill her driver and threaten her maid to make it look as though she was?

Despite the maid's claim, highwaymen were rarely interested in kidnapping young ladies. They wanted their money immediately, then they were on their way. Actually, taking a young woman and holding her for ransom was not how any highwayman he'd heard of normally operated, not in England nor on the continent. The maid clearly did not know that, however.

"I will find her," he said before kicking Merlin into a gallop. He could hear the Hatchets shouting after him, but he ignored them, focused on the road and thinking ahead to the turnoffs. Where might one hide?

Storm clouds were gathering on the horizon as though a portent the danger was not over.

* * *

<u>Lily</u>

Head throbbing, Lily moaned as she slowly came awake. Something cold and wet pressed against the side of her head, where she hurt the most.

"Thank you," she murmured.

There was no answer. Hardly polite. She tried to move her arms, but they were behind her because... because she was sitting on a chair.

*No.* She was tied to a chair.

Lily jerked upright, her head snapping back, and cried out as her headache exploded in a new burst of pain.

"Stop moving about." The frustrated voice brought everything back to her.

The carriage ride back to Derbyshire. The highwayman. Her poor dead driver and his threat to Chastity. Going with him willingly. Trying to knock him off the horse—and failing miserably.

Groaning, she let her head hang back down, endeavoring to appear as pathetic as she could. Sadly, it took very little effort.

"There now. Better." The man sounded very satisfied. Lily lifted her head again, much more slowly, and peeked at her captor through thick lashes. The inside of the cottage was gloomy, and his back was to the only open window, which made him hard to see. The light coming in through the window was not very strong, as if the trees were blocking the sun, or perhaps clouds had rolled in front of it. Possibly both.

It appeared he was still wearing the hat and scarf, though he had pulled the scarf down to cover just under his chin and below. With the poor lighting, she could not see his face any better than she had when he'd accosted her carriage.

Keeping her movements slow, Lily looked around the room. The cottage was sparsely furnished and dusty but showed signs of use, not completely abandoned. A hunter's cottage? There was a table and chairs by the window with drawn curtains, a small stove, cupboard and drawers, and even a bed. Lily turned away from the bed, her blood chilling. So far, her kidnapper had shown no interest in actually ruining her, but she could hardly forget the possibility was there.

Moving to shelves along the far wall, the villain had his back turned to her while he opened a box. Lily immediately pulled at the ropes around her wrists, testing how much give they had. She mentally blessed Evie, who had prepared her friends for all sorts of eventualities. Not just boxing and shooting, but things they thought would never happen to them—like being tied up with rope.

The highwayman had only tied her wrists, and while it was tight enough, he'd used a thick rope that had more give than some she'd gotten out of in the past. It had been a while since she'd practiced, but she was sure she could work herself free if given a chance.

When he turned back around, she froze, watching him warily, but he did not glance up at her as he settled down at the table. In profile, when he was walking, she could see his hawkish nose and dark brows, but when he sat at the table, he did so with his back to the window, putting his entire face in shadow. It felt ominous, so she did her best to press her arms behind her back, pulling and stretching the ropes around her wrists without being obvious.

"Well, Miss Davies, I have a few questions for you." He placed the items he'd gotten from the box on the shelf in front of him, smoothing his hands over the paper and setting the pen against it before looking up at her.

Lily froze as several pertinent facts hit home.

He knew her name.

He spoke like a nobleman.

He wanted her to answer questions.

And he was not writing a ransom note.

She might be in more dire straits than she'd realized.

## Chapter Four

*Nathan*

The biggest problem with the road was all the damn trails that went off into the woods. Thankfully, after a previous mission, he knew which ones actually led to something useful and which ones did not, but that meant there were plenty of cottages and small shelters that would be the perfect spot to hide from notice. He had already checked two of them and was wondering if the continuous stops would bear fruit or if he was falling farther and farther behind Miss Davies.

The storm clouds were getting closer, and soon, he would soon be forced to stop and take shelter if that continued.

At the next path, he paused and stared down at the ground. The dirt on the path was stirred. The oncoming storm would wipe away any traces once it passed, but for now, he could see someone had gone down it. Recently.

Turning Merlin's head, he followed the path into the woods. It was not a very long path, but the cottage was set back well away from the road. Overhead, the sky was becoming darker. Even if Miss Davies was not here, he would need to take shelter. Approaching the cottage, he could see a small, covered shelter off to the right, which served as a kind of stable. The doors were open, and a horse was inside, still saddled.

Nathan turned Merlin back. He would return for the horse, but right now, discretion was the most important thing. He needed to know what was happening in that cottage and who was inside before they were aware of his presence. Just in case. An overabundance of caution had never done him any harm.

Merlin whickered, unhappy to be left in the woods.

"Shh." Nathan patted the stallion's neck. "I will be back, and I promise you will get a reward for today's work, regardless of how it turns out."

As if he understood, Merlin made another noise, sounding a bit like a grumble. Nathan patted him again and took off through the woods, staying off the path in case anyone came out of the front door. Making his way around the cottage, he was aware of the skies darkening overhead, but he would rather be caught in a bit of rain than by the enemy.

\* \* \*

<u>Lily</u>
"What do you know of the Earl of Devon?"

The line of questions the highwayman, if that was what he was, was taking her down did not make sense. On the other hand, none of them had seemed harmful. So far, he had wanted to know her relationship with the Marquess of Camden and his sons—they were neighbors, and her friend Josie was married to the eldest—and a list of her correspondents, as well as how often she wrote them. Then he suddenly veered to asking about the earl, which had nothing to do with anything.

"His Christian name is Lucas Beckett. He is a rogue with few marriage prospects despite his title and will likely need to marry for money, if and when he does wed." The words slid off her tongue. Debutantes were supposed to know such things, though the only reason Lily had bothered to learn anything about the man was, at one time, he had been their suspect for the traitor they were hunting. "Close friend of the Marquess of Hartford and currently residing in France."

"Have you had any communications with him?"

Lily blinked. This line of questioning was even more nonsensical.

"Absolutely not. You already asked who my correspondents are."

She could not help but sound huffy. The longer the questioning had gone on, the less fear she felt. She could not see what his questions had to do with anything. She'd worked her hands free of the rope, holding it as she feigned being still restrained.

The only thing she could think of was this must have something to do with the traitor she and her friends had been hunting. *Traitors*, though the one they really wanted was the mastermind behind it all. For some reason, they must suspect she knew something.

"I did not ask if he was one of your usual correspondents. I asked if you have had any communication with him since he left for the Continent, but I will take that as a no." The highwayman's voice remained calm, measured. "What do you know of the Earl of Talbot?"

"Christian name Sebastian Talbot. Though he came out of mourning in time for the Season, he did not attend and instead sent his younger brother, Captain Nathan Jones, to London. The estate is rumored to be in shambles." Something which made her very suspicious of the man and of his younger brother. She had met the handsome captain during the Season and had found his penetrating gaze to be rather disturbing.

The man was very intense and not friendly. Not only that, but considering some of the things her correspondents had said, there was a serious smuggling operation happening along the coastline of Talbot lands. Smuggling had abounded along the coastlines during the war, but several of her connections with high places in their governments had indicated the smugglers along the Talbot coastline had been willing to take more than lace or brandy—they'd smuggled spies in and out of the country.

Spies against Britain.

If the Talbots had already engaged in treason once, why not again? The captain actually worked for White Hall as a spy, so perhaps it was a double-cross.

Lily did not speak any of her suppositions aloud. She did not know what her questioner was looking for, and she had no concrete proof for any of her thoughts. That her friends had outright dismissed her suspicions had hurt and made her second-guess herself. They did not want to believe it about someone their 'Uncle Oliver' trusted. Lily had a more cynical mindset.

"And Captain Nathan Talbot?"

Lily shrugged, ignoring the way the man's face flashed across her mind's eye. Far too handsome for his own good, despite his unfriendly expressions.

"A second son, he joined the army and this past Season came to London to help sort through his brother's affairs in the wake of the earl's inheritance."

Though the room was growing darker, despite it being afternoon and the highwayman's face completely cast in shadow, she had the sudden feeling he was smiling at her. A shiver ran down her spine. Her instincts were screaming at her that it was not a nice smile. She pressed herself back against the chair.

"You forgot to mention he is also a spy, working under the direction of your neighbor, the Marquess of Camden, and that the Marquess of Camden is the crown's spymaster." The silky tone of the man's voice made him sound more threatening, not less.

All the hair on Lily's arms and the back of her neck stood up in reaction to the smooth menace, as well as his words. Though she and her friends knew those things, they had been sworn to secrecy by Evie when she had first told them about her uncle. Even Lily's godparents did not know.

"You seem to be leaving out a few pertinent details, Miss Davies. I wonder what else you have been leaving out."

Lily sucked in a breath as he got to his feet, slowly, leisurely, as though he had all the time in the world. His movement was accompanied by an ominous crack of thunder, and a moment later, she heard the first splats of rain falling on the cottage's roof.

"Perhaps we need to loosen your tongue."

It was a threat, delivered in a tone that said he was looking forward to doing so. Lily did not know what he intended and was not going to sit to find out. She had hoped Chastity might find her way back to London or flag down a passerby to send someone to help, but her hopes had already dwindled when the highwayman had moved off the main road to the cottage, and at that moment, they died completely.

No one would be able to see the path into the woods in a downpour.

There would be no rescue. She was entirely on her own.

* * *

<u>Nathan</u>
Creeping around the house, Nathan ignored the crack of thunder. The sound of voices was coming from the back, and he realized the window was open.

"No!" Miss Davies' voice was clear, and there was the sound of flesh hitting flesh.

"You little bitch!"

Nathan dashed back to the front of the house and threw open the door. The rain was already coming down harder, but he barely noticed as he barreled into the cottage. Thunder rolled overhead as the two in the cottage turned towards him. They were grappling next to a chair that had fallen to its side on the floor.

"Bollocks," the man cursed, shoving Lily aside. With a small cry, she fell over the chair, her skirts tangling about her legs, rousing Nathan's protective instincts as much as her first cry had, despite knowing she might be a traitor. If she was, and this was her associate, they were clearly not on good terms.

*Or she is innocent and was actually kidnapped for some nefarious reason.*

A conjecture he would examine more closely when he had the time to think about it.

For now, he rushed forward, meeting the brute halfway. He lashed out with his fist, nearly connecting, but the other man dodged. Nathan was ready for a bout of fisticuffs. What he was not prepared for was the man to lurch to the side, spin around Nathan, and run out the open door into the storm.

And it *was* a storm. The deluge coming down was so strong, he could barely see out the door. Dammit. He needed to get to Merlin.

"Why did you let him get away?" Miss Davies' tone was strident.

Nathan turned to see her struggling to her feet. She appeared unharmed, but he felt ungentlemanly watching her try to untangle her skirts from her legs and the chair.

Quickly moving closer, he reached out his hand and assisted her to a standing position, trying to ignore how dainty her hand felt in his. Though it was possible she was innocent, he was not ready to give in and trust that everything was as it appeared to be. Only careful contemplation of new information would help him come to a new conjecture.

"Are you hurt?" he asked brusquely rather than answer her question, which he did not consider worth his time. He had not *let* the man get away. He had not expected the man to want to get away at all.

"No."

"Good." Nathan turned and headed out into the rain, leaving her standing there with her jaw hanging open. The deluge battered against him as he shut the cottage door firmly behind him and hurried to where he'd seen the other horse hitched up, but the little shelter was empty. It had been too much to hope it wouldn't be, he supposed.

Turning, he hurried back down the path to retrieve a cranky Merlin. The horse was not at all happy about being left out in the rain, and it took all of Nathan's coaxing and soothing promises to get him into the little shelter. Thankfully, it was a very sturdy shelter. Merlin settled once he was inside, happy to be out of the wet. There was no food for him since Nathan had not expected to be out past his morning ride, but there was no help for that. Tying Merlin's bridle in place, Nathan steeled himself to return to the cottage.

He had a few questions for Miss Davies.

## Chapter Five

*Lily*

Watching Captain Jones storm out the door, Lily's mouth dropped open. Of all the nerve! Letting the blaggard get away, then treating her so rudely. Perhaps he had gone out to catch the man. That would be the only excusable reason, she fumed.

The summer storm was battering the small cottage, which was the only reason she did not follow him out. Besides, she did not want to distract him, or likely he would blame *her* for the highwayman's escape.

Lily sniffed and searched around the cottage. Her knuckles still stung from the knock she'd given the highwayman. Shaking out her hand, she searched the cottage for anything that might be useful. With the storm, they would not be going anywhere soon. She paused.

*Oh, dear.*

It would not matter which man she was trapped with overnight— either would lead to her ruination in the eyes of the *ton*.

Well, no help for it now. Hopefully, she was physically safer in Captain Jones' company than she was in the highwayman's. If her luck held, the rain would let up, and she would be back in London with her parents before sundown. Though she had no way of knowing how much time she'd lost when she was unconscious. With the storm clouds, it was impossible to judge the hour by the amount of daylight.

Finding a candle and box of matches, Lily sighed with relief. Some light, at least. She glanced at the fireplace behind where she'd been sitting. There was plenty of wood stacked if they were to need a fire. Hmmm... Captain Jones would likely be soaked through when he returned.

*If* he returned.

Glancing at the closed door, Lily frowned, then decided she may as well get the fire started. If he did not return soon, her curiosity would demand she made at least a cursory search for him outdoors, then *she* would appreciate having a fire. She closed the curtains of the window that had been letting in light and set the candle. Thankfully, the cottage was small enough, even something so small gave her enough light to see by. The fire would be useful for more than one reason.

As she was stacking the wood in the fireplace, the door opened behind her. Startled, she jumped to her feet and grabbed the poker, holding it up like a cricket bat. She had never been very good at the game, but hitting a man was much easier than hitting a ball. The wind gusted in, blowing out the candle she'd set on the table and taking away that bit of light.

"It's me." Captain Jones' voice was tinged with frustration.

"What happened to the highwayman?" she asked, lowering the poker, though she did not let it go. Captain Jones closed the door behind him. She really needed to get the fire lit. Turning her back on him, she finished stacking the wood and struck a match, dropping it onto the tinder in the center.

The light from the fire was much better than that from the candle. She stood to hear his answer, brushing her hands off with a satisfied smile. When she turned around, she shrieked at the sight that met her eyes.

* * *

*Nathan*

His clothes were soaked through, and despite the warmth of the day, there was a distinct chill across his skin. Though Nathan would normally not disrobe in polite company, the state of his coat made it hard for him to move, and he had taken it off while Miss Davies attempted to start a fire.

"What is it?" he asked, turning and looking around, ready to defend himself if the villain he'd chased off had returned.

"Nothing... I..." Her gaze was averted, staring at the wall, then he caught her eyes tending his way before jerking away again.

The fire had actually caught, to his surprise, and was giving off enough of a glow they could see each other easily enough. He looked down at himself since she appeared to be having trouble looking at him, wondering what was the matter. His ivory waistcoat and the fine linen of his shirt were soaked through, clinging to his body, but he did not...

Oh. *Oh.*

As a debutante, Miss Davies had likely rarely, if ever, seen a man without his coat on, certainly not one she did not know. Something he had forgotten. Nathan did not spend time with debutantes outside of the required social gatherings and would not even do that had he been given the option.

"I need to dry my coat," he said awkwardly by way of explanation.

How did one talk to a debutante? Especially when they were alone? He had never been alone with one. While he still needed to question her, he was thrown by the realization, if she was innocent of treachery, this situation would be extremely scandalous. It would be if she was not innocent as well, but in that scenario, he would not feel obligated to care.

Blast.

With her maidenly demeanor as she avoided looking at him, he could not take off his waistcoat. The wet fabric was clinging to him uncomfortably, though taking off his coat had been an improvement.

"Ah, might I approach the fire?" he asked hesitantly. There were no social norms for a situation such as this for him to draw on. When he was forced to interact with debutantes in the ballrooms, he could rely upon the usual subjects to get him through menial conversation—the weather, their families, any recent gossip. The few times he'd interacted with Miss Davies... well, he had mostly watched as she interacted with her friends and the Camdens. Partly because she was beautiful and partly because he found her suspicious.

"Oh, yes, certainly."

Interesting. This was the first time he'd seen her flustered. Even right after he'd rescued her, when her captor had run out the door, she had not seemed this disconcerted.

Passing by her, he noted the blush on her cheeks as she ran her gaze over him again before turning her head away. Going to the table, she sat down, angling the chair away from him. Since he was no longer in her view, Nathan decided he might as well take off the waistcoat. He would dry faster.

Draping his coat and waistcoat to dry as best he could, Nathan stood close to the fire, letting the heat soak into his chilled skin and dry his shirt and pants. Those he would keep on. They were uncomfortable, soaked as they were, but much less so than if he took them off while Miss Davies was present.

"What happened to the highwayman?" If her voice was a little higher than before, Nathan had no desire to mention it.

"Scampered, I believe. His horse was gone when I went to check. I have stabled my horse in the shelter he was using. Once the rain clears, we will return to London."

\* \* \*

*Lily*

Once the rain cleared. So far, it showed no sign of slowing, though she fervently hoped that would soon change. Her reaction to the coatless captain had been both unexpected and unnerving.

She had seen men without their coats, of course. She spent most of her time in the country, and a good bit of that time had been spent with Evie and Evie's cousins. However, Lily had never been as distracted by Elijah, Joseph, or Adam as she was by Captain Jones.

Perhaps she had been too young to properly understand the appeal of the male physique when she had seen them. Or perhaps she had always thought of them as brothers more than anything else. Whereas Captain Jones was practically a stranger.

*A very attractive stranger.*

*Do* not *look at him again.*

Lily did not understand her own fascination. The temptation to take another peek was almost overwhelming, so she distracted herself by asking a question.

"How did you find me?"

It turned out to be a good question, though his answer made it even more difficult to keep her eyes averted from him. She gasped as he ran down the events of the morning from his point of view—the attempted assassination, finding the Marquess of Camden wounded and on the floor of his study. She gripped the edge of the table when he spoke of that, worry for her honorary uncle flooding her. It had not occurred to her that her kidnapping might have been part of a larger plot.

Evie and her cousins must be going out of their minds with worry. If she could have, Lily would have jumped up and demanded they return to London immediately, but the storm was only slowing a little. The rain was still coming down in a hard, steady downpour, though the initial fury had decreased.

When he finally got to the part where he came upon Chastity on the road, she sat up a little straighter—and groaned when he mentioned the Hatchets.

"Please tell me Chastity did not tell them my name."

Captain Jones hesitated, which made her groan again. London had its share of vicious gossips, so the fact the Hatchets were among the worst of them was truly an accomplishment.

"I do not know. She may have. I cannot remember exactly what she said to me or what she said to them prior to my arrival."

That kind of succinct but comprehensive summation was typical of Captain Jones, she was beginning to realize. He did not want to impart incomplete information, a fact which she appreciated.

"I nearly did not find the path to this cottage," he admitted. "But it was fortuitous. Now, you must tell me what happened this morning."

Doing her best not to bristle at his 'must,' since he had been forthcoming enough to answer her query so completely, Lily ran down the events of her own morning. As she did so, her mind was already turning over his report. She wanted to trust him, she truly did, yet...

There was something happening on Talbot lands. He could be involved. Though he claimed someone had shot at him this morning, that could be nothing more than convenience. It would be very suspicious if everyone else was attacked, and he was not.

Riding alone in Hyde Park, shot at by a hidden party... well, there was no way to prove it, was there? Even before the storm, finding any evidence of such a claim would have been extremely difficult. Now it would be downright impossible. Which meant she was alone in a cottage with a possible traitor.

Though since her friends had sent him looking for her, he would be extremely foolish to harm her. Unless he blamed it on the highwayman. But if he was going to do that, why had he attacked the highwayman?

The circular thinking was getting her nowhere. She needed more information.

Finishing her summation of how she had arrived at the cottage, she automatically turned her head to see his reaction to her account.

Her breath caught in her throat. He had taken off his waistcoat, and the fabric of his shirt was thin enough to see through, especially when he was backlit by the fire. Though she could not see everything, she could see enough to know he was certainly not padding any of his clothing, and he had a smattering of dark hair across his chest.

Why that set her cheeks aflame, she did not know. So the man had hair on his chest. That should not be enough to make her blush and lose her voice. Plenty of men had hair on their chests, but she only reacted to him this way.

She had to get out of there.

"I think the rain is lightening up."

"It is doing no such thing."

Though he spoke the truth, Lily scowled. She might have been exaggerating, but it was rude to negate her statement so comprehensively. He did not seem to care. Pure contrariness made her press the point.

"We cannot stay here forever."

"Not forever, but certainly long enough to let the rain slow, if not stop completely." The tone of his voice made it clear he would not accept any other opinions, and Lily felt her temper rise.

"Even that might be too long," she snapped. "The Hatchets will say..." Her voice trailed off, her throat tightening as she thought of the things that vile couple might spread about her.

"There is nothing we can do about them. What we need to do right now is keep ourselves safe until the storm passes."

"Easy for you to say," she snapped. "It is not *your* reputation at risk." With her temper flaring, she got to her feet. Truthfully, if he had been more conciliatory, she would not be so frustrated, but he was talking down to her, just like every gentleman had all Season, and it was making her want to be the ninny-headed flibbertigibbet they—and he—seemed to think she was.

She was so tired of men brushing her off, and here he was, yet another one, unconcerned about her and her future, even though she was stuck with him through no fault of her own.

"Your reputation is hardly the largest concern right now." The condescension dripping from his voice made her want to scream.

Yes, there were a great many other concerns she would like to help with and find out whether her Uncle Oliver still lived, but her reputation was still a massive concern to her! It would affect her entire future.

His complete dismissal of her was infuriating. If she stayed one more minute in these cramped quarters with him, she would surely throttle him. How Elijah maintained a friendship with such a cold, self-centered brute was beyond her, but she had no desire to be trapped with him any longer than absolutely necessary.

She got to her feet and moved towards the door. She would rather walk back to London in a storm than spend one minute more with Captain Nathan Jones.

# Chapter Six

## Nathan

Standing by the fire, Nathan could only shake his head at the vagaries of women. Not only did they not know the Marquess of Camden's fate or her friends, the Marquess and Marchioness of Hartford, but she was worried about her reputation? If there was a scandal, they would have to marry, of course, but her reputation would hardly suffer for that. He was a perfectly eligible gentleman. A wedding between them would be quite appropriate for their stations and immediately clear up any gossip.

Besides, they did not even know yet if such a thing would be necessary, so there was no reason to dwell on it.

When she suddenly got to her feet and walked towards the door, he frowned.

"What are you doing?" She could not actually intend to be going out into the rain, and yet it looked like just that.

"Forgive me for not wanting to stay somewhere with a man who does not value my reputation," she shot back over her shoulder.

The words, questioning both his character and his honor, hit Nathan like a blow to the chest.

"That is not what I said," he snapped back. Zounds. This was why he did not like to speak to debutantes. Well, not just debutantes. If he was truthful, speaking to people, in general, was not his forte. They always seemed to hear what they wanted to hear and rarely paused to think before speaking.

And this particular one was not listening.

Nathan bounded forward, grabbing her arm as she pulled open the door. The rain was coming down as hard as ever, the wind blowing the wet in through the open window and splashing them. Frustration pulsed through him. Bloody hell. He had *just* started to feel warm and dry!

He yanked her back by the arm, causing her to gasp with outrage. Half-expecting a slap, he was somewhat ready when she lifted her hand but not quite prepared for the vicious right hook she aimed at his nose. Barely dodging out of the way, thanks to his training and years of practice, he kicked the door shut as he spun them around.

"The bloody hell?" Where had she learned to do that? Perhaps his suspicions were as warranted as he'd thought.

"Get out of my way! You have no right to hold me prisoner here!"

"You are hardly a prisoner." Though she was daft if she thought he would allow her to storm out into the rain. Where was she going to go? And how? Did she plan to steal his horse? Walk? Both options were incredibly senseless. Or was there something he did not know? The skill with which she had thrown that punch at him...

Whatever the reason, she was not going anywhere. He still had questions for her, and her behavior was growing increasingly suspicious. Even if it turned out he was wrong, what kind of gentleman would he be to allow her to go out into a storm like this on her own? Anything could happen to her.

No. Not under his watch.

"If I am not a prisoner, then move out of my way."

"No." Increasingly frustrated by her mule-headedness, he glared right back. "As a gentleman, I cannot allow you to go out on your own in such intemperate weather. Especially when we do not know where your highwayman has hied off to. It could be dangerous."

Instead of seeing the sense of his words, she glared even harder at him and jerked her arm away. He let her go. Now that he was standing between her and the door, he did not need to hold on to her.

Something about the interaction was setting off instincts normally reserved for meetings of the Society of Sin, the secret and debaucherous club created by the Marquess of Hartford, where members of the *ton* indulged in all sorts of perversions.

A club Nathan had been happy to join. He had always been a bit bossy when it came to intimate relations, and at the club, he had found several new interests, as well as training to be more than a 'bit' bossy with the women he bedded. As Miss Davies challenged him, he brought some of those lessons and instincts to the foreground.

"You are not my father, my brother, or my guardian, Captain Jones. You do not get a say in my actions."

She tried to step forward again, but Nathan was not budging. Crossing his arms over his chest, he stared down sternly at her.

"As the only man present, and the only person with any sense, it appears,"—he ignored her gasp of outrage—"I get a say in your actions."

Dark eyes blazing, she tried to go around him. Nathan had not expected she would be done trying to verbally move him out of her way, but he caught up quickly enough. This time, when he grabbed her arm as she reached for the door, she spun and tried to punch him again.

Nathan dodged. "Stop trying to hit me!"

"Get out of my way."

"If you try to hit me again, you will not like the consequences." There was only so far he was willing to go in the name of chivalry, and he had weeks of pent-up frustration over this woman to work out.

"If you do not get out of my way, *you* will not like the consequences," she retorted, jerking away from him and heading for the window.

Seriously? Nathan groaned inwardly when she reached it and began undoing the latch. Moving behind her, he grabbed her by the waist as she pushed the window open, yanking her back and pulling the window back down—which gave her the opportunity to rush for the door. Cursing inwardly, he abandoned the window and dashed after her, barely catching her before she escaped.

Bloody woman.

"Damn you!" She did not try to punch him this time—instead, she landed a stinging slap across his cheek and did not look one bit sorry about it.

Enough was enough.

Completely fed up, Nathan pulled her over to the table, sat down in the chair, tipped her over his lap, and yanked her skirts up. If he was going to do this, he would make sure she felt it, though he would not bare her to him entirely. This had already gone too far, but he was out of patience.

Lifting his hand, he brought it down hard on her drawer-covered bottom.

\* \* \*

<u>Lily</u>

Of all the outcomes, this was one of the last she would have expected to provoke, if she had thought of it as a possibility at all. Though perhaps she should have. Mary and Josie had both been frank about their involvement with the Society of Sin and had talked of Captain Jones' activities with the club.

She had not expected him to lay hands on *her*.

*Oh, really? Exactly what response* were *you trying to provoke by acting like a madwoman?*

Lily was the calm one. Out of all her friends, she was the least likely to do things like trying to run off in the rain or punching a captain of the army in the nose. She was the one who took the time to think and analyze before deciding on a course of action.

Something about Captain Jones got under her skin, and her emotions were harder to control than usual. There were good reasons for not wanting to spend overmuch time in the cottage with him, but if she was completely honest with herself, the moment he had told her there would be consequences for hitting him again... it was as though he had unleashed something within her.

She'd wanted to know what the consequences would be.

Not quite able to bring herself to do what he had told her not to do, she'd slapped him. She'd almost expected the 'consequences' would turn out to be nothing more than a threat.

Which she would have found disappointing.

She had not expected to react like this to being spanked.

Mary and Josie had spoken about it, and she had found their testimonies to be almost unbelievable.

Now, she was finding out for herself.

The intimacy of being over a man's lap, feeling his strong thighs flexed beneath her stomach. Having her skirts flipped up and knowing he could see, and feel, more of her than any man ever had.

The shocking sting and lingering burn of his hand coming down against her upturned bottom hurt far more than she had imagined.

The first swat took her breath away, and she did not suck in another breath until his hand had come down twice more, and she was finally able to yelp in both shock and consternation.

There was no measured pattern, no consistency in the force, and therefore, no way of predicting where each swat would land or how much it would hurt.

The experience of being so physically imposed upon knocked Lily off her usual axis, stunning her mind with shock and making it impossible for her to think. Her thoughts came to a grinding halt as the physical sensations overwhelmed her.

"You will sit, and you will behave until such time as we can leave!"

Captain Jones' voice penetrated the fog in her brain, and she realized he had been lecturing her as he spanked her. She had not heard a word he'd said until the last sentence.

Four more swats, then she was suddenly put upright again, a rush of dizziness spinning her head around. She had not even had the time to protest. Staring blankly at him, she did not resist as he turned her around and seated her in the chair he had just occupied.

Despite the brief time he had been sitting, it was still warm from his body. Or perhaps it was her own bottom's warmth she was feeling. Lily stared up at him, feeling very... odd. Her mouth opened. Closed.

She should protest his brutal treatment. Rage against his handling of her person. Instead, she was speechless. Her mind was too busy categorizing and absorbing the sensations, which had happened too rapidly for her to do so as they occurred.

The warmth in her bottom had somehow spread throughout her

body. She pressed her legs together. There was an odd throbbing between them. She felt odd everywhere, in fact. Even her chest. Her nipples felt... itchy.

Was this what Josie and Mary had been describing?

\* \* \*

*Nathan*

Bloody hell. He'd traumatized the debutante.

Miss Davies was staring off into space, her eyes unfocused, lips slightly parted as if she could not believe what he had just done to her. Nathan had to press his lips to keep from apologizing.

He had warned her there would be consequences, though he should have outlined exactly what those consequences would be. If he had been at a Society event, that would have been expected. On the other hand, how did one tell a debutante that he was going to spank her if she did not behave?

*How does one go about spanking a debutante? One does not. Yet you did it, anyway.*

Because he had been driven to the last of his patience.

Which was not really an excuse. Nathan had never reached the end of his patience before, no matter the provocation. Ladies who tried to provoke him were always disappointed.

Except Miss Davies. Perhaps it was because the stakes were so high, whereas, at the Society, there was very little risk. This was real life, though, not a game.

Shifting movement caught his eye, and he turned his head to see Miss Davies was still staring off into space, but she was also now squirming on the chair in a very familiar manner—like a naughty, well-punished member of the Society.

His cock jerked to attention as he realized she was not traumatized. She was aroused.

Blasted hell. Now, so was he.

## Chapter Seven

*Nathan*

If there was anything more torturous than being stuck with an aroused woman who was a debutante possibly involved with treachery, whom he could not touch and should not have touched in the first place, yet was wildly attracted to, Nathan did not know what it was.

And the rain was not letting up.

He kept away from her, well on the other side of the cottage, staying by the fire and trying to pretend she was not there. Unfortunately, his body had no interest in such pretense, and every soft sound she made was met with a throbbing reaction from his cock. His balls were aching as his erection went untended.

He had not been this sexually frustrated since he was a youth, still trying to figure out how his body worked. If it was not raining so hard, he would go out to relieve himself.

*If it was not raining so hard, I would have never been trapped in this situation in the first place.*

What to do now?

Trying to make conversation while he had an erection and she was still sitting on a hot bottom and wriggling with arousal did not appeal, but the silence felt just as awkward.

And the damn rain was still not letting up.

Nathan's stomach growled.

Damn. How long had they been there? With the rain pouring down, it was impossible to tell the position of the sun, and he did not have his pocket watch with him. He had been feeding the fire, so he could not even tell by how much the fire had burned down, though if the amount of wood he'd used was a sign, it had been longer than he'd realized. He had gone through quite a bit without realizing it.

"I think it must be getting close to suppertime." It was not a conversation starter, not really, but he did not want to startle her when he got up to search more of the cottage. Miss Davies jerked in surprise before looking at him. There was a deep blush on her cheeks when she lifted her chin and answered him.

"Yes. I did not see any food when I was looking earlier, but I did not check everywhere."

As if by silent agreement, they searched through opposite sides of the cottage. Nathan looked through the boxes and tins on the shelves on his side while Lily opened the drawers by the bed.

"Hardtack and some dried meat," Nathan said, looking up to see how Lily would react. She made a face, but she was busy pulling sheets and blankets out of the drawers. "What are you doing?"

"I am going to make the bed." Her tone sounded a bit aggrieved, and she kept her gaze averted from his. "Since it appears we are likely to be stuck here overnight."

Blast, she was right. If it was late enough for supper, and the rain had not let up, it was late enough they would make it back to London or anywhere else. They would be stuck together in the cottage tonight.

Nathan supposed he should start preparing himself for marriage to Miss Lillian Davies. Preparing himself to bed her would be far too easy, but he doubted she would happily take a suggestion to further their intimacies in preparation for marriage. There was always the chance, somehow, they might get out of making that final leap, but not if they actually did the deed.

Of course, now that he had the thought, he could not stop thinking about it. Could not stop remembering the glimpses of her pale legs, the feel of her body pressed against his lap, her squirming atop him, and her skin warming as he laid his hand down on her bottom. Could not stop glancing over to watch her graceful movements, notice the curls caressing the back of her neck, and watch her bend over to drape the sheets across the bed, so her bottom was pointed directly at him.

\* \* \*

*Lily*

The most infuriating thing about this entire situation was how hot she felt all over while Captain Jones remained utterly cold. Cold physically, cold emotionally, and cold to her plight. The man did not care that her reputation would be ruined after this. He did not even seem to care that the highwayman had gotten away.

Her friends had told her she could be cold, but compared to Captain Jones, she was like a summer breeze. The man must have ice in his veins. Even after he'd spanked her, his expression had remained distant. Her reaction had been the exact opposite, and it grated that she had been so affected while he had not been.

If she was alone, she would already have her hand between her legs, rubbing herself. Josie and Mary's descriptions of being spanked and the aftereffects were far more accurate than she had thought they would be. She had made an exploration of her body and read quite a few books about sexual relations—including a fascinating one with pictures from India that had been tucked away in her favorite bookstore—but none of her previous explorations had made her feel as desperate as she did right now.

Had a man been the missing element?

What a lowering thought... especially considering the man in question.

Perhaps it was truly the spanking she had responded to and not the man. That would certainly be preferable.

*Would it really?*

Lily hesitated. In this case, yes. Though still uncertain why she had reacted that way... Surely, that could not be the case for every woman, or there would be no need for a secret club where members could indulge in such activities.

Clearly, she would need to try it again. With a different partner, preferably one who did not infuriate her.

Though she was unsure of whether she would be welcome at the Society of Sin as a debutante. Perhaps this was one way Captain Jones had helped her. Surely, a society dedicated to sin would be willing to accept a ruined debutante among its members. If she was going to be tarnished with assumptions, she might as well make them true and enjoy herself.

Especially since one of her best friends was its founder and another best friend was a member with her husband. They could help her pick out a good partner for her experiments with sin and pleasure. Someone other than Captain Jones. Even if he was handsome and being over his knee had set her body aflame.

There must be other handsome men who could ignite the same fire within her.

Bending over to set down the sheets, Lily made a small growling noise under her breath. Whoever decided to push the bed up against the wall rather than leaving space to walk around it had certainly not been thinking in terms of convenience.

"I'm going to get us some water," the captain said abruptly.

Lily straightened, turning to see him scoop up a bucket and stride over to the door, opening it and walking out into the rain.

Her mouth dropped open.

The man was completely nonsensical. He'd just gotten dry!

*Do I have time to... No. No.*

If being spanked by him had been embarrassing and her reaction shameful, him coming in to find her with her hand between her legs, trying to give herself some relief from those reactions... The very thought had her body turning hot and cold in equal measure. Absolutely not. She was not actually ruined yet and would fight against that fate until there was nothing left to do. She would not give in before she even knew if there was a chance she might continue on as she had.

Shaking her head, she finished making the bed. He still wasn't back, so she made a small pallet on the floor with blankets as best she could. He returned before she was finished.

"Why did you not stick your arm out with the bucket?" Her tone was more than a little aggrieved as she looked down at the water he had dripped across the floor when he'd returned to his previous stance in front of the fireplace... since he needed to dry off *again*.

"I wanted to check on Merlin." He stared into the fire, not looking at her as if she was unimportant. Certainly less important than his horse.

Though her heart did go out to the poor creature. It was not truly cold, thankfully, despite the rain, but she doubted the accommodations were comfortable and did not have any food for the animal, unless... She glanced at the hardtack.

"Do you think Merlin would like some of this?" she asked, picking it up.

Captain Jones finally glanced up, looking to see what she was talking about. Something in his expression changed. Softened, if ice could soften.

"Yes, once we dampen it, I will see if I can get him to eat some." He glanced at the bucket of water by his feet. "We should move some of this into cups for us to drink before soaking the hardtack."

The short conversation, then getting the food ready, finally allowed her body to quiet. Sitting down and feeling the soreness of her bottom made her blush again. Thankfully, he did not seem to notice. Over dinner, they talked about innocuous subjects, such as their friends.

Things like spankings, the Society of Sin, and the traitor they were hunting were not mentioned.

She sincerely hoped that was not because she was alone in a cottage with the traitor in question.

*** 

*Nathan*

Two of them.

One bed.

Which he was not going to think about because she had thoughtfully made up a pallet for him on the floor. Of course, his mind couldn't help but fantasize about what might have been under other circumstances. Especially now that he'd had the beautiful debutante over his lap and realized she'd become aroused by the spanking.

This was going to be a torturous night.

More than just the traitor was now hanging over their heads. There was also the possibility of marriage.

He would not give up his bachelorhood unless he absolutely had to. Thankfully, he was not the heir, and marriage was not one of his duties. He only had to marry if and when he wanted to or if an unfortunate situation arose, such as the one he now found himself in.

Was it so unfortunate, though?

She was beautiful. He was attracted to her. *And* she took being spanked very well. There were worse things to base a marriage on, as the members of the *ton* demonstrated on a regular basis.

*Why are you even thinking about marrying her? You should be thinking about ways to escape it!*

Right.

"Well, I suppose it must be time to sleep." Miss Davies glanced at the bed, at him, then down at her lap, where her hands were fretfully smoothing her skirts.

"Yes. Hopefully, we'll be able to get an early start in the morning." Early enough to return to London without anyone seeing? That was the most likely way out of having to marry the woman.

He supposed he could abandon her and let her either stay in the cottage on her own or return to London by herself, but her reputation would be ruined, regardless, and he was too much of a gentleman to have that on his conscience. His honor would not allow it.

No, the most likely outcome of this entire excursion was marriage.

Certainly not what he'd expected when he'd started the day.

Taking off his waistcoat, he kept his back to Miss Davies. He could hear the rustle of fabric and wondered if she intended to sleep in her traveling dress. Should he offer to help her undress?

*No.*

Let her be. If she asked for his assistance, that would be one thing, but she seemed remarkably self-reliant.

Lying on the pallet, which was lumpy and did not do much to cover up the hardwood floor, Nathan sighed. There was an answering sigh from the bed, then the candle went out.

"Good night, then," he said, figuring it was only polite. There was a moment of silence before she responded.

"Good night."

## Chapter Eight

**L**ily

The cottage's bed was not comfortable, and neither was wearing her dress to bed. Lily was also not used to sleeping in a room with someone else. Every move Captain Jones made—every soft snore, every time he rolled over—she jerked to awareness. Finally, pure exhaustion had her falling into a deep slumber, but she did not feel particularly well-rested when she woke.

By the light coming in through the thin curtains, it was early morning. Lily jerked awake, sitting straight up in bed. At the foot of the bed, Captain Jones was standing in nothing but his shirt and pants. Lily blushed.

"Sorry," she squeaked, lying back down and turning her head away.

"Give me a moment." His voice was deeper, rougher than usual. Because it was the morning. "I'm decent."

Apparently, decent meant he'd put on his waistcoat. Both of them were decidedly rumpled. While Captain Jones went to fetch the horse, Lily brushed out the fabric of her skirts as best she could, but it was truly a lost cause. Sighing, she walked out to the front of the cottage, closing the door behind her and waiting for him to come around with the horse. She had to admire the stallion he was leading. A beautiful bay with a shining amber coat, he was sleek and well-muscled, his good breeding showing in every line of his body.

"He's beautiful," Lily breathed, watching as the stallion came to an obedient halt at Captain Jones' command. The two of them made quite a sight, despite the captain's unkempt appearance, though she had to admit, she did not find the dark scruff along his jawbone to be unattractive, even if it was not fashionable. "Will he be all right carrying both of us?"

"For the ride back to London, he should be. I will give him a handsome reward at the end of it."

To Lily's amusement, Merlin snorted and bobbed his head up and down as if to say, 'you'd better.' Even Captain Jones unbent enough to chuckle.

They were so preoccupied, the sound of a shout made Lily jump. She had not been paying attention to the path, much less whether or not someone was making their way down it.

"There she is! I see her!" The voice was unknown, and she frowned as she turned her head to see a man on a horse who looked vaguely familiar. The triumphant tone of his voice made no sense to her, and she could not see who he was calling to behind him. "My God, and with Captain Jones after all. Is the highwayman gone then?"

If Captain Jones had been ice before, now he was a glacier, his body rigid. The way he was looking at the other gentleman was not at all friendly.

"Long gone," he said.

"Ah, well..." The man looked behind them at the cottage, his eyebrows rising. "Then you two spent the night together?"

She did not need to recognize him to recognize the gleam in his eye, and her stomach turned over. London was full of malicious gossips, those who delighted in the misfortune of their peers and loved to talk about it.

Perfect.

There was no escaping ruination now.

Captain Jones walked up beside her, wrapping his arm around her waist and causing her to jump.

"Lord Hatchet, I am sure you are not insinuating anything untoward about my fiancée."

*His what?* Lily clenched her jaw, barely keeping from shouting the words. The effort to maintain an even expression was even more difficult. Truthfully, it was probably shock more than anything that kept her quiet.

Not one word—*not one word*—all night, even though he knew she was worried over her reputation! Would it have killed him to talk to her about it first?

"Your fiancée?" Lord Hatchet's eyebrows rose in suspicion, and she thought there was a bit of disappointment as well.

"Of course. Why do you think I was so frantic to reach her yesterday?" Captain Jones tightened his hold.

Lily forced herself to smile sweetly at Lord Hatchet before turning her gaze to her erstwhile fiancé. If he had bothered to look at her, he would have seen pure murder in her eyes.

"Thankfully, I rescued her before anything terrible happened."

In one fell swoop, he'd managed to save her reputation. Not only had he pronounced them engaged—which did not entirely forgive them spending the night together unchaperoned, but no one would care once they were married—he had also reassured the others she had not been ravished by the highwayman. Lord Hatchet struggled to cover his disappointment at the lackluster gossip he'd been presented. The loathsome man.

When Mary and her husband, the Marquess of Hartford, came riding up the path behind him, Lord Hatchet turned at the sound. Lily felt a surge of relief at the sight of her friend. They appeared unharmed. Of all her friends, they were the only ones Captain Jones' had no information on. Perhaps they had been left out of the attacks?

"There you are! Thank goodness," Mary said. Lily was clearly not the only one who was relieved.

\* \* \*

*Nathan*

The rigid way Miss Davies was holding herself did not bode well for his future, but it was well-locked in now. If it had been their friends who had found them first, they might have been able to come up with... something. Lord Hatchet's presence made that impossible. Nathan had seen the other man's excitement at having such a juicy bit of gossip to chew on.

Miss Davies rushed from his side to embrace her friend. Nathan had to admit his own surge of relief at seeing the pair, especially since the Marchioness did not appear to be upset or in mourning. She was as close to the Camden family as Miss Davies was, so that must mean the Marquess of Camden still lived.

The tension he'd been holding in his chest all night relaxed, leaving him feeling like a cloth that had just been wrung out.

At least something was going right.

The urge to get back to London, as quickly as possible, to get caught up on everything was rampant, but he knew he could not let on. Not with Hatchet there.

"Thank you for joining in the search," he said casually to Hatchet, drawing the man's attention away from the two women and their whispering. "I would have expected you to be well on your way to your estates by now." Hopefully, he would think Miss Davies' distress and the Marchioness' relief at finding her was entirely due to her ordeal and nothing else.

If gossip got out about the attack on Camden House, Nathan hoped this would be all Hatchet remembered. Or if he did realize it, he would think the two things were entirely unrelated.

"Yes... well." Hatchet looked uncomfortable at the reminder he'd been less than gracious to Miss Davies' maid. "Once I realized you were taking the situation seriously, I could hardly do any less. It bothered my conscience, so I turned back to London to inform Miss Davies' parents and offered my services, along with Miss Davies' friends. I daresay, none of us expected to find you alone here."

"We thought you might have gone on ahead to the next town," Hartford confirmed. He'd gotten down off his horse, unlike Hatchet, and was holding the leads to his and his wife's horses. "The Camdens and Davies went ahead to look, and we stayed behind to search the paths, just in case."

"If it had not been for the storm, I would have certainly made an attempt," Nathan said, trying not to sound too grim. If they'd been able to make it to the next town, they could have found an inn and a woman to tend to Miss Davies, and he would not have to marry her.

Or if Hatchet had not shown up with the search party, that was likely the story they would have concocted.

Unfortunately, his presence made everything much more dire. And he'd told the Davies. Of course, he had. It was the right thing to do, but... damn.

Nathan was well and truly trapped.

* * *

<u>Lily</u>

"What do you mean there's no other option?" Lily's voice was shrill even to her own ears as she stared at her mother in the mirror. Her mother had insisted on tending to Lily, which in her mother's world meant brushing out Lily's hair. It was rather soothing if not very helpful to her situation. "Surely, we can come up with... something."

"You do not know the Hatchets well enough to understand," her mother replied grimly. "If you do not marry Captain Jones, they will not only bandy about bits of the truth, they will add in all sorts of embellishments and speculation about why the wedding did not happen."

"They're awful," Mary confirmed from her seat on Lily's bed. She was there, along with Josie and Evie—who was dressed for her station and not as a maid for once. Thankfully, Uncle Oliver was recovering, though he'd been gravely injured. Evie had announced she would take care of him, which meant retaking her place in the family.

"If Captain Jones had not stepped up, they would have told everyone they know, written to every acquaintance they have, and your reputation would be in tatters. As it is, Captain Jones and Rex managed to convince Hatchet he was part of a rescue party for the captain's fiancée. Now he gets to proclaim himself a hero rather than focus on you."

Since Lily had seen the man's disappointment for herself, she could hardly argue with their assessment. The little she had seen of him had shown him to be one of the worst of Society.

"It will also keep him from focusing on anything else he hears about," Evie murmured. She was staring off into the distance, her dark eyes worried, but she'd insisted on staying with Lily. Her cousins currently had care of her uncle, and Captain Jones was giving his report, which had rendered her presence there unnecessary for now. "The servants know not to gossip, but..."

Keeping an attack on a Marquess quiet was not an easy endeavor. Especially since it happened at the same time as an attack on another Marquess, though it was unlikely anyone would know about the assassin who had attempted to breach the Hartford's house. The man had not been prepared for Cormack, Hartford's butler, unlike the man who had been sent to Camden House. Cormack had dealt with the intruder's attack with lethal resistance, something Mary said he now regretted since he blamed himself for not leaving the man alive to question. Unfortunately, Camden House had not fared quite as well, and they had lost both a footman and their butler.

Surprisingly, Josie was silent, which was not her normal state. She was on the bed, sandwiched between Mary and Evie, hands twisting on her lap. The three of them in a row were a rather devastating combination of beauty—Josie's blonde ringlets and bright blue eyes, Mary's quieter, paler auburn beauty, and Evie's dramatic contrast of dark hair and green eyes. Unfortunately, the momentary thoughts did little to distract her from the issue at hand.

"I do not want to marry Captain Jones," Lily half-wailed. She shot her friends a look. She could not talk about it in front of her mother, but her friends knew she suspected his family.

"Do you think you have another option?" her mother asked matter-of-factly. It was a pragmatic question. If Lily could come up with an alternative that did not cast the family into shame, her mother would present it to her father, and the three of them would find a way to make it happen.

Lily knew the truth of that deep in her heart, which made her feel marginally better, even though it did not help the current situation since she could not think of a single other option.

"Give me some time," she started, and Josie snorted.

"You do not have time, Lily." The words were not unkind. Josie and Lily had always been blunt with each other, and this was no exception. "Lord Hatchet will have told his wife by now. Word will be spreading. If it was the beginning of the Season, perhaps we could do... something, but the best way to cut off any untoward gossip is for you to be married immediately before the rest of the *ton* leaves London. That way, when they go, they'll carry the news of your last-minute wedding to Captain Jones with them, which will curb any gossip." As Josie was a master at dealing with the social side of the *ton*, including gossip, her opinion could not be easily discounted.

"Special licenses are not that easy to come by," Lily argued, rubbing her forehead and ignoring the chorus of snorts that came from her friends.

"I believe your father, godfather, the Marquess of Hartford, and Lord Camden are planning to visit the Archbishop this afternoon when Captain Jones goes to make his petition," her mother said mildly.

Lily groaned. With her godfather being the Duke of Frederick, it would have already been hard for the Archbishop to say no. With the Marquess there as well, along with the son of another Marquess who was currently injured, she thought it very unlikely Captain Jones would come away empty-handed.

Apparently, she would be getting married.

She stared at herself in the mirror.

This was not how she'd expected her Season to end.

## Chapter Nine

*Nathan*
Finally alone.

Nathan collapsed in his favorite chair in front of the fireplace in his library. His thinking chair. It was comfortable in all the right ways, well-worn without falling apart, like putting on a favorite pair of boots, except it cradled his entire body. The afternoon with the Archbishop, along with Lily's godfather, Elijah, and Rex, had been necessary but exhausting.

"Would you like something to drink, Sir?" Connor asked from the doorway. His butler was relieved to have him back home but knew better than to hover.

"No, thank you, Connor. You may retire for the night." He needed to be clear-minded while he thought through all the implications of the past forty-eight hours.

In the army, he'd been known for never being without a plan. A well-structured plan made life flow easier, and a well-structured plan always came with contingencies. Not once had he considered the possibility of marriage this Season. Certainly not with someone he suspected of being involved with treason.

On the one hand, this was the perfect way to keep an eye on Miss Davies' activities and correspondence.

On another hand, what was he to do if he found her culpable of treason? As her husband, it would be his duty to protect her.

After careful consideration, staring into the empty fireplace, and remembering the night before, Nathan came to the realization he did not believe Miss Davies was purposefully involved in any treasonous activities. Unwitting involvement, however...

She had a goodly number of correspondents, and though she seemed bright enough, their conversation last night had hardly been unusual. Certainly, nothing that would inspire a French government official to foster an acquaintance. Which made him wildly curious about what she might be speaking about with her contacts across Europe. Was she passing along gossip? Points of interest about her godparents? Something must be inspiring her contacts to encourage her to keep writing to them.

Perhaps it was merely that she was willing. As the goddaughter of the Duke and Duchess of Frederick and neighbor to the Spymaster to the Crown, she would certainly make an enticing target to those with nefarious intentions.

Those who spoke to her during the Season had indicated she was 'too smart' for her own good and labeled her a bluestocking. From what Elijah had said, she always had her nose in a book, which would be enough to cause the more vicious among their set to deride her. From his own, admittedly limited, interactions with her, Nathan had seen nothing of the sort.

Hopefully, they could find common ground and muddle along well enough.

She had been headed to the country, so perhaps she preferred it there. Nathan's duties would keep him in London a while longer, but she might like to go on to Talbot lands ahead of him.

Surprisingly, the notion did not appeal.

*Well, I will not be able to keep an eye on her if she is on Talbot lands and not here with me.*

*It's also hardly fair to ask Sebastian to keep an eye on my new wife with all the duties he has to attend to at home.*

Yes, he would need to keep her in London with him for the time being. Close by his side where he could watch her closely.

Perhaps touch her.

*Admit it. You want to get your hands on her again.*

That was hard to deny. Nathan had always been the curious type. Tomorrow, they'd be married, and she would be his wife. The idea of leading an innocent like Miss Davies down the path to where pain and pleasure could collide was incredibly alluring. He'd dallied with plenty of women who knew what they wanted but had never been with a virgin.

Would her blushes be hotter?

How far would she be willing to be led?

The spanking had aroused her—would tying her up induce a similar reaction?

How would she react to a longer, more intense spanking? Or a spanking with something other than his hand?

Would the level of shock at new perversions help or hinder her arousal?

What would she look like tied down, legs spread wide apart, while one of his machines drove her to ecstasy over and over and over?

Nathan cursed, realizing his pants had become decidedly tight and uncomfortable against his arousal. Reaching down, he undid the laces and did what he'd been unable to do last night—he gripped his cock and pumped, hard and fast, with visions of Miss Davies dancing in his head.

So prim. So proper. What would she look like in ropes or spread out and flush with arousal and passion? How wet would she have been if he'd touched her cunt last night after spanking her?

His hand moved up and down his shaft, eyes shut as he leaned back against the chair. With his other hand, he deftly reached into his pocket to pull out his handkerchief.

Debauching an innocent. Something that had not appealed to him before, but if Miss Davies was that innocent and soon to be his wife.... The things he could do to her.

Picturing her on her knees before him, her lips parted to receive his cock, while he sat in this very chair, he imagined pushing into the wet heat of her mouth. Perhaps with ropes wrapped around her, tying her hands behind her back and framing her breasts, running between her legs for her to rub her most sensitive bits against.

"Bloody hell!" The force of his orgasm surprised him. His cock throbbed against his hand, spraying the interior of the handkerchief the way he imagined spraying himself across Miss Davies' breasts. He could see her face in his mind, eyes widening with shock, letting his seed flow over her skin to drip off her breasts.

Spent, Nathan slumped in the chair, breathing hard as he shuddered in the last throes of his orgasm.

Perhaps marriage to Miss Davies would not be so bad. He would need to keep an eye on her, of course, but he could certainly make this work. Particularly if she responded to the rest of his interests the way she had reacted to being spanked.

\* \* \*

*Lily*

Tossing back and forth in her bed, Lily rolled onto her back and stared up at the ceiling. She was having as much trouble sleeping tonight as she had the night before.

*It is the night before your wedding, you ninny-headed twit. Of course, you are having trouble sleeping. You went from considering a life as a spinster to having a fiancé and a far-too-fast wedding in one night!*

Far too fast for her, but not too fast for the rate gossip spread among the *ton*. Josie had been correct. Despite the number of people who had already left London, and although Lady Hatchet had supposedly been sent ahead home by her husband, several curious callers had come by the house where she and her parents were staying.

Everyone had mentioned her 'adventure' and the curious fact that her engagement to Captain Jones had not been previously announced.

Nosy busybodies.

Thankfully, her friends had been there for her, as well as the Duchess of Frederick, to bolster her with their support. Mary had also brought her aunt, Viscountess Hood, and her cousin by way of marriage, the Duchess of Manchester. Their presence had also made it difficult for the busybodies to take any glee in her situation.

With not one but two Duchesses present—smiling charmingly and declaring how happy they were for her and Captain Jones—every lady who had the nerve to visit went away with an understanding of the 'correct' story. Even though the wedding was rushed a bit for the sake of her reputation—to silence those who would gossip maliciously, you understand—their visitors left with the understanding that captain and Miss Davies' courtship had begun during the Season and was reaching its culmination faster than expected because of events outside of their control. Namely, her attempted abduction by a highwayman and the Captain's brave and romantic rescue.

Each one of those visiting ladies was smug when they left, feeling as though they had been given privileged information, which previously had only been known to the family. If Lily was the sort for hysterics, she would be screaming.

All this work to save her reputation when nothing had even *happened*. It was enough to drive a woman mad.

*Nothing happened except being turned over his knee, you mean.*

Yes. Well. That was hardly enough to actually ruin her, but she knew what mattered was the perception of facts, which was maddening in and of itself. Though not half as maddening as her reaction to remembering the spanking. She should be past this already.

*Like Josie and Mary, you mean?*

Both of them were spanked by their husbands, and according to them, spanking was the least of the perversions practiced by the Society of Sin. Nathan, especially, was known for his inventions, actual machines that serviced the women the same way a man would.

Lily flushed hot all over, then cold as she wondered whether he would expect to continue those activities with other women while he was married to her.

Well. That would be the first thing to put her foot down about.

*Because you only want him to do those things with you?*

Well... yes. If they were married. Faithfulness might not be fashionable among the *ton*, but the marriages Lily had grown up seeing had all involved loyalty. She expected nothing less from her own marriage and would make sure her new husband was aware of that expectation. Even if it meant having to let him practice his desires on her.

From everything Josie and Mary had said, letting him do so should at least be enjoyable.

Lily shivered as the memory of being over his knee slid through her mind again. The way it had felt to be so easily manhandled. So at his mercy. Why had she liked that so much?

Her nipples were pebbling again, the ache between her legs growing, and she was shifting beneath her covers for a different reason entirely. Tomorrow would be their wedding night. Would he spank her again?

Would he want to practice his perversions on her immediately?

Her hands moved over her breasts, which felt swollen and tight, and her nipples were sensitive to the touch as her fingers moved over the fabric covering them. Pressing her legs together, she moved them back and forth, teasing herself. Lily had found, through much experimentation, how she liked to be touched.

How different would it be when *he* was the one doing it?

Rougher.

It would be rougher.

He had spanked her, after all.

The pain was gone, but she could still remember how it had felt.

The sting. The lingering heat. The way her body had wanted more when it was over.

Pushing her bedsheets down, Lily tugged the hem of her nightdress up and pressed her fingers between her legs. She was hotter and wetter than she ever remembered being. Her fingers stroked against the slick, swollen flesh of her womanhood, which felt even more pleasurable. Writhing against the sheets, Lily bent her knees, so her feet were flat on the bed, and rubbed at the little spot that always felt so good. There was a tiny nubbin of flesh there, exquisitely sensitive, and the more she rubbed it, the better it felt.

Lily gasped as she thought about Captain Jones rubbing that little spot, his large, rough fingers touching her sensitive flesh, touching her where no one else had touched her...

Crying out as pleasure exploded through her and hot bliss surged through her limbs, she rubbed and rubbed and rubbed through each wave of ecstasy until the incredible feeling finally ran its course, leaving her limp and breathless. Breathing heavily, Lily let her hand fall away and her legs slide into a supine position.

In the aftermath of her climax was a feeling of lethargy. Pushing the skirt of her nightgown down, she pulled her sheets over her body. She turned on her side, closed her eyes, and let herself fall into sleep, Captain Jones' face following her into her dreams.

## Chapter Ten

*Nathan*

It was his wedding day, and the entire thing felt like a farce.

The brightest spot of the day was the Marquess of Camden's presence, even though he had to be rolled into the church in a bath chair, his face far paler than normal. Nathan was not sure the man should be out and about, but he was glad to see him well enough to do even that. His sons and niece hovered by his side.

Miss Stuart's presence had caused several double-takes by the Duke and Duchess of Frederick, as well as Miss Davies' parents. None of them said anything at the outset, of course, but they clearly recognized her and were wondering where she had been all Season.

So was Nathan, but that was not his primary concern today. A quick question to Elijah had confirmed her cousins were not entirely sure either, and Elijah had not wanted to talk about it. It was the parental surprise that made Nathan realize all of Miss Stuart's friends had shown a lack of surprise at finding her in London. Including his bride. Perhaps he could get a fuller accounting from her later.

*Really? You are getting married, and your thoughts are on questioning your bride about her friend?*

Well, his priorities were a bit torn, considering the events surrounding their sudden engagement. The wedding was going through, regardless, but his mind tended to be preoccupied with questions, not certainties. When Miss Davies appeared at the back of the church on her father's arm, his mind stopped wandering and focused entirely on her.

She was stunningly beautiful. The dress she was wearing befitted a bride, a stunning concoction of white lace and silver edges that clung to her figure in an attractive manner while still being perfectly modest. The lace on her dress perfectly matched the lace of her veil, and the bouquet she held was made up of white roses and baby's breath.

Despite himself, Nathan's breath caught in his throat at the vision she made. If he had ever contemplated becoming married, he would have been happy to find himself wed to such a beauty.

Her expression needed work, though. She appeared uncertain and not entirely happy., which was not unexpected, given the circumstances. He hoped to improve her mood. If nothing else, their mutual friends should make settling into a relationship themselves easier. He hoped.

** * *

*Lily*

Borrowing Josie's dress had been a mistake. It did not fit her correctly. The bosom sagged a little, the skirts were a bit too long and dragged on the ground, and it made her feel itchy all over. Though it was better than borrowing one of Mary's dresses, considering Mary was nearly a head shorter than her. And the itchiness might be more mental than physical.

It simply did not feel like *her* wedding dress, even if Josie had handed it over with a cheerful, "Something borrowed!"

*Something old, something new, something borrowed, something blue.*

The blue was the sapphire drop necklace she wore, the old were her shoes, and the new were the earrings her mother had given her that morning as she was getting dressed.

Married in a borrowed wedding dress. Somehow, that was fitting to the occasion, even if it was very uncomfortable.

Trying not to cling to her father's arm, Lily peeked at the altar, where her groom was waiting. Captain Jones looked handsome in a dove grey morning coat, which set off his dark hair and eyes. His shirt was crisp white with a high, starched collar, and the blue of his waistcoat matched the sapphire of her necklace.

Had he known? Or was it a coincidence?

Her feet tripped a little over the hem of her dress.

"Careful, sweetheart." Her father's voice was a supportive murmur. "There is still time to make a run for it. You do not have to marry him. Your mother and I will support you."

Lily blinked back tears. Her parents were not the type to bow to the social strictures of the *ton*. They had been welcomed into the fold because they were sponsored by the Duke and Duchess of Frederick and their merits as a scholar and a gardener, but they had only come up for the Season for her. They would be perfectly happy back in Derbyshire.

However, the gossip would make its way there, eventually, especially if she ran out on her wedding. That would make it spread all the faster. She liked to think their friends at home would be understanding but knew enough about human nature to know not everyone would. The ruination of her reputation would have far-reaching effects her father did not anticipate and she could not calculate. She would not put her family through that.

"No. Thank you. I want to do this." She was stretching the truth. In a different situation, she certainly would not be getting married today, but she was living with the circumstances she had been given. Fate had hemmed her in and cut off any honorable route for escape. With things the way they were, she knew this was the best option for her family.

Hopefully, it would not turn out to be a personal disaster for her.

Nodding, her father escorted her down the aisle. He trusted she would tell him the truth. They had always been a very frank family. Perhaps she should feel bad about not being entirely truthful, but the world was not made up of black-and-white truths but of shades of grey.

Finally reaching the end of the aisle, her father placed her hand in Captain Jones'. Looking into his face to see his dark eyes blazing back at her with desire, she felt as if she had been more truthful than she'd realized. Perhaps this was not the man she would have chosen, but if not for the possibility of his family being involved in treason, he was not a bad option.

\* \* \*

*Nathan*

Wondering what Lily and her father said to each other halfway up the aisle, Nathan took his bride's hand in his. Even through their gloves, the touch was electric. There was no denying the attraction between them anymore. It had only grown since their night in the cottage.

Which was not the worst thing to base a marriage on.

The ceremony sped by in a flash, ending with a touch of his lips to hers—he held back and gave them a mere brush, not wanting to make a fool of himself in front of their gathered audience. Everyone knew this marriage was out of necessity. Doing more than a brush of lips would show far too much of his hand.

For all that their wedding brunch had been hastily put together, there was no sign of it. The food was delicious and the decorations beautiful. If only his bride had any interest in talking to him instead of Elijah, who was seated on her other side, it would be just about the perfect wedding brunch.

"Are you staying here in the capital?" Lady Stuart asked. Elijah's new wife, as well as being one of Lily's close friends, was seated next to Nathan. A vivacious blonde beauty, she had given Elijah a run for his money this past Season, before and after they married.

"Yes, for now. I would like to return to Brentwood Manor when I can, but there are still things I need to do for my brother here." Truthfully, he had completed the most urgent of Sebastian's requests and had planned to help more with the hunt for the traitor. Now that they all had been attacked and his own marriage arranged because of it, he was more determined than ever to find out who was behind the schemes.

Looking at Miss Stuart, he was reminded her marriage had also been the result of one of the traitor's schemes. She'd been set up for scandal, meant to serve as a distraction for the spymaster. The attacks this time had been deadly... well, they must have touched a nerve with their recent investigations.

Most of which had pointed to the Russians, despite Nathan's deeper suspicions of the French. He would need to spend some time thinking over the implications. Everything had moved like a whirlwind, and he had not had the time to re-evaluate the situation.

"Lily loves the countryside." Lady Stuart sighed. "But I will miss her."

"I am sure we can arrange visits between us. Perhaps we can have a house party. I will ask... Lily." It felt odd to use her Christian name. The idea was sound, and it would be good for his brother to see people. Sebastian would have enjoyed the Season far more than Nathan had. It seemed a cruel irony that the brother whose presence was needed on the estates was the more social of the two, and the one who could travel to London was the one who would prefer a more secluded existence.

Though, he had enjoyed his time with the Society of Sin while he was in London.

Lady Stuart snorted.

"I am sure Lily will enjoy setting up a house party," she replied, but the solemn expression and twinkle in her blue eyes indicated the exact opposite. "She does so love social events. I am sure she would be delighted to host one."

Ah. Yes. Well. Perhaps since it would be a social event of their friends. He would allow her to choose the guest list. Everyone he might invite was either already at their wedding or part of the Society, although he doubted too many of the latter would be welcome. Not unless it was an event *for* the Society, and he did not know how she would feel about those activities.

When they had more time alone, he would have to ask her how much her friends might have told her about the Society.

\* \* \*

<u>Lily</u>

Sitting between her new husband and Elijah, Lily found she was uncommonly nervous. Despite having spent a night alone together in the cottage, she had no idea what to say to the man she had married. What *did* one say in such a situation? They hardly knew each other, which was not uncommon among the *ton*. With the number of matches arranged between families, there was not a guidebook about how to muddle along once the deed was done.

She could not stop thinking about her fantasies from the night before, could not stop looking at his hands and wondering what tonight would have in store for her, which did nothing to help settle her nerves.

So, she concentrated on talking with Elijah instead, choosing the familiar over the unknown. Captain Jones... no, she should call him by his Christian name now that they were wed, no matter how odd it felt to think of him as 'Nathan.' Nathan seemed content to talk to Josie, thankfully. She was still acutely aware of him by her side, his large body taking up her peripheral vision, but talking to Elijah, she could distract herself.

A little.

"Has Evie said how long she will be staying at Camden house?" Lily asked, her gaze straying to her friend. It felt odd not to have to sneak off to the retiring room to see her, the way they all had for Mary's and Josie's weddings.

"While my father recovers is what she said," Elijah replied, turning his head so his gaze followed hers. "I mean to see she stays after as well. It's time for her to return to the family."

"Does that mean including her in the family business?" The reason Evie had disappeared was her uncle and cousins had tried to keep her out of the search for the traitor. Evie had not appreciated being left out, so she'd left and initiated her own hunt, using her friends.

Evie had also been posing as a maid at multiple households throughout the Season, something her uncle and cousins were still unaware of, as far as Lily knew, though they'd known Evie was somewhere in London. Lily knew Elijah had been searching for her unsuccessfully.

"If we must." Elijah's tone was dour, and he gave her a sidelong glance. "It seems impossible to keep you ladies out of it at this point."

"We have contributed greatly," Lily pointed out. "At least half of what you learned has been due to *our* efforts."

He sighed, which was not the same as acknowledging her point, but

Lily decided to count it as a win. At some point, the Stuarts would have to learn to let Evie be Evie. She was never going to fit into the mold of a polite young debutante.

"Do you know what is going on between my cousin and Anthony Browne?" Elijah's question surprised Lily.

"Something is going on between them?" She looked, and yes, Captain Browne's attention was on Evie whenever she was not looking at him. More interestingly, Evie's eyes wandered his way whenever he was not looking at her.

That was enough to pique Lily's curiosity. Maybe it was not such a bad thing that they would be staying in London for a while longer, even though she'd been yearning for the countryside.

"Something definitely is." Going by Elijah's expression, he was not happy but was not sure what to do about it. Well, this should be interesting.

## Chapter Eleven

Nathan "Welcome to Talbot House." Nathan led Lily into the foyer of the house. She blinked, looking around and appearing suitably impressed, as far as he could tell. She was hard to read, other than noting she seemed nervous. "This is Connor and Mrs. Potts. They run the household."

"Mrs. Jones," Connor murmured with a bow.

"Ma'am." Mrs. Potts bobbed a curtsy and beamed at Lily. She'd been a mainstay in the household since Nathan was a small child and had watched out for both him and Sebastian after his mother died and his father's vices began to rule him. Nathan had not realized how happy she would be to see him marry, regardless of the circumstances. "We would like to be the first of the household to wish you happy."

He should probably warn Sebastian in case this started to give her ideas, though she would not be returning to the manor with him. She would have to wait until Sebastian came to London, so his brother had some time to prepare.

"Thank you, and thank you for the warm welcome," Lily said with a smile.

"It would have been a better one, but we did not have much time to prepare." The look Mrs. Potts gave Nathan made it clear where she placed the blame, although he was not sure what she thought he could have done differently to change his circumstances. Still, he knew better than to argue with her. "Let me show you to your room, so you can make yourself comfortable before supper."

"Thank you, Mrs. Potts." Lily released Nathan's arm and stepped forward.

He had to make an effort not to show his disappointment. It made sense to have Mrs. Potts show her around. Likely, it would make her more comfortable. His new bride tried to hide it, but she was clearly nervous. Nathan could only assume her anxiety was over the upcoming evening and the wifely duties she would be expected to perform.

For his part, he was very much looking forward to that part of being married. His fantasies of leading her innocent body down the path to his preferred perversions and depravities had taken hold of his imagination and would not let go. Tonight, he would keep things straightforward, as she had no experience at all, but eventually…

Wandering down the hall to the library, Nathan headed for his thinking chair. This time, it was not because he wanted to fantasize more about his wife. Now that she was under his roof, he did not need to fantasize. He could indulge in the reality soon enough.

No, he needed to think about the revelations from the brunch, the thoughts he had not been able to dwell on while in the middle of social surrounds. Most notably, he needed to think over how the traitor's tactics had drastically escalated between the Stuarts' wedding and today's event.

He settled into his chair, leaning back and closing his eyes so he could concentrate.

The scandal that had precipitated the Stuarts' wedding had been well thought out and well-executed. The traitor had shown their hand more than once. Setting up the former Miss Pennyworth for a scandalous situation, using a note it appeared Elijah's younger brother had written, just as Joseph was about to propose to someone else.

It could have been the scandal of the Season had Elijah not been present and immediately stepped in to marry Miss Pennyworth. Although once she was Lady Stuart, it had not ended there. The two of them had chased down the threads from the scandal until they'd found the man who had given her the note.

Unfortunately, he'd been beaten to death not long afterward, so no further answers were forthcoming from that quarter.

So, what had precipitated these assassination attempts? Something they had discovered? Something they were close to discovering? And why had Miss Davies been kidnapped instead of killed?

*Not Miss Davies. Lily. Your wife now.*

The more Nathan thought about it, the more he realized the only possible conclusion was either she was in league with them, or there was something the traitor wanted to know from her. Which meant she was likely still in danger.

*Good thing I'm planning to keep her close.*

\* \* \*

<u>Lily</u>

Talbot House was beautiful. It was not hers, of course, but where they would be staying. On the other hand, since Nathan's brother was unwed, that made her the current lady of the house, did it not?

She was not entirely sure of her position in the household.

"This is where the captain sleeps," Mrs. Potts said, pointing out the door as they passed it. The pride in her voice as she used Nathan's title was clear. "Your bedroom is the next one. The earl's room is at the end of the hall, along with the future Countess', when he has one." The anticipation in her voice made Lily think the housekeeper was hoping that time came sooner rather than later. The older woman glanced at Lily. "The accommodations on the estate are more spacious. You and the captain will have your own wing there, and the captain made mention he would be looking for a house of his own, eventually. Likely, he would move up his search now."

Would he? Lily had no idea. They had not had the time to discuss such niceties, such as where they would live or if they would even live together.

She let out her breath on a sigh as Mrs. Potts opened the door to her room. All her things, which had been hastily packed up the day before, had been delivered and were sitting against one of the walls within the room. It was a very nice room, even larger than the one in the house her parents had rented for the Season. The décor was a bit too pink for her—Lily preferred blues and greens—but she could live with it for a while.

At least she could redo this room without having to worry she would be stepping on the future countess' toes. She would have to work on carving out a place for herself within the Jones household. Something she had not had time to stop and think about, considering all that had happened.

"Would you like me to ring for your ladies' maid?" Mrs. Potts asked.

"Oh, yes, please." Relief suffused her. Chastity would be a welcome familiarity in this sea of new and different, and Lily would be far more comfortable in one of her own gowns. Josie's borrowed wedding dress was just another reminder of how her life, and her plan for her life, had changed over the past few days.

"Thank you for the tour," Lily said.

"Of course. I have taken the liberty of preparing a menu for tonight's supper. Tomorrow morning, would you like to go over the menu for the next week?" Mrs. Potts' smile of expectation was impossible to refuse, even though deciding menus had never been one of Lily's interests. Still, she was the lady of the house, and it was her duty, one Mrs. Potts' clearly expected her to take up. Lily would not disappoint her.

"That would be lovely, thank you."

Mrs. Potts left, and Lily heaved a sigh of relief. Moving to the bed, she sat and looked around a room filled with her things, yet entirely unfamiliar to her. How odd her husband, whom she barely knew, would be one of the most familiar things in the house.

\* \* \*

*Nathan*

Supper was a delicious but slightly awkward affair. Nathan was unused to eating in the dining room, at one end of the very long table, across from someone. It made conversation a bit awkward. He'd never been one to stand on ceremony, but he did not want to disappoint the servants, who clearly felt this was what should transpire on the evening of his wedding. They wanted to impress Lily, and he did not want to spoil their effort.

However, he thought both he and Lily were relieved when dinner came to an end. With so many listening ears, he had decided against talking about his thoughts on what kind of danger she may still be in. He also wanted to question her more on what she might know and ensure she had told him everything about the questions the highwayman had asked.

Perhaps the listening ears were not such an inconvenience since such matters should probably not be discussed on their wedding night. Hardly the stuff of romance, and while Nathan might not be highly accomplished at courtship, he knew that much.

"I suppose I shall leave you to enjoy a drink," Lily said, getting to her feet. When Nathan rose as well, she froze, eyes wide in surprise.

"Actually, that is not one of my habits, though I indulge when the occasion calls for it," he said, smiling. "It is not something I do on my own. Would you like an escort to the library, perhaps?"

"Oh... I... yes... the library." Lily floundered over her words, and he realized she must have expected him to suggest they retire immediately. "Yes, that would be lovely, thank you."

Though his body was ready to jump right into bed with her, he thought giving her some time to get more used to his company would be best. They had not seen much of each other this afternoon when she had unpacked her belongings, and he was busy thinking over the implications of the traitor's actions. Mrs. Potts had told him Lily had been enamored of the library during her tour, so he hoped that would be a good starting point for them.

She did have a reputation as a bluestocking. So far, although their conversations had not been any different from those he normally had with debutantes and ladies among the *ton*, the possibility of more remained, and he was interested to see what books she would be drawn to. Perhaps they could even find something in common, though his hopes were not high.

Offering her his arm, he took more enjoyment than he would have expected over such an innocent touch.

Which reminded him of something else he'd pondered that afternoon.

"I meant to ask you, who taught you how to box?" A little smile curved her lips when he looked down at her, though the rest of her expression remained serene.

"Evie. She taught all of us to box, fence, and shoot. She was determined we not be without the means to defend ourselves if need be." The corner of Lily's mouth quirked downward as if a thought occurred to her that was not as pleasing. Nathan could only imagine she was thinking of the time Miss Stuart had spent on the streets of London after her parents died and before her uncle found and claimed her again.

It was not common knowledge, but Nathan knew because of Elijah's confidence in him. Clearly, Lily knew as well. Which made sense and also explained the closeness he'd seen between the four women. They trusted each other with their secrets, and in turn, Miss Stuart had trusted them enough to recruit them to her cause when she decided to hunt for the traitor on her own. The wisdom in such a maneuver was up for debate, but he had to admit, so far, the women had shown themselves to be useful.

"You are very good," he said truthfully. Complimenting women was part of the courtship dance he could do, and he much preferred to commend a woman on her skill at something rather than her beauty. Though Lily was beautiful, and he had noticed women expected compliments on their looks, acknowledging their activities or skills caught their attention.

As expected, Lily's smile became a little more sincere.

"Not good enough to match you," she murmured, though she did smirk.

"There are few who can," he answered honestly. "You came far closer than most." Reaching up with his free hand, he rubbed his cheek where she'd slapped him. "And you did get me, eventually."

She giggled, and the little sound was music to his ears. Yes, they would get on well enough. First a trip to the library, a way to connect with her, then they could retire, and he could indulge in his desire for her.

## Chapter Twelve

**L**ily

The Talbot House library was not overly large, but it was full of books Lily did not have at home. There was some crossover with the Shakespeare and classics collections, but her parents' library was mostly dedicated to gardening, plants, and travels, all the things they preferred to focus on. Lily was interested in those things as well, but there was only so much botany she could take, which was how she'd ended up with such a large network of correspondents.

She'd always been most interested in history, not only what had happened but why it happened. What were the motivations? What caused mass groups of people to act a certain way? Or one individual to betray everything, including their country? Not that she thought researching such matters could inevitably lead to the traitor, but she was incredibly curious about what would cause someone to take that route.

She had not expected to spend much time in the library on her wedding night.

The captain—Nathan—smiled as he escorted her into the room.

"We have a much larger library at the country house, but this is fairly representative of the collection," he said, waving his arm grandly.

"Is there anything in particular you recommend?" She was curious where he might try to steer her.

"It depends on your interests, of course, but if you have any questions, I have read every book in here."

Lily blinked in surprise, coming to a halt in her steps.

"Every book?"

"Oh, yes." Nathan flashed her a smile. It really was a charming smile, but there was something in his eyes that made it look not quite genuine. "My favorite room in the whole house has always been the library."

"Mine, too."

It felt as though there was something he was not saying, but Lily decided not to press. Letting go of his arm, she wandered to look more closely at the titles now that she had the time. Nathan stayed in the center of the room, watching her. Feeling his steady gaze made her skin prickle, but she did her best to ignore it.

Still.

As much as she loved books and loved learning from books, she had expected to be learning something far different tonight—and from a hands-on tutor, not from reading. She sighed inwardly as she looked over the titles, slowly heading toward the far back corner.

"Ah, perhaps these?" Nathan's voice cut through her perusal.

She turned to see him standing on the opposite side of the room from where she was headed. There was a tightly suppressed emotion in his voice she could not identify, but it roused her curiosity. She got the impression he had not expected her to wander so far into the shelves—especially the particular shelves in front of her. He was looking to distract her.

"What are those?" she asked, still moving in the direction she'd been headed.

"Lily." He practically growled her name.

Coming to a halt, she looked over her shoulder. There was something menacing about his stance as if he was about to spring across the room to grab her, and...

Well, what would he do then?

"Yes?" She smiled sunnily at him, very aware she was poking the beast. Unfortunately, it was in her nature to push and prod until she knew where a line was drawn. Just as she had that night in the cottage.

The memory heated her blood and made her cheeks flush. This was even more exciting since she had a good idea of where it would end... except they were married now. He could take even further liberties with her person if he chose to. The liberties her friends had whispered to her about.

Lily took another step closer to the shelves he apparently did not want her exploring.

\* \* \*

*Nathan*

His wife seemed determined to test him, and Nathan was trying very hard not to let her have the upper hand. However, he had forgotten about some of the folios in that corner.

Etchings were the least of his worries. The designs for several of his... machines... were tucked away there, the earliest models. Designs he had discarded once he'd improved them, though he kept them to see the progress of his work.

Normally, visitors would not be given free rein of the library, and until he'd actually seen Lily moving toward that corner, he hadn't remembered that there might be an issue. It figured that was where she was most drawn to, and her blasted curiosity would not allow him to distract her.

Did she want him to spank her?

*Wait... does she want me to spank her?!*

"Lily, are you already breaking your vow to be obedient?" The threat lay heavy in his voice. She was well on her way to earning a spanking on her wedding night. That had not been his intention, although he was beginning to think it was hers.

Especially with the expression that flickered across her face at his question.

Curiosity. Desire. Interest. All quickly hidden behind a mask of innocence, and all the more ludicrous after what he'd seen before it descended.

How very intriguing. Nathan could feel his palm itching, fingers beginning to twitch. He'd been anxious to get his hands on her, but now that desire was transforming, expanding to encompass more fantasies than he'd thought he would fulfill on their wedding night.

"I will be obedient when it makes sense to be." Her tart tone was at odds with her wide-eyed expression. "There is no reason I should not be able to explore the library as I please."

"Lillian, if you do not come over here, you will find yourself over my knee again."

Instead of coming to heel, she sniffed derisively.

"Seriously, Nathan, you are being unreasonable. What on earth could be here that you do not want me to see?" Before she finished speaking, she turned and pulled one of the folios off the shelf—the most recent one that had been consigned there.

Nathan sprang forward but not before it fell open in her hands.

\* \* \*

## Lily

If it wasn't for Nathan's restraint in stopping her, she might have thought she had stumbled upon proof of his family's involvement in treasonous activities, but his attitude had not been quite dire enough for her to believe that. Lily did not believe he would have stopped at mere warnings if that had been the case.

No, there was something he did not want her to see, but it was nothing criminal, of that she was sure.

When she pulled the folio out, and it fell open in her hands, she could see him moving toward her out of the corner of her eye, but she barely paid attention. She was far too fascinated by the drawing the folio opened to.

It was of a woman, completely nude, tied to a table with her legs spread. The table did not have an ordinary configuration. There was a split, which allowed for a large machine to be placed between her ankles. From the machine, a long piston emerged, with something on the end of it that was inserted into the woman's vagina.

Lily's mouth dropped open in awe and horror. Was this a rendering of one of the machines Mary and Josie had talked about? Her eyes scanned the image, widening when they came to the woman's face.

Before she could say a word, Nathan snatched the folio from her hand, closing it with a snap and cutting her off from seeing anything more.

She looked up at him, breathless and more than a trifle shocked. Towering over her, he glared down, but the threat and menace emanating from him were sexual in nature, not violent. What she had just seen had the opposite effect than he had intended. She was not intimidated; if anything, she was more aroused.

"That was me," she said, the words coming out in an odd monotone. Part of her still was unsure she had seen what she thought she had.

"What?" Nathan stared at her as though she was babbling nonsense, which sparked her temper.

Though she had only seen the face of the woman in the drawing for a moment, it was enough of a likeness, she could hardly be mistaken. She saw the same face in her looking glass every day.

"The picture! The woman... she looks like me!" Lily was not about to let him brush this under the rug. Her blood was simmering beneath her skin, her body heating in reaction.

*Is that how he sees me?*

The question was answered by consternation and bafflement on his face as he flipped open the folio to where she had been looking, then utter shock when he took a good look at the sketch she had found.

"That's... ah... that's not..." He stumbled over his words, his gaze flashing between her face and the sketch.

Lily raised a haughty eyebrow.

He had not realized he drew her face on the woman, but the likeness to her was irrefutable whether or not intended. Truthfully, it gave her a bit of a thrill. Not only to see her likeness in such a compromising and exciting position but to know she had been on his mind, even if he had not realized it.

Perhaps there was more to this marriage than she'd initially realized.

* * *

*Nathan*

How the devil had he drawn Lily's face on the woman?

This particular drawing had been sketched not long after they'd first met, but Nathan would have sworn he was not thinking of any woman in particular when he'd made it. He certainly had not realized the resemblance until the drawing and Lily were right in front of him, and he could no longer ignore it.

Some part of his subconsciousness must have been thinking about Lily when he'd been working on his latest creation.

Now, they both knew it.

Glancing at his wife, the smugness in her expression, in her delicately arched brow, made his palm itch even more.

She thought she had the upper hand.

"It does look a bit like you," he conceded, enjoying her gasp at what amounted to a dismissal of the fact. The drawing looked more than a 'bit' like her, and they both knew it. "But you should not have seen it in the first place. I told you there would be consequences."

Before she could protest, he slotted the folio back in its place on the shelf and bent over. Lily gasped as she went over his shoulder, her hands landing on his buttocks before she snatched them away with another gasp, as though the touch had burned her.

Nathan turned, giving her a little heft that knocked the air from her lungs as he carried her through the library into the hall. She finally found her voice again, though she used it to whisper furiously rather than shout—quick thinking of her since there was a good chance they'd attract attention from the servants if she yelled.

"Put me down this instant!"

"No."

The refusal was swift, firm, and he did not bother to add any additional arguments. He had warned her, she had ignored him, and now she was going to pay the price. If the servants saw her being carted off like a sack of potatoes over his shoulders, so be it. It was late enough, most of them should be in the back of the house, where they slept.

"Nathan!" Her voice was a harsh whisper now. "Put me down! I can walk perfectly well on my own!"

He applied a firm, hard slap to her rump, making her gasp and wriggle on his shoulder, necessitating another adjustment that sent the breath puffing from her lungs. Nathan grinned. This was far more fun than it had any right to be.

Who knew marriage to Lillian Davies, now Jones, would be so enjoyable?

He was looking forward to the rest of the night.

First the punishment, then the pleasure.

## Chapter Thirteen

### Lily

It occurred to Lily, as she was carted through the house over her new husband's shoulder, she may have made a miscalculation. In her efforts to determine where the line was, she did so under the assumption she could predict—to a reasonable degree—Nathan's reactions. Obviously, that was not the case.

She had expected to be spanked in the library.

An endeavor which still would have carried the possibility of the servants overhearing their activities, but they would be unlikely to interrupt. It would be embarrassing if she ever found out someone had overheard, but she was unlikely to ever know. That was completely different than the risk of being seen as he carried her through the hall over his shoulder!

And swatted her on the way!

The skirts of her dress meant the swat wasn't painful, but it turned her cheeks brighter red as she desperately tried to look around to see if there were any witnesses to her undignified position. From her limited vantage point, there were none to be seen, but she was well aware that could change at any moment. Something she had not factored in, not realizing Nathan would be so brazen!

Before she started testing where his lines were regarding her behavior and how far he could be pushed, she should have established where his lines were in general.

"Here we are."

A door opened, and she was relieved to lift her head and see semi-familiar surroundings. He'd brought her to her bedroom. When instead of setting her down, he kicked the door shut behind them and made a beeline straight for the bed, Lily began to wriggle on his shoulder.

"Put me down!" Now that she did not have to worry about someone coming across them in the hall, she had no problem vocalizing her objections again. To her surprise, he obeyed, and she found herself swaying on her feet as the blood rushed from her head. The dizzying effect was enough to make her nearly fall over.

She was not given a chance to find her bearings. As soon as he set her down, Nathan sat down on the edge of her bed and reached for her. In her disoriented state, she was hardly in a position to resist, so she went upside down again—this time over his knee, just as he'd threatened.

"Nathan!"

Her husband flipped up her skirts, and Lily found herself mentally transported back to the cottage. With her thoughts so discombobulated by her position, it felt as if her fantasies and her reality had collided, and her body responded. Between her legs throbbed, and her nipples had hardened to little points of arousal.

This time, Nathan was not deterred by her drawers. He pulled the thin fabric down, divesting her of even that bit of shield to her modesty and her bottom. Thus, when the first swat fell, it was on bare skin.

Lily shrieked, jerking on his lap, in response to the shocking, stinging intimacy. It was even more acute than at the cottage, though she would have thought a thin bit of fabric would not make much of a difference.

It turned out she was very wrong on that count.

\* \* \*

*Nathan*

The spanking at the cottage, while indicative of how Lily would react, was nothing like this.

For one, Nathan had no compunction about holding her tightly in place—as tightly as he wished—while she wiggled and squirmed against his erection. The throbbing evidence of his arousal did not incur the slightest bit of guilt on his part. Now they were married, she was his to do with as he pleased, and while he would much prefer she enjoy their activities together, he had every right to punish her as he saw fit—which made his cock ache even harder.

While he'd never thought having a wife would be a point of arousal for him, it turned out her being so completely his spurred a possessive desire within him. Holding her was even more exciting, knowing she would be going nowhere afterward, and there would be no need to part. It inspired emotions Nathan had never felt before.

He was sure of one thing—he needed to impress upon his wife the seriousness with which she should take his warnings.

"The next time I tell you to stop, you will stop, or there will be consequences. You will listen," he told her before bringing his hand down again hard on her bottom.

Lily shrieked, her legs kicking, and he tipped her farther forward, so her feet could find no purchase. She had to put her hands out and brace them against the floor so she would not fall—not that he would let her fall, but the force of gravity would make it feel imperative to hold herself up. Thus, her hands were out of the way, unable to protect her tender backside and leaving Nathan free to work his will upon her creamy skin.

Peppering hard, swift swats all over her upturned rump, he thoroughly enjoyed hearing her shrieks of outrage slowly turn pleading as her ivory skin pinkened. By the time he'd covered her bottom and begun on a second round, his hand coming down on already chastised skin, Lily was wriggling and letting out unhappy little sobs, she immediately tried to bite back.

To his amusement, she did not plead for him to stop.

He had a feeling pride was the cause for that lack, but it certainly did not bother him. He would not have acquiesced, even if she had.

Once he'd laid down a second row of hard smacks, he paused to offer her a way out. It was their wedding night, so he would consider it a gift.

"Well, my dear, would you like to apologize and promise you will do as your told?"

"Bugger off!"

So much for offering an olive branch. Nathan went right back to spanking her saucy bottom without an ounce of regret, enjoying the way her pink flesh rippled as his hand came down again and again.

\* \* \*

<u>Lily</u>

She hadn't meant to say that.

However, the utterly patronizing tone of his voice when he'd asked if she was ready to apologize and promise to do as she was told... everything in her balked. Despite the sorry state of her bottom, which was red-hot and throbbing, even more so now that he'd returned to his task, laying his hand down over already flaming flesh.

Tears trickled down her face as she sobbed and kicked, to no avail.

"I'm sorry!" she cried out, forcing them from her mouth. Pride was well and good, but that did not mean she had to be rude. The smarter tactic would have been to apologize and let him feel superior for a bit. "I'm sorry!"

To her surprise and relief, the spanking halted. His hand curved over her buttocks, his touch even hotter against her already blazing skin, yet somehow soothing. Lily could feel the press of his manhood against her side, digging into her soft stomach, a declaration of how much he was enjoying his domination over her.

Between her legs, the evidence of how much her body was reluctantly enjoying itself had gathered, leaving her slick and hot, even though he had not touched her there yet.

"Are you?" It was no surprise he did not sound convinced.

"I am sorry I was testing you," she admitted, albeit grumpily. "But I do not think I should have to promise to obey you in all things. What if you ask something unreasonable? If you had told me you did not want me to see your sketch of me, I would have known what was there, and my curiosity would not have been so piqued."

"It is not... never mind."

His aggrieved tone made her smile, despite the tears, and for a moment, she did not mind being over his knee since it meant he couldn't see her expression. So, she had found an advantage to this position. There was a moment of silence as if he was considering her words. His hand stroked her bottom, though it did not seem to be with any intent, more as though he was caressing her without thinking about what he was doing.

"You are correct. I gave you insufficient information. I suppose I was testing you as well."

Lily heaved a sigh of relief as he pulled her up, then stiffened when she landed on his lap. Sitting was not comfortable in the least. Her bottom was throbbing beneath her, pressed against his hard lap, but with his arm around her waist, there was very little she could do to adjust her position.

Sitting on a man's lap was also very odd, in and of itself. Especially since he'd somehow arranged her so her skirts were not under her bottom, leaving her bare skin against his trousers, rough against her sensitive nates. Her breasts were mere inches from his face, which made her nipples harden beneath her dress, rubbing against the fabric from within.

The myriad assault on her senses left her breathless.

Nathan studied her expression, and she stared back, trying to organize her flyaway thoughts into some semblance of order while her body was struggling to sort through the assault of physical sensations.

"I will be clear about why I want you to do something if you will promise to be obedient once you understand my reasoning." Though he sounded perfectly reasonable, Lily narrowed her eyes. Despite her throbbing bottom and her absolute certainty, she did not want to go back over his knee tonight—no matter how much some parts of her body reacted to the punishment—she would not make any such promise.

"I promise to consider your reasoning."

To her surprise, her answer caused Nathan to chuckle.

"I suppose that is as good as I am going to get for now, so I will be satisfied. One day, I hope you will trust and know me well enough to know I do not issue idle commands."

His hand stroked down her back, making it hard for her to think, hard to assimilate his words, then made it completely impossible as his lips claimed hers for the first time since their wedding ceremony. It was immediately apparent the kiss they'd shared earlier that morning was a bare shadow of what was possible. Lily's lips parted in surprise, and Nathan's tongue moved inside, stroking against hers and exploring her mouth.

She responded tentatively.

While she had been kissed before, it had not been open-mouthed. Her previous kisses had been more akin to the one they'd shared at their wedding. Intriguing and exciting for what they were, but without the thrilling invasiveness, the commanding desire of this kiss.

This kiss... all the heat that had been building inside her swirled in response, filling her to the brim with an aching need, the lingering pain in her bottom did nothing to dissipate.

She squirmed on his lap, her thighs pressing together as the need between them increased. When his hands brushed over her body, one sliding up her stomach to cup her breast, Lily moaned.

The spanking had heated her bottom, but this was akin to being set on fire.

Rational thought had flown, unable to compete with the new, overwhelming sensations that swamped her. There was no defense against them. She had never felt anything like this. Never sat on a man's lap. Never had a man's hands running over her.

She gasped when she felt her dress loosen. She had not realized he'd been undoing the ties. The front of her dress gaped, sliding down, and Lily felt her cheeks heat with a blush. Yet Nathan's kiss kept her so busy, she could not concentrate on trying to keep herself covered.

The dress slipped down, and the next thing Lily knew, she was on her feet, and Nathan was tugging her clothes from her body.

"Wait!" Her voice came out as a squeak, her hands flying to her bosom, covered with nothing more than a chemise and her corset loose and sliding down to join her dress on the floor. How the devil had he done that so quickly? "I need... I need..."

"Relax, angel, I know what you need." Nathan's voice was a husky growl, not soothing in the least. His words seemed to roll over her skin, making all the little hairs stand on end and sending a shiver up her spine.

Now that she was nearly naked, he spun her around and laid her on the bed. As Nathan lay atop her, the thin fabric of her chemise was absolutely useless, doing nothing to dampen the sensation of his hard, hot body against hers.

Claiming her lips again, this kiss was utterly unlike the one before. While their lips and tongue danced the same way, she could feel every inch of him pressed against her. Her breasts were crushed to his chest, his hard body was between her legs, keeping them from closing, and his manhood rocked against her needy pussy. Lily whimpered as he kissed her deeply, clinging to his shoulders as his hands slid down her sides, caressing and stroking, teasing before they cupped her breasts.

Kneaded.

Thumbs brushed over her hard nipples, then pinched hard enough to make her cry out.

The pain was indistinguishable from the pleasure.

Writhing, Lily wanted nothing more than to thrust her hand between her thighs and rub herself to completion, but Nathan's big body was in her way. He felt so good where he was, she moved her hips, rubbing against him as best she could. Her sensitive bottom moved against the sheets beneath her, reigniting the sting from her spanking. Even that pain was transmuted, turning into sweet ecstasy that made no sense, yet was undeniable.

She felt utterly wanton, her desire far stronger than she would have ever imagined.

Now she understood her friends' preoccupation with their new husbands and bedroom activities.

Nathan's lips pulled away from hers and began to mark a heated path of kisses down her neck.

## Chapter Fourteen

### Nathan

Keeping control of his own desires was far more difficult than Nathan had expected. He was used to the practiced, appreciative, but ultimately expectant sounds and movements of the ladies who attended the Society of Sin events. His wife, on the other hand, had no such expectations. Everything he did to her, every way he touched her, was completely new, and her reactions were genuinely startled.

It was incredibly easy to observe and mark what she liked best. Subterfuge or flattery for the sake of his ego or for her own purposes were not considerations.

Having never been with an inexperienced woman, much less a woman with no experience, Nathan was finding it remarkably educational and enjoyable. Every touch elicited a gasp. A caress was met with a moan. And a pinch with a small cry.

When he began kissing down her neck, his hands pushing her chemise up to bare her body to him, Lily whimpered, arching her back and thrusting her breasts into his hands. His cock was aching behind the placket of his pants, but he did not dare undress, not until she was ready for him. He was already struggling to keep the slower pace he felt was necessary for a virgin.

Especially since he wanted her to thoroughly enjoy the activity and be enthusiastically in favor of engaging in it on a regular basis.

Nathan had not given it much thought until now, but the idea of having a wife and a mistress did not sit well with him. The thought of Lily being one of those women in the Society who dallied with men other than their husbands sat even less well.

He'd seen how successful Elijah and Josie's marriage was, and even the leader of the Society of Sin, Rex, had settled down happily into marriage with his wife. Nathan wanted the same, even if he had not chosen this marriage or this wife. Now that he had her, he wanted the relationship his friends had.

Which meant he wanted a wife who enjoyed being in his bed.

Tonight would be crucial in assuring her future interest.

Leaning on his elbow, Nathan sucked lightly on the sensitive skin between her throat and her shoulder, sliding his hand up over her stomach to cup and massage her bare breast. The chemise had not provided much protection, but he delighted in the feel of her satiny skin against his palm, her tightly ruched nipple so easily pinched between his fingers.

Without his lips against hers to muffle the sounds, her moans and gasps filled the room. She moved beneath him, rubbing against him, and he could feel the wet slick of her covering the front of his trousers with her arousal, making his cock throb as it ached to plunge into her heated embrace.

Nathan's lips moved farther south, along with his body, so he could kiss her breasts, taking one budded nipple between his lips and sucking hard. Lily cried out and arched beneath him, her hands sliding into his hair and gripping as if she didn't know whether to pull him away or clasp him closer.

As his mouth went to work, one hand still on her breast, the other moved between her thighs to her hot, wet folds.

*  *  *

*Lily*

If Nathan's lips on her neck had been breathtaking, feeling them on her breast, the hot suction of his mouth closing around her nipple was devastating. Her senses reeled from the glorious sensation, and her pulse pounded so loudly, she could hear her heart racing, driving her utterly wild.

When fingers delved between her legs, touching and stroking her so intimately, so pleasurably, she thought she might actually die.

*La petit mort.*

The little death. That was what the French called a climax, but the ones Lily had given herself had not made her think it entirely apt.

Now... *now*, she understood at last.

Nathan's fingers moved through her soft folds, touching the little nub at the apex of her womanhood that ached and pulsed. Having his hands on her was exquisitely intoxicating, and she was dizzy with the sensations. Every part of her body was throbbing, pulsing with need.

His mouth moved on her breast, abandoning one nipple and seeking the other, leaving the first cool and wet while heat and suction pulled at the second. Lily cried out as his finger pushed inside her. Though she had touched her insides before, she had not found it to be particularly enticing and had not explored much.

Now that it was Nathan touching her there, his finger rudely pushing in and invading her, it felt entirely different. It felt like a claiming, as though he was planting his stake in her body. The finger pushed deeper, moving back and forth easily in her arousal, stroking her insides, while the heel of his hand pressed against her exquisitely sensitive clitoris, rubbing it even as he stroked her from within. The combination made her inner muscles clamp down, her body quivering from the stimulation.

"Nathan! Oh God... please..." The words began to tumble from her mouth. Until now, she had been unable to utter anything comprehensible, but as he toyed with her, pushing her closer to climax while he dominated her senses, she found herself pleading for the ecstasy she knew was imminent. This would be far more powerful, far more overwhelming than any pinnacle she had managed to reach on her own. "Please... I can't..."

Her fingers fisted in his hair, pulling, and she gasped as he ignored the tug and began moving his lips down her stomach. Using his tongue, he traced tiny circles on her skin, moving closer and closer to the curls covering her mound. Lily felt fainter with every inch he advanced.

Another finger pressed inside her alongside the first one, stretching her. Again, the pain and pleasure mingled together, making her unsure of which sensation she was experiencing.

The movement inside her, along with Nathan's rapidly approaching tongue and lips, was driving her closer and closer to the apex. Lily cried out again when, his fingers still pumping, he dipped his head between her thighs, and his lips closed around the sensitive nub of her clitoris.

The ecstasy shattered her.

The tumultuous sensations coalesced and broke apart, like fireworks lighting up the night sky—and behind her closed eyelids, she saw the flares of light. Tears trickled down the sides of her face, not from pain, like during her spanking, but from the sheer intensity of her pleasure.

It hummed along every nerve, breaking her apart and putting her back together again, buoying her on waves of sensation that ebbed and flowed until she was satiated and boneless on the bed. Mindless and unable to piece together a single coherent thought.

*Nathan*

Touching, tasting his wife, Nathan was determined to learn every inch of her, inside and out. Her pussy quivered around his fingers, the tightness of her sheath swiftly loosening as she became more and more aroused. Looking up the length of her body, he could watch every undulation, every change in expression.

Pert pink nipples wobbled on her upturned breasts as if begging to be touched, tugged, and played with. Her grip on his hair tightened as he laved his tongue over her clitoris, coaxing more sweet juices from her eager channel.

The salty-sweet taste of her arousal was his new personal ambrosia.

The sound of her breathy moans and passion-filled cries were his new favorite symphony.

Pumping his fingers, it was all too easy to imagine how her body would feel around his cock. The clench. The massage. The wet heat and delicious slick cream of her arousal coating his entire length.

Watching Lily climax as he worked his tongue and fingers on her sweet cunt, Nathan's willpower was quickly unraveling. She was exquisite. The very picture of an arousing houri, there to stir his passions and drive him mad with lust.

When she finally went limp from her pleasure, no longer responsive to the stimulation, Nathan quickly finished taking off his own clothes without giving up his spot between her thighs. He was just finishing undressing when her eyelashes fluttered, and her dark eyes opened, staring up at him.

Their gazes met.

Caught.

Held.

The head of his cock pressed against her pussy.

Lily's eyes widened. Her lips parted. Nathan pushed forward, and her eyes went even wider as he slid into her body.

She felt as amazing as he had thought she would, her cry catching in her throat as he thrust in, spearing her on his cock and stretching her open. The sensation was silky heaven wrapped around him, gripping him tightly as her muscles clenched and squeezed, adjusting to being filled as she'd never been before.

Nathan drank in the sight of her reaction, the subtle play of expressions across her face, then pulled back and thrust forward again, burying himself inside her.

* * *

*Lily*

The sensation of having something so large, so thick, moving inside her body was almost more than Lily could bear. The movement of Nathan's manhood stimulated flesh that was already swollen and sensitive from her climax.

"Oh!" She arched her back, and her hands pressed against his chest.

The muscles flexed beneath her palms, the wiry hairs rasping over her skin.

Nathan leaned forward, and her elbows bent, hands gliding over his shoulders and around his neck to hang on for dear life as he pumped in and out of her. The movements started off slow, but she could feel the repressed power behind his thrusts, the desire in his corded muscles and hard body. She felt impossibly full. Each time he buried himself inside her, she could scarcely breathe because there was no room for the air.

Her body clenched around him, increasing the friction, and Lily sobbed out her pleasure as it wound tighter and tighter inside her. Having already experienced one colossal orgasm, Nathan was driving her toward another, but she did not know how it was possible. How could she hold so much ecstasy in her already satisfied body?

"Lily... bloody hell... Lily..." The guttural groan that fell from Nathan's lips along with her name made her muscles clench again.

The movement of his hips was faster, harder, driving into her with a force that rocked her on her axis. He leaned forward, and her breasts bounced in the space between their bodies, nipples rubbing against his chest and the wiry hair rasping over the sensitive buds. Every time he buried himself inside her, his body rocked against her sensitive lips and clitoris.

She could not tell if there was any pain or if it was all pleasure. Every muscle in her body tightened, pulling taut, as he moved within her. The peak came quickly this time, a fuller, more powerful, more encompassing climax that seemed to start deep within her core and ripple outwards.

Lily screamed with the force of it, unable to bear the intense sensations in silence. Her nails dug into Nathan's shoulders, and her legs wrapped around the backs of his thighs, clinging to him as though he was her only port in a storm. She tried to hold him as close to her as possible, but he was not done thrusting, each powerful movement sending her soaring higher and higher.

Like Icarus, she was coming too close to the sun, and Nathan was all that kept her from tumbling down into darkness.

The closer she held him, the more his body rasped over her sensitive flesh. When he buried himself inside her for the final time, it drove the breath from her lungs. She could feel every inch of him throbbing within her as hot fluid pulsed and filled her as he shuddered.

When his weight came down atop her, she felt oddly protected beneath him.

Was this what it meant to be married?

## Chapter Fifteen

### Nathan

Sleeping beside a woman was not something Nathan was accustomed to, and by that token, neither was waking up beside one.

He came awake all at once, his usual way. Nathan had never been slow to wake in the morning, though the feeling of a warm woman curled up in his arms made him wonder if he was still dreaming. Then he remembered yesterday had been his wedding day, and the woman in his arms was his wife.

Also a woman he had recently suspected of assisting a traitor. Not that he still thought she was, at least not knowingly, but he was surprised he had slept so soundly beside her.

She was sleeping soundly as well, not stirring when he extricated himself from around her. Nerves were rising. What did he say to a woman in the morning? It would be easier to withdraw and meet her later once he'd had more time to think.

Sliding out of bed, he made sure to cover her up, noticing with some interest a small red smear on his cock he could not see in the darkness last night. There had been one on the bedding when he'd wiped her down with a damp cloth before she'd pulled him down and curled up against his side.

He'd only intended to stay long enough for her to fall asleep, but he'd ended up sleeping as well.

Returning to his bedroom, he realized he had not missed it. Eyeing the large, four-poster bed, he also realized he would not mind seeing her in his bed. His cock twitched at the mere thought of it, easily rising to the occasion, the way it often did in the mornings.

Last night had been her first night, and his understanding was virgins were tender after such an experience. So rather than returning to her room and waking his new wife the way he wanted to, Nathan rang for his valet and began his morning ablutions.

By the time he headed downstairs to the dining room to break his fast, he could hear movement in Lily's room, so she would likely be joining him. Anticipation, along with nerves, rose in his breast. He really needed to figure out what to say to her, but what did one say after deflowering a virgin he was now married to?

*I hope you enjoyed your evening?*

Nathan wished he could ask Elijah.

Walking down the stairs, Nathan's steps slowed as he heard voices coming from the front room. Voices he recognized, including Elijah's.

"Captain, you have some visitors." Connor bustled up to him from the other direction, his expression worried. "I told them it was not an appropriate time to come calling, but—"

"It's alright, Connor," Nathan reassured him. Though Connor was used to Nathan not being a stickler for the ton's social rules, he was clearly worried. Nathan knew Elijah would not have left his uncle's side and descended on Talbot house the day after Nathan's wedding if there was not a real need. Whatever had drawn him and the others here, it had to do with the traitor. "Can you have Mrs. Potts set some extra places at the table? I'm sure our guests will be hungry."

Connor stiffened rather than immediately running to do as he was bidden.

"Do you... will Mrs. Jones..." Connor stumbled over his words, causing Nathan to pause. Right, he had forgotten about Lily for a moment and what her expectations might be.

Oh, well. She might be angry, but Nathan did not think Elijah would blithely interrupt their first morning together without good reason.

"Do we have guests?" Lily's voice rang out through the foyer from the top of the staircase, and Connor and Nathan looked up.

Wearing a practical gown of lavender and cream, her hair done up in a simple twist, she looked every inch the lady of the house. Knowing what she looked like under the modest day dress was arousing—even though she was well covered—was like knowing a secret no one else did.

"Yes, ma'am, my apologies, but they were very insistent." Connor was still wringing his hands when Lady Stuart came barreling out of the drawing-room, quickly taking in Nathan and Connor's presence before turning to look up at Lily.

"Good morning. Sorry to interrupt your first morning as a married couple, but I insisted you would not want to be left out."

\* \* \*

<u>Lily</u>

"Left out of what?" Lily asked as she descended, trying to act normal when she was very aware beneath her skirts she was... sore. Everywhere. Her bottom from the spanking and between her legs from the lovemaking. While she did not feel differently as a person, she reacted differently as soon as she saw Nathan's eyes on her.

In truth, the presence of her friends was a relief. She smiled when Elijah, Rex, Mary, Evie, and Captain Browne followed Josie into the hall.

"We are making plans," Evie said briskly, just as Elijah opened his mouth, causing him to send her a glare. Captain Browne was also glaring at the back of Evie's head. Hanging back, he seemed more like an outsider than part of the group. Lily hid her smile at the way Elijah and Evie were already clashing, both of them sure they should be in charge. This was going to be interesting now that they were together. "The assassination attempts, your kidnapping... we must have gotten too close to the traitor to precipitate such drastic action."

"We already knew that, considering the stiff that turned up after being questioned by Elijah," Captain Browne muttered. At the sound of his voice, Evie's shoulders went back, but she did not turn or in any other way acknowledge his comment.

Yes, the man whom Elijah and Josie questioned turning up beaten to death had already been a large clue they'd gone down a track toward the truth, but they thought it had dead-ended with that man.

"His name was Jacques," Josie said, shivering. Elijah had not been the only one present when the now-dead man was questioned. The man had set her up to be ruined, though he claimed he had not known what was in the note he'd given her. Though he'd been French, he claimed he'd been paid by a Russian to pass along the note.

He'd also said he was supposed to tell anyone who came to question him that an English lord had been the one to bribe him. The only description he'd been able to give had been a dark-haired Russian of average height and weight, which could be applied to most of the visiting delegation. Nothing in what he'd said to Josie and Elijah had seemed revealing. In fact, when he'd turned up dead, they'd all assumed it was so he could not be revisited and plumbed for more information.

Unfortunately, the man who had actually attacked Josie had also been murdered before he could be questioned. They'd been left hanging in the wind... or so they thought.

"Clearly, the villain we are chasing must think the dead man told us something more useful than we realized," Lily said as she reached the bottom of the stairs, thinking out loud. Nathan stepped to her side, offering his arm, and she jolted before taking it, doing her best not to turn pink when they touched and knowing she failed.

"Exactly," Evie said with a sniff. She joined Lily on her other side as they moved down the hall to the dining room. "Which is why we must meet to discuss it. Obviously, yesterday was not the right time, and of course, the wedding had to be done as quickly as possible because of the social ramifications, but now we need to figure out where to go from here."

Lily glanced at Nathan from the corner of her eye to see what he made of Evie's declaration, but his expression was unchanged other than clenching his jaw. That could be because he did not want to be ordered about by a woman, or he was upset their first morning together was being overtaken by the investigation, or perhaps because he had gas. Really, there was no way to tell.

Truthfully, she was a bit relieved to have their friends there as a buffer since she did not know what to say to him. Last night had been a revelation that left her feeling unaccountably awkward and vulnerable. Despite the intimacy they'd shared, they were still mostly strangers to each other.

To her surprise, Nathan claimed the place next to her at the dining room table. She'd thought he'd want to sit with his friends. On the other hand, she also realized she was pleased he'd chosen to sit next to her.

They were married now, after all. It was a small thing but one that gave her a small rush of pleasure.

\* \* \*

*Nathan*

Though their guests were entirely unexpected, Mrs. Potts and the household staff coped astoundingly well, providing an abundance of food. Nathan had the sneaking suspicion they would have done so even without the guests, which would have been far too much for only him and Lily. Perhaps it was just as well they had guests.

Looking around the table as they were served, Nathan had to admit everyone's chosen seat appeared to be rather revealing. He had wanted to sit next to Lily, even though it would not be considered fashionable to cling so closely to one's wife. Since his guests were uninvited and it was the day after their wedding, he had decided to forgo caring about the social niceties.

Apparently, so had everyone else.

Elijah and Rex had chosen to sit next to their wives as well. Anthony and Miss Stuart, on the other hand, were sitting on opposite sides of the table, as far from each other as they could get, even though it left the configuration lopsided. Once again, Nathan wondered what was going on between the two of them—or had gone on—but that was hardly the most pressing matter.

"How is your father?" Nathan asked Elijah. "I was glad he could make it to the wedding yesterday."

"Improving daily," Elijah said, glancing at the footman who filled his coffee cup. "Though he is chomping at the bit to be released from his chair."

Miss Stuart snorted indelicately, shaking her head. "What my cousin means is my uncle is being a holy terror and grumpy from being confined. I will be interviewing nurses today." The young lady's brilliant green eyes met Nathan's. There was a strength of will there he did not think he'd seen in anyone other than the Marquess of Camden's. While she might be a woman, she clearly took after him in temperament.

In fact, pitting them against each other, Nathan would probably put money on her.

"Good luck with that," Elijah muttered under his breath, then shook his head when his wife elbowed him in the side. "If anyone can manage it, it's you, but I think you'll likely end up having to play nursemaid."

"We'll see." Miss Stuart had a glint in her eye that said she was more than up to the challenge.

Nathan felt sorry for whatever nurse she managed to find; the poor woman would be caught between Miss Stuart and the Marquess—the proverbial rock and a hard place.

Once everyone was served and had their food and drink, Nathan dismissed the staff, instructing them to close the doors behind them. While Nathan trusted his people, he also knew how easily loose lips could scupper the best of intentions. This conversation would be too delicate for him to risk having his servants about.

"Now that we're alone, let's go over what we already know," he suggested, and Elijah nodded.

They were in the middle of discussing Elijah and Josie's interrogation of Jacques and whether or not it was the Russians or the French who they needed to be most concerned about having a connection to the traitor—as usual, Lily insisted they should not trust the Russians, and Nathan was beginning to lean to her side based on the evidence—when the door to the dining room flew open.

Every head at the table turned, and Nathan got to his feet, frowning. He'd given a clear order they were to be left alone, which meant whatever the reason for the interruption, it was dire.

"What happened?" he asked, then blinked as a familiar face walked in after Connor.

Harker, his brother's butler, ran Brentwood Manor. He looked even older than he had the last time Nathan had seen him, less than a year ago, as though he'd aged ten years in the last few months.

"Harker? What is it? What's happened?" The words spilled out of his mouth, his brain working frantically to tell him something as alarms sounded in his head.

"My lord... I..." Harker's voice trailed off as everyone around the table gasped. There was only one reason Harker would be calling Nathan 'my lord,' the only reason he could. The reason Nathan had subconsciously known the moment he had seen Harker, the only reason Harker would have come to London. He knew before Harker even said the words, though he hoped Harker would say anything but.

"Your brother is dead, my lord. You are now the Earl of Talbot."

## Chapter Sixteen

**L**ily
The announcement stunned the room into utter silence. Of course, she'd realized by Nathan's reaction to the man something was seriously wrong, but she had not expected *that*.

Beside her, her husband fell back into his seat as if his legs could no longer hold him. His face was white as a sheet, all the color leeched from it, and he stared in front of him with unseeing eyes.

Elijah jumped up, taking control of the situation and escorting Harker to one of the chairs. The older man looked as though he was on the verge of collapse as his eyes filled with tears. Casting a glance around the room, Lily could see Connor and Mrs. Potts hovering in the doorway, both wringing their hands. Mrs. Potts was crying, big fat tears rolling down her face.

Lily's heart went out to her. She beckoned the woman to her and requested tea for everyone, which would give Mrs. Potts something to do. Looking relieved at having a task to attend to, confirming Lily's instincts for the situation, Mrs. Potts hurried off.

With Harker settled in a chair, when he confessed he had ridden through the night to reach London without stopping, Elijah insisted the man eat something. Lily bit her lip. She was not sure how old

Harker was, but surely, he was too old to have made such an extraordinary effort. Why had he not sent someone younger?

Everyone waited in silence, exchanging glances while Harker ate. Evie and Josie bent their heads together to have a quick, whispered conversation no one else could hear.

Mrs. Potts returned with the tea, and the clink of cup against the saucer seemed to stir Nathan. He sat up straighter, blinking as if coming back to himself. Reaching out, Lily placed her hand over his where it rested on the table, steeling herself in case he jerked away. Instead, she found her fingers suddenly held in a very firm grip, although he did not look at her. Turning his head, he pinned Harker with a glance, and when he spoke, his voice was oddly hollow.

"What happened?"

"That's the thing, my lord." Harker's expression was full of grief but also an emotion Lily could not define as his grief was so overpowering. "That's why I came myself instead of sending someone... I think he was murdered."

Gasps went up around the table, everyone exchanging glances. The only one who didn't look around was Nathan, his gaze fixed upon Harker. They were all wondering the same thing—was Nathan's brother murdered around the same time as the attempts against all of them?

Connected? Or an almost unbelievable coincidence?

"Whoever did it wanted it to look like an accident," Harker continued grimly, his brow furrowing, and Lily finally pinpointed the other emotion. Anger. Deep, deep anger approaching rage. "He was out for his morning ride, and Devil came home riderless. We all went out to search."

The sincere mourning in his voice plucked at Lily's heartstrings, and she tightened her grip on Nathan's hand. Even though she had never met his brother, even though she barely knew Nathan, she grieved for his loss.

"Devil would have never thrown Sebastian," Nathan said with utter certainty. Lily could not feel the same.

Why would a horse be named Devil? She could scarcely imagine it was a biddable horse. The more accomplished riders of the *ton* had a habit of choosing steeds that were not always easy to control.

However, Harker nodded his agreement with Nathan's statement. Lily held her tongue and listened since she had not known horse or rider.

"We found him by the beach, head dashed in on the rocks." Harker's eyes were unseeing, as if his words had conjured the memory and it had risen before him.

Sitting next to Nathan, so acutely attuned to his reactions, she was sure she was the only one who heard his quick, pained intake of breath at the picture Harker painted.

"We brought him home." Harker's eyebrows came down again, his anger rising as more tears glistened in his eyes. "Which was when I checked Devil over. Someone had put something under the saddle... something sharp. I found some blood on him. If I hadn't been looking so closely, I would have missed it."

"And whatever it was, was gone?" Nathan asked. His voice was turning brisker, more considering.

Lily realized he was distancing himself from the events, turning off his emotions so he could analyze the situation. She recognized it within him because it was something she so often did herself.

Harker nodded. "Most are shocked Devil would have thrown Sebastian... but they do not know..." Harker's voice trailed off, the anger rising over his grief again, the two emotions seeming to choke him. He cleared his throat. "I did not tell anyone. I did not know whom to trust. Which is why I came myself."

By her side, Nathan had gone utterly cold. Whereas Harker's rage was hot, Nathan's was cold and calculating. She could practically feel him working through the ramifications.

"Nathan, did your brother know anything about..." Now it was Elijah's turn to let his voice trail off because of the number of people in the room who had no idea about their self-appointed mission. Indeed, other than Uncle Oliver's injuries, she did not think Nathan had told any of his staff about the multitude of attacks on all of them.

"No." Nathan shook his head sharply. "He had enough duties to attend to, and I did not want to distract him with other matters." A muscle in Nathan's jaw worked. That seemed to make it less a possibility that his brother had been targeted because of the traitor, though the timing was still far too close. "Harker, you need to rest. We will pack up the household and return to Talbot immediately. I will ride on ahead of everyone—"

"I will go with you," Lily interrupted and sat up straighter. Out of the corner of her eye, she saw Harker jerk, then his gaze came to rest where her and Nathan's hands were still connected, his mouth dropping open in shock. Well, that answered her question of whether or not the man knew about Nathan's marriage. "I... I should go with you." Meeting Nathan's gaze head-on, she lifted her chin.

"I will think on it," he said, then pressed his lips together

He would do more than that. Lily did not need to ask to know he wanted to investigate his brother's death. However, he should not do it on his own, especially with a household full of suspects. More than that, he would need to attend to the duties of his earldom, which would not leave much time for investigating his brother's death on his own, much less any connection to the events here in London.

Nothing this week was going as planned, but Lily was determined to rise to the challenge.

\* \* \*

<u>Nathan</u>

If the events of the past few days had not felt real, that effect was now doubled. Nathan sat heavily in his thinking chair, aware of the others still in his house. Lily was overseeing the packing of their things, along with her friends. Harker had gone to rest. Elijah, Rex, and Anthony were still in the dining room, having some kind of discussion.

Another time, he would have been right there with them, offering his opinion, but he was having trouble caring.

*Sebastian is dead. I am the earl.*

Though he'd known he was his brother's heir, it had never occurred to him that he might actually one day inherit. Sebastian had not wanted to marry immediately, but he had wanted to marry. He'd wanted children. It had been his duty but also his desire.

Now, somehow, Nathan was living the life Sebastian was supposed to have.

Married.

The earldom.

One day children.

Hell, the way his life was going, a child could already be on the way.

And Lily wanted to accompany him home.

*Out of the question.*

There was a murderer there.

*There are murderers in London. The reason you are married is she was kidnapped.*

If he left her in London, Elijah and the others would watch over her. He could insist she went to stay at Camden House.

*Ah, yes, because Lily and her friends have shown an abundance of obedience.*

Nathan gritted his teeth as his jaw clenched and unclenched. If he left Lily here, the likelihood was she would continue searching for the traitor with her friends. With Elijah chomping at the bit to avenge his father's injuries, he would hardly be able to corral both his wife and Nathan's. Rex was useless on this matter—he let Mary lead the way as long as she kept him by her side for safety. His focus would always be on her safety first, not Lily's, and Nathan could hardly blame him.

Another time, he would have asked Anthony without hesitation, but right now, Anthony was distracted by Miss Stuart to the point, Nathan was unsure how reliable he would be.

*Besides, if she stays in London, you will be wracked with nerves, waiting to hear if something has happened to her.*

Perhaps she truly would be safest at his side—away from the hunt for the traitor, away from the organized assassins and kidnappers. There was only a murderer to contend with at Brentwood Manor. The thought made him sick, though he supposed it was marginally better than a traitor intent on kidnapping or killing her. All the staff had been there for a long time, and it was unlikely anyone else had been able to get close enough to his brother's tack to put in something sharp that would cause Devil to rear and throw Sebastian.

He was grateful Harker had the same thought and the wits to look for proof. By the time Nathan would have arrived, finding anything under Devil's thick coat would have been impossible, and all traces of blood would have been curried away. If it wasn't for Harker's quick thinking, there would have been no proof it was anything other than an accident.

Though Harker could be lying, Nathan dismissed that possibility immediately. There was no reason for him to lie. Harker had spent most of his life protecting Sebastian and Nathan from their father. Nathan trusted the man implicitly.

Yes, taking Lily with him to Brentwood Manor was the wisest course. Harker could keep an eye on her when Nathan could not. He'd been floored to discover Nathan had married but had been delighted and teared up again. Apparently, Nathan's letter to his brother on the subject had not reached the manor in time, or perhaps Sebastian had not had a chance to read it and tell Harker before he'd been murdered.

In some ways, Harker had been a father to Sebastian and Nathan, just as Mrs. Potts had often acted as a maternal figure. Nathan was glad to have been able to give him a bit of good news in the wake of Sebastian's murder.

Getting to his feet, Nathan left his chair and crossed the foyer to where his friends were gathered in the drawing-room. They knew to leave him alone when he needed time to think. As he approached, they looked up with varying degrees of relief and sympathy. Rex, who he'd known for the least amount of time, looked the most worried.

"I have decided to take Lily to Brentwood Manor with me," he announced.

"Are you certain?" Elijah frowned, concern written across his face. Whether it was concern for Nathan or Lily was unclear. They had been friends for a long time, but Lily had grown up next door to Elijah, and he'd known her since she was a little girl. "We can keep an eye on her here if you like. She can stay with Josie and me."

"No." Nathan shook his head. "I have thought it over and think it makes the most sense to bring her home with me. That will leave you one less lady to contend with during the investigations here."

"He has a point," Rex murmured, with a little twist of his lip. "Otherwise, if Nathan leaves, we will be outnumbered now that Evie has come out of hiding."

"Adam could... no, never mind." Elijah sighed. "Lily can push both my brothers around without much effort, especially if Evie backs her. I think you are right, Rex. We will have enough to contend with now that Evie is directly inserting herself into affairs." He met Nathan's gaze. "You leave this afternoon?"

"Yes, as soon as Lily is ready to go." It would take all afternoon and part of the evening to reach the manor. "Harker will join us tomorrow, and the rest of the household will follow. We will close up here, but feel free to make use of the house if you need to at any point."

"Thank you." Elijah grimaced. "Unfortunately, it may be to our advantage to have an empty house where we can gather."

Right now, they did not know who they could trust. It was a bad situation all around, no matter which way Nathan looked at it.

## Chapter Seventeen

*Lily*

L This week was bordering on the absurd. Lily had scoffed at penny dreadfuls Mary and Josie found so enjoyable, pointing out how ludicrous the situations were... and now she was living through such far-fetched events, she could scarcely believe it. Assassination attempts, a highwayman kidnapping, a rushed wedding due to scandal, then a murder turning her husband into an earl and herself into a countess. If it was not so tragic, she might have laughed, but Nathan's grief was very real, even if the series of events were farcical.

Sitting in the carriage, she looked out the window to where her husband was riding. They were moving at a fast clip—as fast as the carriage would take them. While Lily was a good rider, Nathan had insisted she ride in the carriage since they would be going over terrain unfamiliar to her and likely would be arriving after dark. She was surprised he had decided she could accompany him without a fight, so she acquiesced to his request without protest.

Their friends were staying in the capital, though they would come out for the funeral.

She could tell he wished they were moving faster, but he stayed close by the carriage as they traveled, his head turning this way and that. Lily pressed her lips together as she realized he was watching out for highwaymen. God forbid they had to go through *that* again, although she did feel a good deal safer with Nathan out there watching over their travels.

"Do you see anything, miss? I mean, ma'am... I mean, my lady." Chastity had been nervous the moment she climbed into the carriage but had insisted on accompanying Lily to the manor. Lily couldn't fault her maid's bravery, but a worried Chastity was putting herself through unnecessary stress.

"Just the earl watching over us." She gave her maid an encouraging smile.

Lily knew part of her desire to ride had been her *lack* of desire to be trapped in a carriage again. Like herself, Chastity relaxed, remembering they had what amounted to a guard traveling with them. Lily also suspected their coachman had some hidden talents. She had seen the glance he'd exchanged with Nathan when her husband had helped her into the carriage.

"He seems like a very good man," Chastity said, her eyes glowing. Lily's maid had more than a bit of hero worship, and Lily did not blame her.

"He is," Lily agreed.

With every passing hour, she was becoming more and more certain he could not possibly have anything to do with the traitor. No matter what her correspondents had said about the smuggling operation on Talbot lands. If someone had been bringing in human cargo—spies from France—during the war, she could not imagine Nathan knowing about it, much less being involved, not now that she knew him better. Whether his father or brother was involved...

Well, she would find out. Lily did not mean to let her investigations into the traitor go by the wayside. While Nathan worked to find his brother's murderer, she would continue her mission to uncover the traitor.

The thought the two might be connected had occurred to her, but she could not see how.

\* \* \*

## Nathan

By the time Brentwood Manor came into sight, lights glowing softly in the windows, Nathan's nerves were shot. He had been on high alert all day, wondering and waiting to see if they would be attacked on the road. Every dust cloud from another horse or carriage had his muscles tensing.

It was exhausting.

The sight of home did nothing to soothe him. His feelings about Brentwood Manor had always been complicated, thanks to his father. While Nathan loved the estate and the beaches, the house held more than a few bad memories. Being there with Sebastian as the earl had been better before his brother had sent him to London, but now Sebastian was dead.

Nathan had sent a runner on ahead of him to let them know he and his countess were on their way, so the rooms should be prepared for them. Nathan had specifically asked for his old rooms to be prepared. Eventually, he would have to move into the earl's but... not yet. The loss of Sebastian was still too new. Too raw. He could not sleep there. Not tonight.

He'd asked for Lily to be installed in the room next to his rather than putting her in the countess' rooms. Hopefully, she would not mind. Nathan did not think so—she had seemed more shocked than pleased at finding herself a countess. He did not have to worry she'd been a title hunter.

The household came bustling out to greet them, including Mrs. Potts' daughter, now Mrs. Moore, who had been serving as Sebastian's housekeeper while Nathan had Mrs. Potts for the London House. She looked like a younger version of her mother, with big blue eyes and the same auburn hair before Mrs. Potts went grey. Her bottom lip trembled at the sight of him, and Nathan stepped forward to give her a hug as soon as he handed Merlin off to one of the hostlers.

"Oh, Nat." Grief thickened her voice, and she hugged him back. "I cannot believe he's gone." Her husband, Matthew Moore, came up behind her. Nearly as tall as Nathan, with dark blond hair and dark brown eyes, Moore had also grown up on the coast and had been training under Harker to become a majordomo or butler, with an eye to eventually taking over the position from him. Connor was supposed to be for Nathan's household. Now they would have to figure out a new arrangement.

"Our heartfelt condolences, my lord," Moore said, opening his arms when Valerie turned back to her husband, trading Nathan's embrace for his. Valerie had been a pseudo-sister to Sebastian and Nathan after her mother had taken the two boys under her wing.

"Thank you." Aware of the carriage rolling up behind him, Nathan turned to see his wife peering curiously at the three of them. He supposed he should have probably told her about the Moores... and any number of things about Brentwood Manor. If he had ridden in the carriage, he could have done so, but the idea of being so confined had made his skin itch.

He would have to make up for it now.

Helping Lily out of the carriage, then her maid, he turned to make the introductions. Valerie curtsied and looked as if she wanted to hug Lily as well, her expression one of wonder. Lily smiled at her, but Nathan could tell she was curious about the relationships in front of her. Little wonder. Nathan would have to reassure her, out of all the people available as suspects, the Moores were at the bottom of his list, though it could not be denied, whoever had done it was someone he and Sebastian would have trusted.

"You really got married? I almost thought it was a joke when Bryce arrived with your instructions." There was a faint note of accusation in her voice.

"Matters had to proceed rather quickly. I wrote Sebastian, but..." Nathan's voice trailed off.

"Oh, he received a letter, but he waited to read it after he went for his ride, and... well..." Valerie looked away, more tears welling in her eyes. Pressing his lips together, Moore put his hand on his wife's shoulder, and she turned back into him for another bout of crying.

"We have your rooms ready for you... your old rooms, as requested." Moore curved his arm around Valerie's shoulders, bolstering her while she got her emotions under control again. "Let us help you get settled in."

*** 

## Lily

The manor's housekeeper was not at all what Lily had expected, though she bore a startling resemblance to the London manor's housekeeper. Mrs. Moore explained she was Mrs. Potts' daughter when she showed Lily to her room with Chastity trailing anxiously behind them. The housekeeper was beautiful and obviously familiar with Nathan, but Lily could not determine if she should be jealous. The woman was married to someone else, but it had been a bit startling to come up in the carriage and see her in Nathan's arms.

"Best wishes on your wedding," Mrs. Moore said, hovering at the door as Chastity unpacked Lily's things. Clearly, she wanted to stay and talk. Since Lily was curious as well, she had no objection. There was no need for her to explore the room since it was nearly a mirror to the one in London, except larger and with some additional furniture and a window seat. Since it was dark, there was no view to be seen.

"Thank you. I am sorry you were caught unawares." Lily shrugged ruefully, smiling. "I was kidnapped by a highwayman, and Nathan rescued me, but we were caught in a storm and had to take shelter overnight with no chaperone, and... well..." She made a face. "A lady's reputation is everything, even if nothing happened." The derision in her voice was clear.

Mrs. Moore appeared to be enthralled.

"A highwayman?" There was a touch of disbelief in her voice. Lily could not blame her.

"It was awful," Chastity interjected, shaking her head. Her hands shook as well as she pulled another of Lily's chemises from the one bag they had packed for her. "He killed our coachman, then took Miss, I mean, my lady. We were too far from London for me to walk, and I have no idea how to drive a carriage. Then the first people to come upon us were those awful Hatchets—begging your pardon. Thank God Captain Jones, I mean, my lord, was not too far behind them since I am sure they would have left me there on the road without thinking twice about it."

Mrs. Moore's eyes widened as she listened to Chastity's matter-of-fact recollection of events. Once Chastity got going with a story, it was often hard to stop her, and she had probably bottled up far too many of her emotions about this particular event over the past couple of days. She seemed relieved to have been able to vent some of them now.

"You did wonderfully," Lily told her, crossing the room to put her arm around the young woman's shoulders. "It was an awful situation, but we made it through."

"Unlike our poor coachman." Chastity shook her head. "It has been the most unbelievable week."

Good to know she and her maid were in agreement on that front.

"It really has." Lily sighed, pressing her fingertips to her temple and rubbing the spot that ached. "But it could have been much worse."

Uncle Oliver, Nathan, Captain Browne, Elijah and Josie, Rex and Mary... any of them could be dead right now—probably should have been—but by luck and skill, they'd come through.

"Well, I am glad things did not turn out for the worse," Mrs. Moore said, shaking her head. "I will admit, I never expected Nat to get married before Seb, but of course, as a matter of honor, he would also never let a lady's reputation be ruined if he could help it."

"Nat and Seb?" Lily asked, fascinated.

Mrs. Moore's cheeks turned a bright red that outshone her hair, then she clapped a hand over her mouth before pulling it away to speak.

"My apologies, my lady—" she started to say, but Lily shook her head, holding up her hand.

"No, no, please do not worry yourself. I am not upset at the familiarity, just curious." Lily prided herself on being observant, and from what she could see, there was no reason to be jealous. The more she saw of Mrs. Moore and her reactions, the more she was certain there were no romantic feelings between the woman and Nathan and never had been.

"They... after their mother died, God bless her soul, the boys spent a lot of time with my mother," Mrs. Moore explained. "They were like the big brothers I always wanted."

"And you were the little sister we never wanted," Nathan said, appearing in the doorway with a smile on his face. Lily was even more intrigued. It was a sad smile, but a smile nonetheless. Clearly, the bond between the two of them remained.

"Then you should have left my mother alone," Mrs. Moore retorted, causing Lily to giggle. Straightening, Mrs. Moore brushed at her skirts and graced Lily with a small smile. "I should go. Would either of you like a tray sent to your room?"

"Yes, please. Send them here. Lily and I can eat together." Nathan nodded his head toward a small table that was set up with two chairs in front of her window.

"I will have it sent right up." With another smile for both of them, only a trifle strained, Mrs. Moore whisked away.

## Chapter Eighteen

### Nathan

Now that he was at Brentwood Manor, Nathan did not know what to do first. He had rushed out to the coast with all haste, but there was really nothing he could actively do until the morning. Devil was in the stables, settled down for the night, it was too dark to visit the spot where Sebastian's body had been found, and he did not know where to begin questioning people.

Still, he did not regret coming out in a rush. This way, he could get started first thing in the morning rather than having to travel for part of the day.

"Would you like me to handle the funeral arrangements?" Lily asked, her tone subdued as she nibbled on her chicken. The supper Valerie had brought them was substantial, but neither his nor Lily's appetites appeared to be.

"Yes, thank you." Nathan looked at his own half-finished plate, his stomach turning over. Someone would need to handle the preparations, and if Lily took it on, he could focus on finding his brother's murderer. "I will send word to the vicar in the morning. I believe Reverend Darvill is still installed for the Brentwood parish."

"What else would you like me to do?"

Even though she was trying to be helpful, the question made

Nathan's chest squeeze. There should not have been anything for her to do. They should not even be here. Yet they now had an estate and manor house to run. The number of things they had to do, in addition to seeking justice for his brother, was monumental.

Nathan had not been trained for any of it because he was never supposed to be the earl.

"Familiarize yourself with the house, I suppose," he said, rubbing his forehead. While his head did not ache, it felt tender, as though it could start at any moment. "Val can show you most things. Damn, I'll have to introduce you to the neighbors at some point."

"We'll be in mourning, so they will not expect a big to-do," Lily pointed out, and the band around Nathan's chest loosened a touch. "I will likely meet most of them at the funeral. A larger gathering will have to wait."

Though he was very knowledgeable of his expectations as a guest, the rules of hosting social gatherings were not familiar, but they would be necessary now that he was the earl.

Suddenly, his marriage to Lily seemed even more fortuitous rather than being an unfortunate necessity. She knew the ropes. She'd been in London for her Season, looking for a husband among the *ton, and* would have been trained to run a household. Hopefully, that would help get them through the coming days while he learned what he was supposed to be doing.

When his friends arrived, he would have a multitude of questions for them. Rex was already a marquess, and Elijah would be one day. Both of them had been trained to the positions, so he would have to utilize them while he had them at hand, though he doubted they could remain overlong since their hunt for the traitor would take them back to London.

He already wished he could go with them.

\* \* \*

<u>Lily</u>
Nathan was a thousand miles away in his thoughts. Biting her lip, Lily tried to decide what to do. Neither of them was hungry, despite

their travels today. Being alone in her bedroom made her particularly aware of the activity they could be engaging in, but she was unsure whether Nathan would want to.

If how to behave as a wife had been a mystery to her, how to behave as a wife and countess to a grieving husband was even more so. Making arrangements for a funeral was probably within her capabilities, though she had never had to do so before. Mrs. Moore and the curate would direct her.

Hopefully, her mother and father would join them soon. Lily had hastily scrawled a note for them before leaving London, telling them of the earl's death and that she was accompanying her husband to Talbot lands.

"How do you find your room? Is it adequate?" Nathan asked, looking around as if he had just noticed where they were.

"Oh, yes. It is lovely." Plenty of space to spread out in. She was looking forward to reading in the window seat. Hopefully, the view was pleasant.

"It is not the countess' room." Nathan looked away from her. Guiltily? Sadly? Mrs. Moore had already told her that. "I am not ready yet."

"Of course," Lily said soothingly. Touched by the show of emotion on Nathan's face, she reached out to put her hand over his. "We do not have to make the change any time soon."

Blowing out a long breath, Nathan's hand turned to grip hers, fingers tightening. The sorrow in his dark eyes pierced her heart, making her chest ache with sympathy for his grief.

"Thank you." His voice was low. Husky. As though he was holding back tears.

Unable to stand it any longer, Lily stood abruptly and moved to him, ignoring his startled expression. Plopping down on his lap, she pulled his head against her breast. For a moment, she thought he would push her away, then his arms came up and around her waist. She felt his shoulders shake, his hold tightening to the point where she could barely breathe as he finally let loose his grief in her embrace.

Tears flowed down her cheeks with sorrow she had not had a chance to meet his brother, sorrow he was so alone without family, sorrow he had held himself together for so long without expressing his grief.

Running her fingers through his hair, she murmured soft reassurances, fairly certain he was not hearing a word she was saying but hoping something in her tone would break through. While they may be newly married, Lily would have to be cold as ice not to be affected by his emotions.

Her tears slowed before his, and her cheek rested against his hair, letting him hold her to his heart's content.

* * *

*Nathan*

Arms wrapped tightly around his wife, the flare of grief slowly ebbed, leaving Nathan feeling drained and oddly aroused. Likely because his wife was snuggled up against him, her fingers gently trailing through his hair. Guilt arose as well—how could he feel this way when his brother was gone? He also understood physical reactions did not necessarily align with emotions.

Right now, despite his grief, he felt very much alive with Lily atop him, touching him, comforting him. He knew he needed to return to his own room. He was feeling too raw, too emotional, to be a gentle lover tonight. The things he wanted to do to her, she could not possibly be ready for.

"I should return to my room," he said abruptly before realizing how sharp he sounded. Wincing inwardly, he tried to soften the statement. "Thank you for... your comfort." Awkward, but the best he could do under the circumstances, distracted as he was by his arousal.

Lily wriggled on his lap as she straightened, looking down at him with a small frown on her beautiful face.

"You want to return to your room?" She wiggled again, rubbing her bottom against the physical evidence of his desire, her confusion obvious. "But... I thought..." A pink blush heated her cheeks, which made Nathan's cock harden even further.

"Not tonight." Nathan shook his head. Something in her expression changed, and she started to pull away from him. Sensing he had hurt her, Nathan found himself holding on so she could not retreat fully. "I cannot be gentle tonight, Lily. I am not fully in control of myself."

"Who says I need gentle? You were certainly not gentle last night when you spanked me."

No, he had not been, but that was different.

"That is not the roughness I am speaking of," he replied, a low growl in his voice. His hands, already round her waist, tightened. Bloody hell, he was tempted. Losing himself in her, dominating her, seeing how far he could push her... but she had been a virgin yesterday. He did not want to frighten her, much less hurt her.

"You mean the kind you indulge in at the Society of Sin?" Lily settled back onto his lap, no longer trying to draw away. Her matter-of-fact question took him completely off-guard.

"How do you know about—?" He cut himself off before he could finish the sentence.

Lady Stuart and Lady Hartford... of course. He did not know why they thought the Society to be an appropriate conversation for their debutante friend, but they should know better.

On the other hand, perhaps it meant she was not as unaware of what he wanted as he'd thought.

The question was how much they had told her.

"What did your friends tell you?"

\* \* \*

*Lily*

That Nathan immediately guessed where she had gotten her information was no surprise. He was astute and very good at putting the pieces of a puzzle together, much like her.

"They told me about some of the activities. Like spanking. And your machines." Saying the words made her want to squirm even more on his lap from embarrassment, but if she was to convince him she could handle his desires, she could not balk at the first fence.

Nathan's hands stilled, which made her realize he'd been stroking her back. In her distraction and embarrassment, she had not noticed until the movements ceased.

"My machines?" His eyebrows flew up, and he blinked before chuckling and shaking his head. "Perhaps I should thank them for helping me avoid an awkward conversation."

Nathan seemed so self-assured, so knowing he felt awkward as well was a relief and a revelation. She would have never guessed he worried over bringing up something like his inventions, though when she thought about it, she could understand why he would.

"I do not want to use a machine on you tonight, Lily." His dark gaze caught hers, hungry and hypnotic, making her breathless. "I want to pin you down to the bed and torment you. Make you beg. Make you scream for me while I take you as hard as I want, for as long as I want."

The breathless feeling intensified as though her lungs had seized, her entire body clenching at his words.

"How would you torment me?" she asked in a choked voice, pressing her legs together. Her body was heating, and she was far more aware of the gentle caress of his fingers along her back than she had been a few moments earlier. Beneath her dress, her nipples pebbled into hard points that pressed against the fabric of her chemise, which suddenly felt itchy.

"I would tie you to the bed, so you were completely helpless." Nathan's gaze bore into hers, his words painting a depraved picture that roused her desires even more. "I would squeeze and pinch your breasts and nipples, suckle and bite them until you begged for mercy. Maybe use a whip or crop on them. And when I finally relented, I would do the same to your ass and cunt, until you were red and stinging all over. Only then would I fuck you, without one thought of your pleasure, using you as hard and rough as I could for my own satisfaction."

The cold, callous tone of his voice should have been a bucket of cold water over her body. What he was describing sounded nothing like what they had shared on their wedding night, nothing like what her friends talked of, yet Lily felt her body respond as if he'd whispered sweet, seductive poetry in her ear.

"Then do it," she whispered.

"You do not know what you are asking for." His eyes glittered. Hard. Unyielding.

"Then show me." Before he could speak again, Lily bent her head and kissed him full on the lips. She might be walking to her doom, but she took the path willingly. Eagerly, even. She wanted to know what it would feel like to be the woman in the picture he'd painted with his words, if the reality would make her feel the way his words did.

Nathan's hands paused as she kissed him, and for a moment, she thought he would push her away, but then his grip tightened. He opened his mouth, taking over the kiss and wrenching the bit of control she'd had away from her.

## Chapter Nineteen

*Nathan*
*He was at war with himself.*
*She wants it.*
*She does not know what she wants, and she certainly does not know what she is asking for.*
*Then show her. See if she can handle it.*
*If she cannot?*
*Then we will both know.*

Though Nathan was fond of experiments, he was hesitating. There were more measured, more scalable options for this experiment, rather than rushing into everything headlong.

*This is not everything, is it? It is one thing. And she was aroused by my words. Excited, even.*

When he wanted to try something, if someone told him he did not know what he wanted, he would never let that stop him. So why should he stop Lily? Especially when it was exactly what he wanted as well.

Pulling her more firmly against him, he shifted her on his lap, feeling her gasp when her legs parted so she was straddling him, which pushed her skirts up, revealing her legs. The gasp was a reminder of why he was hesitant—despite her bold words, her experiences were extremely limited. She did not know how much she could actually handle, and neither did he.

*If she wants to test her limits, why not let her?*

Why not, indeed.

Resolution set in. It might test his control, but even getting some of what he wanted tonight was better than none, was it not?

Letting himself kiss her the way he wanted, he claimed her lips as he slid his hands down to her bare legs. He gripped the tops of her thighs, his thumbs pressing into the soft flesh near her pussy until she gasped and squirmed, then slid back up again.

Reaching behind her, he undid the buttons of her dress, the laces on her corset, still kissing her. His cock was hard as a rock as he pulled the dress and corset over her head, leaving her half-naked and straddling his lap. Despite the hot blush that suffused her cheeks, she did not try to cover herself. Pulling her chemise off and clad only in her stockings, his wife was now otherwise naked, straddling his lap, with her body completely vulnerable to his hands.

Undoing his cravat, Nathan kissed his way down her neck as he pushed her hands behind her back and wound the short length of fabric around her wrists. He would not tie it tightly since he would change her position soon, but this would give her an idea of what it would be like to be restrained to the bed. The helplessness. The inability to do a thing as he touched and tormented her.

And he meant to torment her.

Nathan wanted to hurt her. Wanted to hear her cries of pain. Wanted to feel the hot slick of her arousal that erotic torture elicited.

"Oh..." Her voice was breathless as she tugged her wrists.

Nathan watched her expression as he filled one hand with her bare breast, thrust out at him, thanks to the way her hands were tied behind her. He had her right where he wanted her.

\* \* \*

*Lily*

Finding herself naked on Nathan's lap while he was fully clothed was oddly exciting, making her feel even more out of control. Sensual. As though she had become a wanton creature, an object of desire, which was not how she had ever seen herself. Josie had always been the beautiful one, the one whom men tripped over their feet to be near, the one who collected suitors as easily as she did poems about her beauty.

The way Nathan was looking at her, the feverish light in his eyes, made her feel like Aphrodite. Lily had always related more to Athena, never dwelling too much on beauty or physical pleasure, but Nathan made her feel like she was the only woman in the world.

When his hand cupped her breast, fingers tightening in an almost punishing grip, she gasped and squirmed even more on his lap. His other hand cupped her buttocks from behind, keeping her secure on his lap, which she needed. With her hands tied behind her back, she felt more off-balance than ever.

He watched her closely, studying her, as his fingers closed around her nipple and tightened to a painful pinch. Lily knew he was testing her, seeing if she would protest his rough handling, and she was determined not to. If she did, the road would stop here, and she wanted to travel its full length.

Despite the harshness of the pinch and the way the little bud throbbed in his grip, another part of her anatomy was throbbing as well. The sensation of pain and pleasure went straight to her core, feeding the growing desire there, stirring her passions. Running his hand along her side, Nathan slid his touch from her buttocks to her other breast, so he was tormenting both. Now she knew what he meant by torment.

Rough caresses, squeezing the soft flesh to the point of pain, pinching her nipples so tightly, her back arched, and she bit back a cry. Her inner muscles clenched, and hot need pulsed through her alongside waves of pain. When the tight grip on her nipples released, the little buds still throbbed, and when Nathan bent his head to take one between his teeth, the sharp scrape was nearly more than she could bear.

She writhed on his lap, gasping and shuddering, tugging at the fabric around her wrists without really meaning to. Being unable to move her arms added to her arousal, knowing she was helpless against him, made her even hotter and wetter.

Mouth on her breast, teeth biting and scraping against soft, sensitive flesh, he thrust his hand between her legs. Two fingers pushed into her roughly, stretching her hard and fast, and Lily cried out. This was what he meant by rough. Their wedding night, his touch had been firm but gentle.

This was wilder. Rawer. Far less refined.

And it roused her passions even more than his gentleness had.

\* \* \*

*Nathan*

Cock throbbing in the confines of his trousers, Nathan was far rougher with Lily than he had meant to be as she responded to his attentions. The little buds of her nipples had turned dark red from his pinches and nips. He could hear the pain in her gasps, yet she did not ask him to stop. When he touched her pussy, he found her utterly soaked, proof she was enjoying this as much as she had their wedding night.

Shoving two fingers inside her, he enjoyed the clench of her muscles, the way she moaned and arched. He pulled away so her nipple was stretched between her body and his teeth. Nathan refused to let go, causing her to whimper as she ground herself against his hand. Spreading his legs to force her legs wider, he felt her shifts of movement as she maintained her balance. He pumped his fingers and rubbed her with the heel of his palm, feeling her curls sliding against his skin.

This was not all he wanted to do to her.

Sliding his fingers out of her, he held the slick digits up to her lips. Lily's eyes widened as the musky scent of her arousal filled the air between them.

"Lick them clean," he ordered in a husky voice. This would not be painful, but if she resisted, he would have a good reason to punish her, and if she was obedient, it was another indicator of how far she was willing to go... how submissive she would be to him.

Her little pink tongue flicked out nervously, her gaze skittering up and down between his eyes and his fingers as she tasted herself for what he was sure was the first time. The throbbing pulse of his cock, his desire for her, surged as he watched her. Bloody hell. Innocence was not usually a draw, but there was something intensely erotic about leading her down the path of depravity and seeing her experience such perversion for the first time and gauging her reactions.

"Open your mouth." If he let her go at her own pace, they would be here all night. Lily's eyes widened, but she parted her lips, and Nathan pushed his fingers between them. Her tongue flicked the digits, licking far more productively now that his fingers were in her mouth, then she automatically sucked.

The sensation made his balls tighten as his imagination supplied what it would feel like for her to do the same to his cock. Moving his fingers back and forth in her mouth, it was all too easy to imagine shoving his cock between her lips and feeling her tongue dancing along the underside of his shaft. Right now, he did not have the control he needed for that.

Pulling his fingers away, now cleaned of her arousal, he studied her expression. Pupils dilated, cheeks flushed, lips still parted even though he'd removed his fingers... all the signs of passion remained.

He reached behind her and pulled the cravat loose from around her wrists. This was why he had not tied it tightly. He'd known the moment would come when he wanted her on her back and to tie her to the bed. His other hand ran down her back to her buttocks, squeezing one cheek firmly before he spoke in a husky voice.

"Over to the bed. I want you on your back with your hands above your head." Legs spread, too, but he would wait to give that command. First, he wanted to see if she would follow this one. Naked as she was, being on his lap was one thing; walking where he could watch her—examine every inch of her—would be another.

The realization in her eyes when she got to her feet and Nathan remained seated was as enjoyable as touching her had been. He could see her nervousness, her anxiousness as she turned and walked to the bed, her bottom swaying back and forth enticingly the whole way.

There was nothing as erotic as watching a woman willingly obey his commands, and knowing Lily had no experience with such things, that she was unsure of herself and nervous at the display but doing it anyway made it all the more enjoyable.

*　*　*

<u>Lily</u>

Modesty had been ingrained in Lily since she was young. Walking naked in front of a man, no matter that he was her husband, ran counter to everything she had been taught. Knowing he was watching her, still fully clothed as he sat in the chair, observing her obeying his order, was both exciting and nerve-wracking. Lily had never felt so exposed in her life.

She had also never been so aroused.

The salty-sweet taste of her own cream still lingered on her tongue. Just thinking about what she had done made her blush hotly.

This was something her friends had never talked about. Because they had not experienced the like? Or because it was so exquisitely intimate and simultaneously embarrassing, they could not find the words, could not bring themselves to speak of it?

Lily was not sure she could admit it to them, either.

Lying on the bed and stretching her arms above her head, she licked at her suddenly dry lips, acutely aware of how vulnerable she was making herself to Nathan, but this was what he desired. What he needed. And Lily wanted it. She wanted to learn everything, experience everything he could offer her. Her nipples and breasts still throbbed from his attentions, the little buds a much darker pink than usual and aching.

Hearing the rustle of fabric as he got to his feet, her heart pounded. What was he going to do now?

Was he going to pinch and suckle and bite her breasts some more? She had not begged for mercy yet. Or would he fetch a whip or a crop to use on them?

What did she want him to do?

Approaching the bed, holding his cravat in his hands, he bent to wrap it around her wrists, tying them together again. Lily jerked when she realized he had attached it to the headboard, her eyes widening.

Although sure she could trust him, fear trickled through her, her heart beating faster than ever as Nathan stared down at her.

One hand slid down her arm to her breast, cupping it fully and squeezing. Watching her face intently, he pinched her nipple tightly. She gasped and whimpered, crying out when he twisted it. The tiny bud throbbed painfully, and she bit her lower lip to keep from begging.

Suddenly, she was not quite as sure of herself.

# Chapter Twenty

Nathan
Sweet Lily at his mercy. Totally and completely. She wiggled as he pinched and tugged her nipple, her legs pressing together, indicating her arousal, even as she whimpered in erotic pain.

"Are you sure you still want this?" he asked, his voice low and husky as he gave her nipple another sharp pinch.

Lily gasped.

Writhed.

Looked up at him with hot need in her eyes.

Nodded.

"I need to hear the words, my dear." Nathan moved his hand to her other breast, giving that nipple a nice, sharp pinch. The original nipple he'd been abusing was now a dark reddish color, and he knew changing sides would be more painful than if he continued to pinch the one he'd already been tormenting. Eventually, he would return to it, and she would experience an even sharper sensation.

"Yes! I want this!" Lily's back arched as he tugged her nipple upward, her legs still rubbing together, twisting.

Releasing her nipple, Nathan bent to press a kiss to it. Gentle. No teeth. He enjoyed the way she tensed in anticipation of more pain, but that would be predictable.

"Good girl."

Another hot blush suffused her cheeks. She liked being called that, but from the way she averted her gaze, he was also certain she did not particularly want to like it. There were some independent-minded women in The Society who suffered from the same conflicting emotions. Nathan had always liked them the best. Toying with what they did not want to want was a dichotomy that had always fascinated him.

Doing so with his wife was even more enjoyable.

Moving away from the nipple, he sank his teeth into the side of her breast as his other hand moved back to the first nipple. Lily cried out and writhed as he sucked the soft flesh into his mouth. Nathan had never been able to truly indulge in his penchant for leaving love marks before, but there was nothing to stop him now. No need to hide it.

He was Lily's husband, and he was determined to be her only lover. He could mark her as much as he pleased, as long as he kept it below the neckline of her dress.

Nathan intended to have his fill.

\* \* \*

*Lily*

Feeling faint from the heady mix of pleasure and pain, Lily watched in fascination as Nathan lifted his head to study where he had just bitten her breast. A dark red mark stood out on her skin where his mouth had been, indents from his teeth surrounding it, starkly contrasting with the pale cream of her flesh. She sucked in a breath, unable to tear her gaze away.

It had hurt, but it had felt good, too, much like everything else he'd done to her. She could not bring herself to protest. Part of her even liked seeing his mark upon her.

The bed dipped as Nathan climbed on, his hands and mouth at her breasts, squeezing, pinching, plucking, while his mouth moved around her nipples, sucking and biting, leaving mark after mark. It hurt. It felt wonderful. Between her legs, she ached and throbbed.

Her small cries filled the air, the need in her core growing and growing, making her restless. The inability to reach down and hold him in place, to touch him, was becoming harder to bear.

Mark after mark laid down a trail across both creamy breasts, some darker than others, all of them bearing the indents of his teeth. Her breasts felt swollen and achy, her nipples throbbing from the pinching and twisting of his fingers. When he pinched both of her nipples, lifting her breasts upward so he could bite and suck on the underside of her right breast, the pulling sensation on such sensitive skin was finally more than she could bear.

"Nathan, please!" Lily tried to twist her body, which only succeeded in pulling her nipples within his tight grip. "It is too much!"

A dark chuckle rose in his throat, sending a shiver down her spine, but he released her breasts, leaving her panting on her back. The expression of satisfaction on his face as he looked down at her now-speckled chest was daunting. She could see how much he had enjoyed tormenting her.

Leaning slightly to the side, his fingers delved into the dark curls on her mound, moving downward.

"Spread your legs." The command was so compelling, she obeyed without thinking, and his fingers delved between them. Gasping as he pressed against her wet, swollen flesh, Lily snapped her legs back together, and Nathan growled, giving her nipple another sharp pinch. Tears sprang to her eyes as she made herself open her legs again, giving him full access to what was between them. Nathan's eyes met hers. "You are enjoying this, darling. You are soaked."

Lily bit her lower lip to keep from whimpering as he stroked his fingers around her clitoris but did not actually touch it. Her hips lifted, seeking the stimulation her body craved.

Instead of giving her what she wanted, Nathan pulled his fingers away and spanked her. Right there. On her sensitive lips and clit. Lily shrieked, pressing her legs shut as the sensation throbbed and pulsed through her, the exquisite agony swirling inside her.

She could have told him enough, could have asked him to stop, but she was afraid if he did, he might never start again... and she wanted more.

"Turn over, sweetheart." Nathan helped her with the awkward maneuver, but she could not look him in the eye. Being on her knees with her hands stretched out was something of a relief. Her facial expressions were hidden, and her breasts were somewhat protected from his attentions. They hung down, nipples brushing against the sheets whenever she shifted, but no longer an easy target.

Now, she was sure, it was time for her bottom to take the brunt of his darkness.

\* \* \*

*Nathan*
The small whip, Nathan decided as he looked at the beautiful target Lily's arse presented to him. Between her curved cheeks, her swollen pink pussy was glossy with her arousal. Nathan ached to be inside her, but he wanted to whip her a little first. Turn that pretty bottom pink before he watched it bounce while he rode her from behind. He would be able to do the same to her cunt without worrying overly much about hurting her.

His Lily was a bit of a masochist.

Who knew debutantes could have such hidden layers? Of course, debutantes eventually turned into married women and spinsters, some of whom ended up at The Society of Sin, so perhaps it was all part of nature's course.

Though, by the time they joined The Society, the women were at least somewhat experienced. Membership was by referral only, which meant they had to meet and bed someone who thought they deserved an invitation. Lily, on the other hand, was a complete innocent.

She had no idea the things he could—and would—do to her.

No matter what her friends had told her, her imagination could only take her so far. She could not—would not—know how anything felt, physically or emotionally, until it happened to her.

The power he felt was immense.

Fetching the small whip with its soft falls of leather, each only about a foot long, he returned to the side of the bed where Lily obediently knelt. Her back was curved, breasts hanging down, bottom in the air. With her head turned to the side, he could see the almost dreamy expression on her face.

An expression he recognized from his time at The Society.

She truly was enjoying herself.

Snapping out with the whip, he brought it down on her upturned buttocks, enjoying the flash of shock across her face.

The soft leather would sting but would not truly hurt until he used it on her pussy. A quick little sting, more like a massage, was all she would feel on her bottom. Nathan had no hesitation bringing it down, again and again, keeping one eye on his wife as she moaned.

Her hips lifted as though she was offering her bottom for more punishment, and Nathan smiled.

Perfect.

Turning her alabaster skin a pretty rose pink was no hardship.

* * *

*Lily*

The whip felt nothing like she had imagined.

Far better than the spanking, it was more pleasure than pain, the sting highly erotic as the ends of the whip danced over her skin. She could feel her bottom warming pleasantly, the same warmth trickling through her and heating her core.

"Oh..." Turning her head, she pressed her face against the bedsheets, closing her eyes and shuddering as Nathan whipped her. She had imagined something much harsher.

Perhaps even felt a trickle of disappointment, it did not hurt more.

The ends snapped against her pussy, and she cried out as her body jerked upward.

That sting hurt *far* more, landing against such tender flesh. The warmth was more like a flame licking at her, the sting sinking deeper with a stronger bite.

Yet it did nothing to temper her arousal.

Again the whip snapped against her sensitive nether lips, then again... and again, leaving her confused as to what sensation she was actually feeling. The craving, the burning, the pain were all melding together.

She was sinking into the sensations, drowning in them. Everything burned. Everything throbbed. The desire growing inside her was pulsing, shoving out every other consideration.

Just like before, her thoughts were being scattered to the four winds. With so much stimulation, so many things to feel, she could not concentrate enough to think, to question.

By the time she felt the bed dip behind her and realized Nathan's intentions, it was far too late to stop him, even if she wanted to. Bent over before him, she felt him press into her from behind, like his stallion to her mare. The stretch of her body to accommodate him was intense.

Hands gripped her hips as he slid into her from behind, pulling her back when he thrust. Lily cried out as he filled her, her body clenching around him. His body slammed against hers, against her throbbing bottom and pussy lips, adding another layer of pain to the pleasure. Her fingers dug into the bedsheets, and she gasped and moaned.

He began to thrust, and her breasts swayed, nipples dragging over the bed beneath her, body pulsing around him. Lily sobbed out her cry and shuddered. Her toes curled, the intensity of the ecstasy more than her body could bear, and all of her muscles tensed.

"Nathan!"

A slap landed against her bottom, already sensitized from the whipping, and she screamed as her orgasm slammed into her, crashing through her body. If it was not for his other hand on her hip, she would have collapsed onto the bed beneath her, unable to hold herself up.

\* \* \*

*Nathan*

Another hard slap against Lily's bottom made her clench around him, her inner muscles squeezing his cock as he rode her. The pink flesh of her bottom rippled every time he slammed into her, and his handprint stood out even starker, brighter, on her skin.

"Nathan!" She screamed his name again, then she sagged beneath him.

Leaning forward, he reached under her to grip her breasts, and she screamed again, spasming around him, bucking beneath him as he closed his fingers around her sore breasts. Though he did not pinch her nipples, exactly, her nipples were between his fingers, and he knew she would be feeling it.

The angle made her cry out again, and Nathan felt her reaction. Thrusting deeper, harder, he gave himself over to his desires, letting himself fuck her as roughly as he could while she shuddered in glorious climax. His own desires finally reaching their peak, he buried himself inside her as deeply as he could, pulsing inside her and filling her with his seed.

# Chapter Twenty-One

*ily*

L Waking up sore and alone was quickly becoming one of Lily's least favorite things in the world. Scowling at the empty pillow beside hers, which was still indented from where Nathan had slept, she wondered when he had snuck out. In the middle of the night to finish sleeping in his own room? Or early this morning to get to work, leaving her resting while he was productive?

Either way, she disliked it.

Sighing, she made herself get up and ring for her maid before taking stock of her body. Donning a chemise before Chastity arrived and could see the marks covering her breasts was a must. Lily rather enjoyed looking at them but did not particularly want anyone else seeing them.

It was something best kept private.

At least, as private as she could.

She was still not sure she would tell her friends about them.

It had not escaped her notice that every mark was carefully placed below where even the lowest neckline would fall. Something she was quite thankful for.

Chastity came in while Lily was looking over the options of her gowns. Should she be in full mourning? Yes. Likely. Though she had never met Nathan's brother, she was the countess now. Full mourning would be the most appropriate, and she certainly did not want to get off to a bad start with the staff or the neighbors. Which meant she would need to find a seamstress as soon as possible.

"Good morning." Chastity was cheerful as she threw open the curtains to the large window. "Oh, how lovely."

Curious, Lily walked over to see the view Chastity had just revealed. It was indeed lovely. The room looked out over a small patio with flowers surrounding it and a large lawn that led down to the woods. Quite picturesque. Lily would enjoy sitting on the window seat and reading when she had the time.

"Very nice." For as long as it lasted. Nathan was not ready to move into the earl's rooms yet, but eventually, they would need to. "I shall have to go exploring. Do you know if his lordship is about?"

Shaking her head, Chastity moved to the large wardrobe.

"His lordship was up early this morning and has already gone riding along the coast with Mr. Moore." Chastity glanced at Lily when she tensed. The idea of Nathan riding where his brother had been thrown from a horse... She was sure he would have checked his mount over carefully, but it was still unnerving. "I believe he wanted to see where his brother was found."

"Of course." Yes, he would want to see that. Need to. Chastity and most of the staff did not know the previous earl had been murdered, and Lily meant to keep it that way for now. Though she trusted Chastity and her maid had never been much of a gossip, the least said the best. "Will you bring me a tray in here? I think I would like to break my fast before dressing."

She had very little in the way of dark clothes, certainly nothing for mourning, so she needed to search through her wardrobe for the most appropriate outfits. Any neighbors dropping by unexpectedly today would be understanding, but only for a few days. She should send a note to her mother... and her friends, in case the first note did not reach her mother in time.

Lily was already making a list in her head of what needed to be done today for the funeral. She would also need to make time for her investigation.

* * *

*Nathan*

The smell of salt in the air as they approached the coast did not have the same calming effect Nathan normally associated with it. He was not surprised when Moore led him to the rocks along the beach. He and Sebastian had always enjoyed riding on the beach and sitting on the rocks, watching the waves.

Anything to get them out of the house and away from their father. As the heir, Sebastian had had it even worse than him. Their father's demands for 'the spare' had mostly been that Nathan stay out of trouble and out of his way. Sebastian, on the other hand, had received their father's full attention when the earl was home.

That Sebastian had been killed at the place that had given him the most peace made his death even more tragic.

"Right over here, my lord," Moore said, turning his horse's head. Foxglove, a bay gelding getting on in years, went easily. While Nathan and Sebastian preferred more challenging mounts, Foxglove was a good choice for riders with a more uncertain seat.

The last time Nathan had been home, he did not remember Moore riding. Clearly, he had been working on all his skills as he trained under Harker. On the Talbot estates, especially the coastline, there were many nooks and crannies where a horse was required that a carriage or even a curricle could not reach.

On the other hand, he could not help but wonder if that would make Moore a suspect. Did Moore know about the tampering of Sebastian's saddle?

In a state of shock, Nathan had not questioned Harker as thoroughly as he probably should have before leaving. Still, Harker should be arriving at Brentwood Manor sometime today or tomorrow morning, then he could ask more questions.

He hoped Moore did not need to be a suspect.

It would break Valerie in more ways than one.

Following Moore past the craggy rocks, Nathan reined Merlin in when Moore came to a halt and swung his leg around, dismounting from Foxglove. Following suit, Nathan gripped Merlin's reins and led him forward.

"Right there." Moore's eyes were dark, sad, as he nodded at some of the larger rocks. Unfortunately close to the ocean, the tides had likely scoured clean any evidence that might have been left behind.

On the other hand, Nathan was glad he did not have to see his brother's blood.

"Here, take Merlin." He handed the reins over, leaving Moore with a horse to each hand, so Nathan could get a better look. Walking nearer the edge of the sea, Nathan turned and looked around. The cliffs behind them, overlooking the spot, had rocks along them as well. It would be very easy to hide up there.

There were many hiding spots along the coast. Quarries and caves dotted the landscape. This was smuggling territory, after all.

Nathan vividly remembered his own runs with the smugglers in the area. Most of the operations would have died down after the war, as trade resumed, but for a while, there had been a thriving team. Mostly lace, brandy, and tobacco, all of which were easy to appear to look legitimate.

While the excise men would not approve, joining a smuggling gang's runs was practically a time-honored tradition for the lords along the coast during times of war. Even Nathan's father had not tried to stop him and Sebastian from joining in, though he'd curtailed any other activity that involved them actually mingling with anyone in the lower classes. Valerie had been very careful never to be seen by the old despot for more than one reason.

"Can you describe how he was found?" Nathan asked, turning back to Moore. Unsurprisingly, the other man hesitated. It was not a common question, but Nathan was not a common man. He had seen enough death when he was overseas to last a lifetime and enough injustice to know he could not stand another. "Where was his head?"

"Ah, feet nearly at the sand, head up that way." Moore jerked his own head upward, using his chin to indicate the area. Nathan turned and looked, cocking his head this way and that, ignoring the tightening of his chest as he pictured the scene.

Devil and Sebastian must have had their backs to the rocks, but what would have made Devil rear? There was nothing around here but sand, waves, and the rocks upon which Sebastian had been thrown.

Nathan's gaze was drawn back to the cliff.

Someone could have easily stood atop there and done something to startle Devil. Like throwing a rock. Or shooting at them.

Lips pressing together, Nathan wondered if he would ever know the full truth.

\* \* \*

*Lily*

Letters written, Lily glanced down at her dark green damask and grimaced. It was the best option she had under the circumstances, but she hoped someone could bring her something more appropriate. If not, perhaps there would be a shop in one of the nearby villages.

When her husband returned, she would ask him. Or perhaps Mrs. Moore. She should have thought of that before sending the woman off to hunt down linens for the guests who would be arriving, but that was important, too. She was juggling multiple balls at the moment.

One of which should be trying to find out more about the smuggling operations on Talbot lands and whether any of Nathan's family had been involved in smuggling more than cargo.

Leaving her room, Lily glanced about, but there was no one in the halls. Presumably, the household was readying for the guests that would soon descend. Her family, her and Nathan's friends, and some of his cousins would likely be coming in for the funeral.

They would need to arrange a viewing as quickly as possible. If those coming from London arrived tomorrow, the viewing could be held the day after and the funeral the day after that. Doing the mental calculations in her head of everything she would need to do before then, Lily made her way to the earl's study with only one wrong turn.

As there was no one in the hall and no one knew when her husband was expected back from his ride, Lily had no reservations about letting herself into the room. Closing the door behind her, she took a moment to look around. Yesterday she had not gone inside when Mrs. Moore had pointed it out on the tour of the house.

In the center of the room was a large desk facing the door she had just come through, which meant one's back would be to the large picture window on the opposite wall. However, there were two armchairs arranged, so one could sit and enjoy the view if they so desired. Two smaller chairs were set in front of the fireplace on her left. The entire right wall boasted shelves covered in books, which immediately attracted Lily's interest.

Duplicates to some of the books in the library or an entirely new collection? Her fingers already itched to find out.

That would have to wait. Nathan had already been gone for at least two hours. What his schedule would be, she was not sure, but she did not want to waste this opportunity. Once their guests began arriving, it would be much harder to find the time to go through anything.

She also did not want him to find, then hide evidence of his family's involvement with treachery. While the impulse would be understandable, it would not be helpful to their investigations.

It was better if she was the first to find anything that might be there.

Scanning the room, Lily decided to start with the desk. There were papers still atop it, and it only took a quick glance to know Nathan had not touched them. The first letter in the center of the desk was addressed to Sebastian and appeared to be from Lord Gabriel Warwick.

Quickly reading it, it seemed Lord Warwick was answering some of Sebastian's questions about import/export from the coast. The letter was marked from London. Import/export... could be code for smuggling or could refer to legitimate business. Something for her to look into.

Lily put it back where it had been.

Another envelope on the desk was addressed to Sebastian from Nathan, likely the notification of their impending wedding. Lily's heart ached. She could all too easily imagine Nathan's brother setting the letter aside to be read and enjoyed after his ride... except he never got the chance.

Quickly shuffling through the rest of the papers on the desk, she did not find anything particularly noteworthy, just the usual correspondence of a gentleman of a certain position. To be thorough, she opened all the drawers, checking their contents with as much speed as she could while checking for any hidden compartments. At some point, she would need to search the earl's rooms, but that would likely be easier than the study as her room should be attached to the earl's bedroom once she and Nathan made the move.

"Ah-ha!" Sliding her fingers along the underside of the center of the desk, where one's legs would be when seated, she found a small catch. Opening it only took a moment. A panel dropped down, and a single piece of paper slid onto her lap.

Lily stared at it. A hidden piece of paper? It must be important. The question was whether it was related to what *she* wanted to know.

Putting the panel back, she got to her feet and placed the paper on the desk. A long list of names, with Matthew Moore's at the top, covered it. All men's names. A total of about twenty, the first eight of which had been crossed off. None of the names were familiar to her, which was not surprising, but there was also no indication of what any of it might mean. Her gut was telling her the list was important, even if she did not know why.

Tapping her fingers on the desk, staring down at the list, she did not immediately hear the footsteps approaching the door—and by the time she did, it was too late.

## Chapter Twenty-Two

Nathan "What the devil are you doing in here?" Nathan stared at his wife, who jerked up from where she'd been bending over Sebastian's desk. His desk now.

Wearing a dark green dress that was not quite dark enough to be the true black of mourning, if she had not been in Sebastian's study—his study, dammit, he was going to need to get used to that—where she had no good reason to be, he would have been touched by the gesture. On the other hand, that was Lily, very proper in most of what she did.

However, her expression was one of guilt, a naughty child caught doing something they were not supposed to be doing.

Quiet fury built in his chest. He had just gotten to the point where he thought Lily was trustworthy, that perhaps she was a dupe or innocent of any treacherous activity, and here she was in his brother's—his—study, looking at whatever was on his desk.

"An explanation, Lily, now," he growled, striding forward to see what she was looking at.

Her fingers reached forward as though she was going to snatch the paper off the desk before she caught the look on his face and pulled them back.

Nathan grabbed the piece of paper and lifted it, frowning as he saw the list of names. Moore was at the top, along with several other members of the household staff. All of them had their names crossed out. The rest of the list was made up of men he recognized from when he'd been running with the local smuggling gang. Only the leader, Thom Pennyworth, had been crossed off the list.

"What is this? Where did you get this from? This was not here before." Nathan jerked his head up, glaring at Lily. Before his ride this morning, he had stopped by the study and had looked at the correspondence on his brother's desk. Seeing the unopened letter he'd sent to Sebastian, he had immediately retreated. The list had certainly not been present then, or he would have noticed it.

For the first time, Lily seemed to lose some of her nerve. Her eyes widening in surprise, she glanced down at the desk, then back at him, her pink tongue darting out to wet her lips. Guilt was in every line of her body. Whatever she'd been doing, however she'd found the list, it was clear she did not think he would approve.

"Lily." The desk was between them, but it would not offer much protection if he decided to make his way around it. The idea of bending her over the desk and spanking her held a certain amount of appeal.

Straightening, Lily lifted her chin.

"I ran out of paper when I was writing my letters and went looking for more," she said so dismissively, if he had not seen her previous expression of guilt, he would have thought he was perhaps overreacting.

Unfortunately for her, he had seen her guilt and her fear and did not believe a single word out of her lying mouth.

*  *  *

*Lily*

Blast her husband's timing.

And damn her for not paying more attention to the sounds in the hall.

Though, to be fair, it was not as though she had experience sneaking around and playing sleuth. Evie would be disappointed in her, but she was doing the best she could under the circumstances.

"You ran out of paper." The flat tone indicated he did not believe her for a moment.

"Yes." Lily knew she had already given herself away, so she wasn't sure why she was still attempting to dissemble. "I happened to draw this list from one of the drawers while I was searching for more." Lily made her countenance as innocent as possible, blinking at Nathan with wide eyes. "What do you think it is for?"

Mobile lips flattened into a thin line as Nathan stared at her. Lily would not be surprised if he was tapping his foot on the thick rug, even though she could neither hear nor see it. He was not amused by her current tack. Strangely, that made her feel better, not worse. Where the impulse to prod him came from, she did not know, but it was difficult to shake now that it had dug its hooks into her.

"I think you had better become acquainted with the truth of your own accord because if I have to motivate you to use it, I will." Nathan's voice was low, deadly, his arms crossing over his chest.

Despite her bravado, Lily felt the urge to hide under the desk. Or run past him into the hall—if she could make it that far. Her bottom tingled in warning, anticipating what he was most likely to use for motivation.

Perhaps she could get away with a partial truth?

"I was thinking of helping you investigate your brother's murder," she said quickly. That was certainly one of her aims. That she suspected his brother, or someone in the household, might have something to do with the traitor they were also hunting was not something she wanted to disclose at the moment. He was already angry enough. "I came in to search his desk and see if I could find any clues."

The way his eyes narrowed did not tell her much about whether he believed her claim.

"I see. You did not think to discuss this with me first? I thought your day would be taken up making the arrangements for the funeral and preparing the household." The accusation in his tone was less about her duties and more that he felt she'd lied to him.

Here, at least, she was on more solid ground.

"Mrs. Moore has everything well in hand for the moment, and there was nothing further I could do. Of course, I expect to be exceptionally busy shortly, which is why I thought to search today." Heart pounding in her chest, she watched his expression and the cool calculation behind his eyes, trying to determine if he believed her. She pressed her damp palms against her skirts.

"I see," he finally said, and Lily nearly sagged with relief. "While I appreciate you want to help, the best thing you can do right now is to take over the household and ensure everything is running smoothly and will be ready for our guests and the funeral. Leave the investigations to me."

Not surprising since he had not wanted her and the other ladies to be involved in the hunt for the traitor either, but by now, he should realize how helpful they could be. Now that she was his wife, it was her duty to help him.

Even if she had been looking to see if she could find evidence against his family.

A tiny trickle of guilt threaded through her indignation, but it did not stop her from putting her nose in the air in reaction to his edict.

"If that is what you wish," she said frostily, wrapping an icy demeanor around her as she stalked out of the room. Nathan did not follow her, thankfully. The complicated mix of her emotions was already hard enough to bear; she certainly could not explain them to him.

Retreat was the best tactic.

"Lily?" Nathan called after her.

She paused in the doorway, looking over her shoulder, but he was not looking at her. He was staring at the list as he stood next to the desk. Lily's heart went out to him. Perhaps she should be more forgiving. He was dealing with an awful lot right now.

"Please send Mr. Moore to me."

Lowering her head in a nod, Lily swept out the door, heart pounding. For a moment, she'd thought he was going to call her back to spank her.

There was a small part of her disappointed he had not.

*There is something very wrong with me, and I should examine that impulse when I have the opportunity.*

\*\*\*

*Nathan*

Though he was fairly certain his wife had just lied to him, Nathan decided to let it go. For now.

He could have tried to spank the information out of her, but he thought he would learn more if he let her go on her merry way, thinking he'd believed her lies. Besides which, she was stubborn enough, he was not certain he could spank her hard enough to loosen her tongue.

Lastly, finding out more about the list was more important than what his wife was up to.

He easily recognized his brother's hand, and given a moment to think, his brother must have been investigating something. Something to do with members of the household and the smugglers. Was it possible this list was part of the reason he'd been killed?

Sitting down in the chair, which felt very odd since he'd never been behind the desk before, Nathan frowned as he looked over the list again. What did the crossed-out names mean?

He hoped Moore could tell him.

He should wait till Harker arrived, but the urge to do something was running hot through his veins. This morning's visit to the spot where Sebastian died had stirred more than grief in his breast—he was determined to find out who had killed his brother and why. There was no way he could be comfortable stepping into his brother's shoes without also meting out justice to Sebastian's murderer.

A knock on the door made him look up.

"My lord, you called for me?" Moore hovered in the doorway, looking unsure of himself. They had parted ways less than half an hour ago, so Nathan could understand why the man was wondering why he had been summoned again so soon.

"Moore, come in, please, and shut the door behind you." Nathan flattened the list on the desk, watching as Moore did as he commanded, then came to the front of the desk, standing at attention.

Only then did Nathan realize how uncomfortable he found the positioning. His father had always liked to sit while Nathan and Sebastian were forced to stand and be lectured. Apparently, Sebastian had decided not to change that part of the study's layout, but it would not do for Nathan.

He would get some chairs to place there, like the Marquess of Camden had. Far more comfortable. Though he supposed he could move himself and Moore to the chairs looking out the window, he would feel obligated for a longer conversation if he did so, and he was not yet sure one was necessary.

"Do you know what this is?" he asked, tapping his finger against the list.

Moore leaned forward, his eyes widening as he saw what Nathan was pointing to.

"Yes, my Lord, that's your brother's list. He was investigating..." Moore's coughed into his hand, seeming perturbed.

"Investigating what?" Nathan's tone was short. "I need to know, Moore, no matter how indelicate a matter. This list could be the reason for his death."

Moore's face paled, and he blinked before slowly nodding.

"Yes, my lord, I could see how that would be very possible." His voice lowered. "Your brother was investigating the possibility your father smuggled in spies from France during the war."

Nathan's chest seized.

\* \* \*

<u>Lily</u>

*My God, I was right...*

Crouched next to the keyhole, Lily fervently wished she had not been correct. The sudden foreboding silence on the other side of the door made her long to rush in and comfort Nathan again, though she doubted he would accept it.

He would not like the evidence she had been listening at keyholes.

"Yes, I can believe that of my father." Nathan's voice was so low, so strained with emotion, she barely heard him. "That would explain a great deal about his financial situation."

How awful to know that while he was away fighting for his country, his own father was assisting the enemy. Likely putting Nathan in even more danger. What kind of father had the late earl been?

Anger suffused Lily, but she pushed it back down. It was not as if the man was alive for her to vent her fury upon.

"I take it the crossed-out names have been removed from the suspect list?"

"My understanding was they were the men your brother had spoken to, my lord," Mr. Moore said apologetically. Though his voice was soft, it was clearer and easier to understand than Nathan's, which had turned gravelly. "He kept notes on his interviews with all of us, but I do not know where he kept them."

Interesting.

Something else to look for.

As loathe as she was to leave her spot by the keyhole, Lily decided to depart. That was plenty of information, and it did not sound like Mr. Moore knew very much. If Nathan caught her listening at the door, she did not like her chances of talking her way out of trouble again.

Getting to her feet, Lily hurried down the hall as quietly as she could, careful to stay in the middle of the carpet. She hoped her friends arrived this afternoon because doing this all on her own was not her forte.

## Chapter Twenty-Three

*Nathan*
Betrayed by his own father. It was not the first time. His father had always been a rotter, though the fact he'd betrayed his country while it was at war... all for money... unfortunately was far too believable, considering how often his father ran through his funds.

It explained why the estate had not fallen into a state of disrepair during his tenure.

That did not excuse his father's actions. Nathan knew without asking, it would have been Harker and Mrs. Potts who used any money that came in for the estate. He did not doubt for a moment they did not know where the money had come from, though he would still need to question them. That they had managed to wrest any money from his father's control to keep the estate going was a minor miracle—though his father had often been generous when he won at the races. Unfortunately for the estate's coffers, winning had been a very rare occurrence.

Passing off payoffs from France as winnings from his gambling would be very like his father.

Dropping his head into his hands, Nathan stared at the list in front of him. He would need to start at the beginning—well, start with the name under Moore's—and work his way through it. Retrace his brother's steps, as it were.

A knock at the door had his head jerking up. The door opened to show Moore standing there, an expression of worry and sympathy on his face.

"My lord, your guests have begun to arrive. The Countess' parents are here."

Wonderful. Nathan gritted his teeth. He had not realized how much time had passed while he sat in the study thinking.

"Thank you, Moore. I will be down momentarily." As soon as Moore closed the door behind him, Nathan opened the secret panel under the center of the desk and slid the paper into it. The desk had been built for his great-grandfather, and family lore said he used to hide notes from his lovers there.

Nathan did not know if anyone had used it since, but Sebastian had shown it to him after their father passed on the knowledge to him. It was only supposed to go from heir to heir, but, in a fit of caution, Sebastian had felt the need to share everything he could while Nathan was his heir. Neither of them had expected Nathan to need it, but Sebastian never liked leaving anything to chance.

Now that Nathan was the earl, he supposed he should get started on providing an heir for the earldom as soon as he could. Not that he and Lily had made a bad start of it, but he could not imagine any of his cousins inheriting the title. As far as he was concerned, none of them were suited for it. Robert, who was currently Nathan's heir, had the same penchant for gambling Nathan's father had. He did not trust Robert would take care of the staff or the estate.

Another thing that he now needed to worry about.

Tucking the list safely away to be dealt with later, Nathan left the study to greet his in-laws, hoping his friends would not be far behind.

\* \* \*

*Lily*

"Well, you are looking well." Lily's mother smiled benignly, then leaned in, lowering her voice. "I trust your marital duties were not too onerous then."

"No, Mama, thank you." Suppressing her eye roll, Lily stepped back and gestured to Mrs. Moore. Trust her mother to bring that up immediately. Her mother's explanation of 'the act' had been given to Lily years ago when the mares were breeding. Her mother had not seen fit to expound upon it before Lily's wedding night, to her relief. Sometimes, her mother's matter-of-factness was a blessing, and other times, it was a trial.

"Beautiful house." Her father was looking at the décor, wandering toward the drawing-room. "Is there a library?"

"A very fine one. Would you like to see your rooms first?" Lily was unable to keep the smile from her lips. Her parents never changed, and she would never want them to. In many ways, they did not fit in with the *ton*.

"Yes, please. I went to Jay's this morning and purchased some items for you," Lily's mother said, and Lily nearly sighed with relief. Jay's on Regent Street had a large selection of ready-made clothing for mourning. "I brought some crepe for the house as well."

"Thank you. I am sure there must be someone around here who provides something similar, but I have not been able to explore yet." Lily smiled as a sound from the stairs made her tilt her head back, and she met her husband's gaze. "Here is Nathan."

Nathan had it much easier than she did. He had plenty of dark suits, from what she had seen, and did not need to purchase new clothing, though the black band around his arm made it clear he was in mourning. Once the initial mourning period was over, that would be cast off.

"Welcome to my home," Nathan said as he descended. His gaze caught Lily's, and he quickly corrected himself. "Our home."

"I am sorry it is under such circumstances," Lily's mother said, stepping forward to greet him, her dark eyes full of sympathy. Lily's father came over to convey his condolences as well.

They got through the social patter well enough, then sent her parents with several footmen and Mrs. Moore to show them to their rooms. That had barely been finished when a knock sounded on the door. To Lily's surprise, it opened immediately, and a man stepped through, and she quickly recognized Harker, the elderly gentleman who had come to London to tell Nathan of Sebastian's death.

"My lord." Harker bowed quickly.

"Harker, good to see you traveled well." Nathan lit up, and Lily looked at him questioningly before realizing he likely wanted more information from Harker. Blast. She wondered if she would have the opportunity to listen at the keyhole again. With more people arriving, it was going to be much harder to escape being caught.

"Yes, my lord. The Earl of Durham was kind enough to offer me transport in his carriage," Harker explained.

"Elijah and Josie are here?" Not that Lily had not been happy to see her parents, but she was extremely relieved to hear her friends had arrived. Perhaps Josie could help her.

"Yes, my lady, the earl, the countess, and his cousin, Miss Stuart." Harker bowed to her. Elated, Lily dashed past him as quickly as she could while still maintaining some decorum. Thank goodness—Josie *and* Evie. Reinforcements were here!

* * *

*Nathan*

Nathan approached Harker, secure in the knowledge Lily would have everyone else well in hand. Keeping his voice low, in case there were any curious ears about—sounds in the foyer could echo oddly—Nathan drew Harker a little off to the side, away from the door.

"I found a list of names in my brother's study. Moore said Sebastian was investigating my father." If Moore knew, Harker would, and it was possible he would know even more. While Nathan had many questions for Harker, that one was the most important now that Nathan knew about it. If someone had been helping his father, they could still hang for treason.

There might even be a connection to the traitor he and his friends were currently hunting. The idea made Nathan's stomach clench, but it was not far-fetched. After all, how many traitors could there possibly be?

*Hopefully, not many.*

"Aye." Harker's expression sobered. "That was one of the things I meant to tell you once I was able. Your brother had found evidence in your father's diaries that he had smuggled in spies during the war and helped them get back out." Harker shook his head, disgust contorting his features. "I swear, my lord, I did not know where he was getting the money from. I thought it was from the horse races, as always."

"I do not blame you, trust me," Nathan said, clapping the other man on the shoulder. Harker was no traitor. He and Mrs. Potts had likely been the saviors of the estate. Certainly, they had shouldered the burden of looking after it and the staff while his father ran through his funds and neglected his duties.

"My father was..." There were so many things he could call his father. A reprobate. A wastrel. A failure of a human being, on more levels than Nathan had realized.

"I hope you know you and your brother are nothing like him," Harker said somberly. The words were more reassuring than the man could know. While Nathan did not like to think he was, having third-party confirmation from someone who had known all three of them inside and out was incredibly comforting.

"Thank you, Harker." Nathan choked up a bit but pushed through, clearing his throat of the emotions clogging it. "I will take over my brother's investigations as it seems the most likely motive for his murder."

"I agree, my lord." The concern in Harker's voice was as clear as his understanding that Nathan would not be swayed from his course. "I will help as much as I can, but... please be careful."

The estate could not afford to lose Nathan as well, something he was well aware of.

They did not get further chance to talk. The front door opened again, admitting Lily with her two friends into the room. As before, Miss Stuart was resplendent in a green dress that matched her eyes exactly, a much brighter hue than what Lily was wearing. Seeing her now, every inch the proper young lady, Nathan did not know how she had managed to pass muster as a maid.

Trailing behind the women was Elijah, an expression of faint exasperation on his face. His gaze met Nathan's, and they shared a look of fellow feeling. The women were already chattering far too quickly for Nathan to keep up, especially as they were mid-conversation. Something about the gossip that was running around London. Hardly something Nathan currently felt concerned about, though he knew later it would be important.

Thankfully, he could let Lily and her friends handle that aspect of their current situation. The less he had to do with the social ramifications of everything, the happier he was.

Harker slipped away as Elijah approached.

"How are you holding up?" Elijah asked, reaching out to clasp Nathan's hand, his voice low so as not to draw the attention of the three ladies, who were already making their way into the drawing-room.

Unlike Lily's parents, they clearly prioritized catching up with each other over being shown to their rooms. Considering how much trouble they could get into, Nathan wondered if he and Elijah should follow them into the drawing-room posthaste.

"Well enough. I have some questions for you, but... also..." Quickly, Nathan outlined finding the list as well as what Moore and Harker had told him. Elijah grimaced.

It was indeed a social scandal if it ever got out that his father had betrayed the crown, but Elijah and *his* father knew Nathan well enough to know that he would never have countenanced such a thing if he'd known. Since his father was already dead, all they had to do was keep it quiet for the sake of the family. If his father had been alive, Nathan would have been the first to throw him to the crown's mercy.

"How did your father die again?" Elijah asked, grim-faced.

"Fell from his balcony." He caught Elijah's expression and shook his head. "He was three sheets to the wind... it was not..." While it was entirely possible his father's death had been an accident, was it possible his treacherous actions had had something to do with his death?

Bloody hell.

The plot kept thickening.

## Chapter Twenty-Four

*Lily*

Escorting her friends into the drawing-room, Lily was relieved to hear that not a word was being bandied about London when it came to her kidnapping. Everyone was too agog over her marriage, followed by Nathan's immediate advancement to a title.

"There are a few who have even commented on how lucky you are," Josie said angrily, flouncing over to the couch and plopping down, aggravation in every line of her body. "As if you could enjoy such 'good fortune' when it meant the death of Nathan's brother."

"Of course, there are always a few," Lily replied with a sigh, taking the seat next to her friend. Evie sat down in one of the chairs across from them, her green eyes darting around the room, taking in every bit. Lily had no doubt Evie would know Brentwood Manor even better than Nathan did by the time she left. "That's the *ton* for you."

"Vultures," Josie muttered.

For all that they were part of upper society, no one in their foursome had ever fooled themselves over the cruelties and unfeelingness of the worst of their class. Nor did they agree with those attitudes.

Unfortunately, as women, there was often very little they could do about it either. It was infuriatingly frustrating.

"I suppose I should be grateful they are distracted from my 'ruination,'" Lily said, wrinkling her nose. It grated to have to be grateful that Nathan's brother's death and Nathan's inheriting the title was of more interest to the fickle *ton* than the scandal that preceded her marriage.

"You cannot change the facts, so you may as well enjoy the benefits," Evie pointed out, returning her focus to the conversation at hand. "Anything to report?" She asked in a tone that made it clear she did not expect Lily to have any news.

Lily thoroughly enjoyed leaning forward and, in a low voice, disabusing Evie of the notion she had been distracted from her investigation. She spoke quickly and succinctly, aware her husband and Elijah might interrupt them at any moment.

Evie's mouth dropped open, and Josie gasped when she told them Nathan's father had likely committed treason, and it was possible Sebastian had been investigating that fact at the time of his murder.

"Goodness," Josie murmured when Lily was done. "Who would have guessed?"

"Certainly not me," Lily muttered, sitting up straight as Elijah appeared in the doorway of the drawing-room. His gaze flitted from one face to the next, then he frowned.

How, exactly, he knew they were up to something he did not approve of, she had no idea, but he'd always had an instinct for that sort of thing. Maybe it was Evie sitting up in her chair, gaze fixed ahead of her, eyes slightly glazed, the way she often did when she was arranging facts in her head.

"What are you ladies talking about?" he asked suspiciously.

"The gossip about Lily and Nathan," Josie replied immediately. The statement was not entirely untrue since that had been the initial topic of their conversation.

"Did you know some of the *ton* are calling it luck that I married him right before he became an earl?" Lily asked indignantly, tilting her nose in the air. After spilling his secrets to Josie and Evie, she was not quite able to meet her husband's eyes as he followed Elijah into the room.

Hopefully, he thought it was because she was upset over the *ton*'s cruelty.

Elijah snorted.

"I can guess who might be saying such things. Do not let it trouble you."

"I know you are not taking any pleasure in your increased station," Nathan said, moving around Elijah and along the back of the sofa to put his hand on Lily's shoulder.

The gesture was comforting, which had the side effect of making her feel even guiltier about listening to his conversation with Mr. Moore, then sharing it with her friends. The more she saw of Nathan, the better she liked him, but her ultimate loyalty still had to be to her friends and country.

Had he told Elijah about his findings? Or had he kept silent to protect his family's reputation?

Lily had no way of knowing. He had not told her his suspicions, only talking to Mr. Moore, who already knew, which did not reassure her. He still might have told Elijah. Elijah was a man and a good proxy for the Marquess of Camden, to whom Nathan reported. The knowledge grated since, as his wife, Lily thought she deserved to know.

"Nathan and I have a few things to attend to," Elijah said, looking past Lily at his wife. "We will leave you to get settled in."

"Very well." Josie waved her hand at him imperiously, dismissing him from the room. "I will speak with you later." From the slight change in Elijah's expression, he had quickly caught on that when Josie said she would speak to him, she clearly meant she would question him—and would expect answers.

Was it possible, one day, Lily might do the same with Nathan? The thought was intriguing.

\* \* \*

*Nathan*

Since Anthony had not arrived yet, Elijah and Nathan decided to visit the stables to look over Devil and Sebastian's tack. Eventually, Nathan wanted to question Harker and Moore about the list, but they may as well wait for everyone to arrive. Anthony should be along shortly—and Rex, though Nathan was not sure the lord would have anything particularly useful to contribute.

Nathan, Anthony, and Elijah had worked together for years under the Marquess of Camden. Rex had become involved in the investigations, thanks to his wife. Something Nathan would do well not to forget.

Miss Stuart had been remarkably quiet so far, but she was the one who had recruited her friends in such an ill-advised manner.

Sending debutantes after traitors. Really. The very idea was ludicrous.

*Which means the traitor would likely not see it coming.*

The thought popped into his head and made Nathan scowl even more. While that might be true, it was for good reason. If they were caught in an unfortunate situation, the ladies could hardly defend themselves as well as the men. Just look at what had happened with Lily and the highwayman.

Although she did have a good right hook, which Nathan did not think most debutantes possessed, that had hardly saved her, now had it?

"Whatever Harker saw, it's completely gone now," Elijah murmured, running his hand over Devil's hindquarters. The stallion shifted his weight slightly but settled quickly enough.

"Which was probably the plan." Nathan's jaw clenched. "With everyone rushing out to search for Sebastian and the commotion once they found his body, there was plenty of opportunity to sneak in and remove whatever they'd put on his saddle."

"Do you think it would have been on the saddle?" Elijah mused as they exited Devil's stall. "Is it possible it was a glancing shot that missed both Devil and Sebastian?"

"Possibly." Nathan considered the suggestion. "Seems risky, though. We can go out to the site later today. While there would have been plenty of opportunity for a shot, it would have to be done from a considerable distance."

"Which could explain the poor marksmanship."

Closing the stall door behind them, Devil snorted and tossed his head.

"Sorry, old boy," Nathan murmured, holding out his hand with the slice of apple he'd been saving for the end. The big horse knew he had it, which was why he'd been so well behaved until they were out of the stall. Devil did like his bribes. "We'll let you out for a run later today." Devil snorted and bobbed his head as if he understood Nathan.

"Too bad he cannot tell us what happened." Elijah sighed. "I suppose that would make things far too easy."

"What would make things easy?" Anthony walked into the stables on the heel of Elijah's wish, Rex sauntering behind him. The two of them made quite a sight. Anthony was short and stocky with dark hair and eyes and a perpetually angry expression. In contrast, Rex was a lazy lion of a man, tawny-haired with amber eyes that sometimes seemed to glow and all the affect of a gazetted rake. That he was now married and happily devoted to his wife had not changed his demeanor one bit.

"If Devil could tell us what happened to Sebastian." Nathan relaxed as the other two men came to proffer their greetings and reaffirm their condolences. Now that they were all here, the chances of uncovering their villain were far higher.

* * *

*Lily*

Somehow, all the ladies found themselves in Evie's room by the time Mary arrived. Josie and Evie had updated Lily on the last tidbits of gossip coming out of the capital, some of which did not include her and Nathan's marriage, thank goodness.

"And..." Even though they were alone, Josie turned her head this way and that before leaning in to whisper to Lily. "I think Priscilla knows about the Society of Sin."

"What? The former Miss Bliss? Why on earth would you think that?" Lily blinked in surprise. She could not imagine how the woman would have discovered anything about the Society. Sweet tempered and mild-mannered to the point of being dull, the beautiful Miss Bliss had apparently gone through multiple seasons of boring gentlemen, who settled on someone else for a bride, until she'd met Elijah's brother, Joseph. The two had married earlier this Season, once the scandalous events surrounding Elijah and Josie's marriage had been cleared up.

That was when Mary found them, coming into the room on the heel of Lily's query.

"Is she going on about Priscilla again?" Mary asked, shaking her head and pausing in the doorway. Wearing a dove grey traveling dress and gloves, which she slid off of her hands before coming into the room, her blondish-red hair properly coiffed, she looked every inch the proper Marchioness.

Lily wondered if she should ask Mary for lessons now that she was a countess. Glancing down at her own hands, she frowned at the faint ink stains. Certainly not what a proper countess' hands should look like. She closed her hands into fists, hiding the tips of her fingers in them.

"Josie, you really need to leave that poor woman alone." Mary frowned, shaking her head.

"That poor woman needs to leave me alone!" Josie protested. "She flat out said she knew Elijah was part of a secret society."

"I think she's realized my cousins and uncle are not what they seem," Evie interjected. She had been awfully quiet since arriving, spending her time sorting through the jewelry she'd packed.

Until Evie was ready to talk, Lily and Josie had been doing their best to behave as if nothing was amiss. She had a feeling her friend was worried about Uncle Oliver, who had been left behind in London with his new nurse since he was not well enough to travel yet. Lily did not envy whatever woman Evie had hired for that job.

"That's what she means by secret society. I am sure Joseph has told her nothing about the family business."

Likely not. A large part of Joseph's desire for her as his wife was that he'd always preferred meek and biddable women. Which was why he and Josie would have never worked, even though she'd been in love with him for years. Now that she was married to Elijah, it was clear they were the better match for each other.

Poor Miss Bliss, though. Mrs. Stuart now, but Lily was not sure she would ever be able to think of the young woman as anything other than Miss Bliss.

"I do not think she has an inkling about Uncle Oliver being England's spymaster. I am telling you, she is talking about the Society of Sin," Josie insisted irritably.

"Does it truly matter either way?" This conversation certainly did not, but Lily found herself happy to be distracted by such a trivial matter for a bit.

"Only when one wonders how she found out about it or why she wants to know about it." Josie crossed her arms, scowling.

Evie snorted. "Likely, she overheard one of my cousins talking about it. They are hardly as circumspect as they like to think."

"Or she could be looking for a lover."

That made everyone except Josie laugh. Pouting, she crossed her arms over her chest. Lily did not know the former Miss Bliss well, but she could hardly imagine the insipid miss being anything but horrified once she discovered what activities The Society indulged in.

"They just got married, and it was a love match. I am sure she is not already looking for a lover, if ever," Mary said soothingly. She tended to play peacemaker among them. "Like me, she has a tendency to be overlooked. I would not be at all surprised if Evie is correct, and Joseph, Adam, or even Elijah, was loose-lipped within her hearing."

"She better not be," Josie muttered, still pouting. "Oh, do not look at me like that, Evie, I am not in love with Joseph anymore, but I still want him to be happy."

"As do we all," Mary said pointedly. She sat down on the bed between Josie and Lily. "Now, tell me what is going on. I am sure Evie and Josie have already hounded you for information." Evie glanced up from where she was sorting through her things. She was the only one who did not have a ladies' maid, and she'd refused Lily's offer of one, leaving her to unpack her own things. Evie had always been rather secretive, so it was not surprising and made her room the perfect spot to gather and talk over everything.

"We did not hound her, I will have you know. She immediately offered everything she'd learned."

Mary looked surprised, as Evie first had when Lily had revealed she had information to share.

"Truly? About the earl's death?"

"His death *and* the previous earl's treachery," Josie announced dramatically.

"Well, let me tell her," Lily interjected a bit crossly. It was her story to tell. Normally, all she had to report was that none of her correspondents gave her anything useful. Being able to contribute something worthwhile was exciting, even if she felt guilty about how she had collected it.

Lily quickly gave Mary the same rundown she had given the other two, adding in a few small details she had left out earlier—like the fact Mr. Moore was married to the housekeeper, Mrs. Moore, who had been like a sister to Nathan and his brother growing up.

Once she had finished, all of them turned to look at Evie. When it came down to it, she was their general.

"I... blast." Evie rubbed her forehead. "I need more information. Josie, see what you can get from Elijah. Mary, the same with Rex. Hopefully, Nathan has been more forthcoming with them."

Evie did not mean the words to hurt, but they did a bit. Another reminder Nathan did not see Lily as his confidant. Not in the same way Rex and Elijah saw their wives-but then Rex and Elijah were in love with their wives. She and Nathan were hardly a love match.

So why did it hurt?

## Chapter Twenty-Five

*Nathan*

By dinnertime, everyone was settled into their rooms, and Nathan's cousins had still not arrived. He was not upset they were running late, though he hoped nothing unfortunate had happened to them. While he might not want Robert and his wife, Amelia, to inherit the title, he also did not want misfortune to befall them. He was not that heartless.

By mutual, unspoken agreement, no one mentioned his brother's murder or any investigations in front of Lily's parents. Conversation centered around the house, the estate, the nearby village, the coast, and any other number of far more socially acceptable topics. Her parents seemed keen to investigate the local foliage, and Nathan was more than happy to give them permission to tour the greenhouse and the gardens and take any clippings they might desire. While he did not think they would find anything particularly interesting, it made them happy, and that made Lily smile at him.

Why that was suddenly important to him, he was unsure, but he was aware his marriage did not quite resemble his friends or Lily's parents, for that matter.

But he wanted it to.

That flash of insight had taken him by surprise over dinner when

Lily smiled at him from across the table—much in the way Elijah's wife was currently smiling at Elijah—and Nathan suddenly felt warm from the tips of his toes to the top of his head. Why the sudden change in how he wanted her to regard him?

Was it the marriage? The realization she probably was not involved in treachery? Or sharing her bed?

Perhaps some combination of all three.

Something else for him to contemplate later when he had the time.

"Gentlemen, would you like some port?" he asked as the dinner wound down. After his father's death, Sebastian had procured a few bottles of a decent vintage. Nathan would have to add to their stores, but they had enough for entertaining for now.

"I believe I am for bed," Lily's father said, getting to his feet with an apologetic glance around. "The traveling has done me in."

"Me as well." Lily's mother stood, turning a gracious smile on Lily and Nathan. "It was a lovely dinner."

Everyone said their goodnights to Lily's parents, then looked around at each other. Typically, the ladies would depart to the drawing-room while the gentlemen discussed matters over a drink, but the ladies looked loathe to leave.

"Perhaps we should all converge on the drawing-room for that drink?" Elijah asked, giving Nathan a significant look, then glancing at the footmen.

The drawing-room would certainly be more secure for private conversation. Nathan did not particularly want to include the ladies, but he would follow Elijah's lead.

"Very well." Nathan got to his feet, walking around the table to offer his arm to Lily. If they were going to throw societal conventions out the window, they might as well go all the way, and he wanted to walk beside his wife.

He was rewarded with a dazzling smile that made him very glad he had.

\* \* \*

*Lily*

Once everyone was settled around the drawing-room—the ladies seated and the men standing either beside or behind their chosen lady, except for Captain Browne and Evie, of course—Elijah cleared his throat, and everyone looked at him. Josie and Evie had chosen to sit in the chairs across from Mary and Lily on the couch. Elijah stood between them, so they twisted in their seats to see him clearly. Rex was leaning against the couch beside Mary, while Nathan was behind Lily, so she could not see his expression.

Captain Brown remained apart from everyone, propped against the fireplace, scowling at Evie, who steadfastly ignored him. Blast. Lily had forgotten to pester Evie for more details about her and the captain's past. It was not a priority, but Lily still wanted to know.

Especially when the captain was the only one who did not change his attention to Elijah.

"Now that we are all gathered here, there is some new information that has come to light I believe we should share in the interest of everyone's safety." Though he said 'everyone,' Elijah's eyes flicked to Lily and her friends, not the men. Of course. "Nathan has reason to believe his brother was murdered because he was looking into the possibility of someone in this area smuggling spies to and from France during the war."

Even though the women already knew, they did their best to act shocked in a believable manner. Josie gasped, putting her hand to her breast. Evie's expression hardened, her jaw firming, and she turned to face straight again, her gaze becoming distant, similar to how it had when Lily told her. Next to Lily, Mary gasped as well, though much quieter than Josie, and reached out for Lily's hand, which she appreciated.

Lily was experiencing conflicting emotions. Relief Nathan had told Elijah what his brother was investigating and anger he'd seen fit to tell Elijah but not her. She was also sure he had told Elijah his father had been part of it, or else Elijah would not have worded his own statement so carefully.

Not only anger. Hurt.

"We do not yet know if there is a connection to the man we have been searching for in London, but it means there is danger here.

Everyone will need to be careful." Elijah's gaze flitted back and forth between Mary and Lily before he stepped forward to look down at his own wife. Nodding, Josie smiled up at him.

"We will keep ourselves safe," Josie replied.

Lily had no doubt Elijah was the one who had decided the ladies should be entrusted with this information, not her own husband. Likely because he knew it would be near impossible to keep them from involving themselves in the investigations and worried keeping them in the dark would put them in greater danger.

That the ladies had all been involved in the major revelations and uncovering clues during their hunt did not seem to signify.

Men.

She sighed, then tensed when she felt Nathan's hand come down on her shoulder. His grip was firm but not punishing, yet she knew he was trying to hold her back. Ha... as if he could.

"What would you like for us to do?" she asked Elijah, rather than turning to look up at her husband. She did not trust her expression right now.

"Keep the household running and those who come for the funeral entertained. We will be questioning some people and need to be free to do so," Elijah said quickly. "Also, if you hear anything suspicious, let one of us know immediately."

'Us' being the men.

The ladies glanced at Evie, who nodded. Yes, they would tell her as well, probably first.

* * *

*Nathan*

It was impossible to miss the silent conversation between his wife and the other ladies, not that he got the sense they were trying to hide it. The idea they might step back and allow others, who were better equipped to handle everything, was too much to hope for.

"This is *dangerous*," he said, gripping Lily's shoulder a little tighter to emphasize his words.

"Oh, well, certainly different from before," Lady Stuart replied with a delicate snort. "After all, it is not as if I was attacked at a ball where I was merely minding my own business."

"Or kidnapped by a highwayman when I was on my way home," Lily added. Though she was not looking at him, he did not need to see her face to know she was annoyed with his assessment.

Unfortunately, the ladies' points were unassailable. Both had been doing exactly what they should be and had been dragged into events by circumstances outside of their control.

Nathan already knew Lily was a target since the highwayman had been questioning rather than attempting to kill her. A fact he was suddenly grateful for. Out on the road, without a protector, she had made an incredibly easy target, unlike the rest of them. He had forgotten that with everything else that had occurred since then.

He exchanged a long-suffering glance with Elijah.

Why could nothing be easy? It was tempting to think keeping the ladies away from danger would mean they were out of danger entirely, but it had not kept them safe before.

"As long as you are not running headlong into danger, such as following a man onto the Dark Walk at Vauxhall Gardens," Rex said mildly, reaching out to toy with one of his wife's curls. She blushed deeply, though Nathan could only see one of her cheeks.

Surprisingly, the outspoken Lady Stuart did as well, lowering her gaze from the rest of them. Miss Stuart did not, of course, as she had not been present for that occurrence. Nathan wondered if his own wife was blushing as well. She had gone down that path along with her friends.

Intriguing how Rex managed to set them neatly in their place.

Nathan mentally took note. Rex's tactic was clearly far more effective than Elijah's talking around the subject or his own directness.

"We want to keep you safe," Nathan said, coming around to the side of the couch so he could take Lily's hand and see her expression. She frowned up at him, but not in a disapproving way, more like she was trying to muster an argument. Meeting her gaze, he squeezed her fingers, lowering his voice. "I have already lost enough."

Truthfully, he did not know if he could handle losing her, too.

The very thought made his blood run cold. It did not matter that they had only met this past Season or had been married only a few days—she was his. His to protect and defend, even more so than anyone else under his care.

* * *

*Lily*

Blast the man. How was she supposed to argue with such a statement? It was infuriating, even as her heart pounded faster and part of her wanted to swoon from the romanticism.

Surely, he did not mean it in a romantic way—how could he? They had not been married a week, and besides, she was already his wife, so he hardly needed to court her.

But it felt awfully romantic.

Meaningful.

The intimate moment was interrupted by a loud knocking at the front door that made everyone in the room jump. Outside the drawing-room, she could hear someone hurrying across the foyer.

"Who could that be?" Josie asked.

"Hopefully, it is Robert, finally." Nathan released Lily's hand and turned, an expression of relief on his face. Lily knew he had been worried about his cousins when they did not appear at the expected time. She hoped he was correct—no one else was supposed to arrive today.

Nathan strode right out of the room without looking back.

Exasperated, Lily got to her feet, exchanging a glance with Evie, before going after him. Apparently, he had forgotten he had a wife. She should be there to greet his cousins as well.

Thankfully, her mother's shopping trip before leaving London had provided several suitable dresses, so she was wearing the appropriate black for mourning. While her friends did not care, she wanted to make a good impression on Nathan's cousins. He did not have any other family, from what she knew.

Brushing off her skirts, she nodded to their friends.

"This is probably goodnight, but we will see you on the morrow."

Introductions and getting Nathan's cousin and wife settled in their rooms took precedence over the discussions. She did not know if Nathan was going to keep his cousins in the dark about the truth of his brother's death and his father's perfidy.

In some cases, ignorance *was* the safer course. There was no reason for anyone to think they knew anything, and the second they did know, they would be in danger.

Gliding into the hallway, Lily pasted a demure but welcoming smile on her face. As she walked out the door, everyone turned to look at her. It appeared his cousins had brought quite the retinue with them.

Harker stood stiffly at attention just off to the side while Nathan faced his cousins. At least, Lily assumed the man was Robert, Nathan's current heir. There was a similarity in facial features and build, though Robert's hair was lighter. He also had a pinched expression, though that might be due to having traveled all day.

Beside him was a well-dressed blonde, who Lily assumed was his wife, Letitia. That was the summation of Lily's knowledge about them. Nathan had not been very verbose, and she assumed they were not close.

"And who is this?" the blonde asked, narrowing her eyes suspiciously at Lily. Nathan turned.

"Ah, yes. It is possible my letter did not reach you in time." Nathan held out his hand to gesture Lily forward.

She kept the polite smile on her face despite their frowns. With their late arrival, it had likely been an arduous day of travel, so she could forgive a little rudeness.

"This is my wife, Lily Jones, formerly Davies. Lady Jones, now, I suppose. Lily, these are my cousins Robert and Letitia Jones."

The blonde's mouth dropped open in shock. More than shock, she appeared to be almost angry.

"Wife? When did you marry?" Though his expression had not changed much, Robert's voice was much gruffer than when he'd been speaking to Nathan alone. Neither he nor his wife appeared pleased about the revelation.

Something unsettling turned over in Lily's stomach as she realized being Nathan's heir might have been a position the man was looking forward to.

"Earlier this week," Nathan said, his voice hardening. "The day before I received the news about Sebastian."

"It has been an eventful week," Lily interjected soothingly. Though she did not want to judge the couple by this first interaction, considering they were likely exhausted and out-of-sorts already—and her marriage to Nathan was a big surprise—she would struggle if they kept behaving so rudely. "Our courtship happened quickly. You must be tired, though. I am sure we will have plenty of time to get to know each other and tell you everything over the next few days. Harker? Please show Mr. and Mrs. Jones to their rooms."

"Thank you, you are correct," Robert said, tugging on the front of his jacket and shooting a look at his wife. "It has been a very tiring day. My apologies for our rudeness."

"We understand completely," Nathan reassured him.

Lily was not so sure. Mrs. Jones still appeared unhappy, but she was not going to press it for now.

Still, she wondered if Nathan had considered the possibility his brother's death might have nothing to do with his father's treachery.

## Chapter Twenty-Six

*Nathan*

With Robert and Letitia finally in their rooms and out of the way, Nathan took refuge in the library. He needed some time away from people to think.

It seemed as if danger was closing in on those left of his nearest and dearest, his friends and wife, and he did not know how to keep everyone safe. Having them all in his house added to his feeling of responsibility, even though he knew the burden of a host only went so far. And the majority of his guests knew of the danger.

While nothing further had happened since the day of the assassination attempts and Lily's kidnapping, that only seemed to indicate something *must* happen soon.

Nathan felt safer on the estate, despite knowing his brother had been murdered, until he'd uncovered the list. Now, the more he thought about it, the more it seemed the danger here was greater than he feared.

Someone willing to betray their country would hardly balk at interrupting a funeral gathering.

Clenching his jaw, Nathan flopped into one of the chairs.

It was not the same as *his* chair back at Talbot House in London.

GOLDEN ANGEL

Perhaps he should have someone fetch the chair for him. He could do that now that he was the lord of the manor.

"Dammit, Sebastian," he muttered, leaning back in the chair. "I never wanted this."

It was not his brother's fault, but he did not yet know where to lay the blame.

More disconcerting was realizing just how much Robert *wanted* the title. Robert *and* his wife. Nathan had not missed the implications of their lack of excitement at Lily's introduction. They had covered well enough once they got over the shock, but Letitia was a grasping social climber on the best of the days, and Robert had always felt cheated out of the money he presumed came with the estate.

Not that Robert would have the first idea how to make the estate profitable. His cousin had never seemed to grasp that it required actual work, any more than Nathan's father had. Though his cousin was not a gambler, Nathan still shuddered at the idea of Robert and Letitia inheriting. They might not gamble the coffers away, but they would likely empty them, regardless.

"My lord?" Harker's voice drifted into the room.

Though Nathan wanted more time to sit alone and think, he knew where his duty lay.

"Over here, Harker." Nathan raised his hand, waving the other man over. "Please, sit."

His father would have had a conniption over Nathan asking one of the staff to sit with him like an equal, which gave Nathan petty enjoyment. Anything he could do to spite his father, even in death.

"I am sorry to bother you, my lord, but there are a few urgent matters your brother was attending to that still need attention." His tone and expression apologetic, Harker sat down gingerly, clutching a folio in front of him. Nathan wondered if Sebastian had made the older man stand on ceremony as well.

Considering Sebastian had been thoroughly trained by their father, it was likely. There were some things lords who were trained to be lords took for granted without thinking. Nathan had not been brought up that way, and his time in the military had given him a very different perspective of people than he'd had going in.

Nathan sighed inwardly but knew Harker would not approach him this late, on the night before his brother's viewing, without cause.

"Very well. What was Sebastian up to?" he asked.

"The most urgent matter is the mill."

\* \* \*

<u>Lily</u>

Where the devil was her blasted husband?

Frowning, Lily paced back and forth in her room, the silky fabric of her peignoir drifting around her. She looked down at it and scowled. The flimsy nightgown and robe were creamy ivory, the silk of the nightgown not quite opaque, which was why she put her peignoir over it. She was not brave enough to don the nightgown on its own. The low-cut neckline was made up of lace that covered her breasts—mostly and with quite a few small holes—before turning into silk that cascaded down to her ankles. The lace was itchy, but she had not expected to be wearing it all that long.

She'd thought Nathan would be in her room by now, ready to engage in marital coitus. Then once he was sated and sleepy, she planned to broach the subject of his cousin and whether Robert might be capable of murder to inherit a title.

Instead, she was fairly certain Nathan was not even in his room.

With an exasperated sigh, she clutched her robe tightly about her and went to her door to peek out. She would not care if her friends saw her, though she might care a bit if their husbands did. They were all in another wing of the house and unlikely to leave their rooms. Her parents and Nathan's cousin and wife, however, were in the family wing of the house with her and Nathan.

If only they had moved to the earl's suite, they would not only be in a separate wing, they would also have adjoining doors. Now, she had to worry about Robert or Letitia coming out of their rooms at the end of the hall. Scowling, Lily muttered under her breath, annoyed with her husband's absence.

Gathering her courage, she pressed her lips together and scurried into the hall and over to his door. Though part of her wanted to knock, she was too worried some of the other occupants in the hall might hear, so she turned the knob and looked inside.

Empty.

Blast the man.

Buoyed by an increasing sense of being wronged, Lily abandoned all modesty and went in search of her husband.

Barefoot.

In nothing but a nightgown and robe.

If he was upset when he found her wandering the halls *dishabille*, it would be his own fault.

The first place she checked was the study, but he was not there. Nor was he in the billiards room with the other gentlemen, which had occurred to her as a possibility. She would have expected her friends to kick up a fuss if that had been the case since none of them trusted the men to keep them informed. Gatherings without their wives were almost certainly meetings to discuss matters she and her friends wanted to be involved in.

Huffing, Lily made her way to the library, slowing when she heard the sound of male voices within. It only took her a moment to recognize her husband and Harker. Whatever they were talking about was coming to an end, and someone was coming to the door.

Lily scurried back into one of the dark corners, next to a tall pedestal and vase, hoping if she was still, her nightgown would blend next to the pale stone. The door opened, and Harker stepped out, striding purposefully in the opposite direction from where she was standing.

She could have collapsed with relief.

She waited to see Nathan, but he was not there.

Frowning, she counted to thirty in her head, wanting to see if he would follow Harker out, but it appeared he was not coming.

With a sigh of exasperation, she straightened up. If her husband would not come to her, she would go to him.

\* \* \*

*Nathan*

The door to the library opened, and Nathan barely stifled a groan. Had Harker remembered something else?

Steeling himself, Nathan got up from the chair and turned.

Blinked.

The apparition before him was certainly *not* Harker.

His wife had decided to dress for seduction this evening, and it was working. Did work. Immediately.

The barely-there nightgown peeked through the matching peignoir, which did not do nearly as good a job covering her as Nathan might have wished, considering she was running about the house. She was not even wearing shoes. Dark hair curled about her shoulders and down to her waist, adding to the exotic image she made.

"Lily? What are you doing here?" he asked stupidly. His brain was struggling to work, distracted by the vision she made and his ragingly hard cock.

"Looking for... something to read." She blinked at him, sauntering past and going to the shelves.

Just as she had at Talbot House, she seemed to have an uncanny sense of where the private family collections were. She headed right for his and his brother's folios, the ones he had not taken with him to London. Nathan groaned inwardly. Now that they had guests, he really needed to move those folios elsewhere.

It had been so long since anyone had stayed at the manor, neither he nor Sebastian had thought a thing about placing their private folios in the library once his father was dead. The servants were not going to bother with them. He really should have taken them down from the shelves when he knew guests were coming, yet he had forgotten.

The fact it had taken him this long to remember made him worry he was losing his edge.

*That or so many things happening at once has been too much.*

More likely, that was the case. Nathan had never dealt with change and upheaval well. It took him time to adjust, and this week, he had had very little time. So many major changes all at once within such a short time span, no wonder he was having trouble keeping up.

"Do you have any likenesses of me in these?" she asked teasingly, reaching up for the folio.

"It is not... never mind," Nathan replied, exasperated. It was not supposed to be her likeness, had not been intended to be her likeness, but there was no point in trying to deny the picture looked very much like her. He also did not want anyone else to see it, especially because of how much it looked like her.

Lily opened one of the folios, the schematics for one of the previous iterations of his newest invention. Getting to his feet, Nathan went to her and reached up to pull down several other folios, two of his and one of his brother's. Sebastian had not been as mechanically minded as Nathan, but he had sketched, and Nathan had not had time to look through it yet and was not sure he could. His brother would have never allowed it when he was alive, so rifling through the book would only hammer home the reminder that he was dead.

Besides, there were far too many other things going on. His brother's sketches were hardly a priority.

"Does this machine exist?" Lily asked, running her fingertips over the image in question, ruthlessly wrenching Nathan's line of thinking from his brother to her. His erection, which had begun to deflate, swelled. Was she intrigued by the notion? She sounded intrigued.

That he might see Lily on the receiving end of his invention tonight... the very thought obliterated all else from his mind. Suddenly, he was not tired anymore.

"It does. Would you like to see it?" Though he tried to remain suave, he could not entirely contain his eagerness. Not that it mattered. Lily closed the folio and turned to look up at him, angling herself closer, her breasts almost brushing against his chest.

Tipping her head back, she smiled.

"Yes, I would."

\* \* \*

*Lily*

The machines were in the room on the other side of her husband's chamber.

Machines. Plural.

"My goodness." She breathed out the words, clutching the leather folio to her chest as she walked into the room, wide-eyed and taking in all the equipment scattered around. Obviously, this was her husband's favorite hobby. Walking up to the first machine, she was surprised when her husband swiftly escorted her away from it, heading toward one at the back of the room that looked almost identical.

"Not that one," he said hastily. "That one, ah... the boiler has a tendency to sort of explode."

*Explode?*

"How safe are these?" she asked a bit faintly.

"This one is perfectly safe." Nathan gestured at the apparatus where he had directed her. To her eye, it looked the same as the other, so the differences must be in the internal workings. "I've run it for four hours with no issues with the engine."

That was somewhat reassuring.

Now that Lily was actually faced with the machine and its long arm, she was not so certain.

"Where is its..." She waved her hand where the attachment in the sketch had been. Of course, that had been the least clear part of the sketch, pictured as already having been inserted into the woman's body.

"The dildo?" The smile that spread across Nathan's lips was pure wickedness. "I have an assortment." Turning, he walked over to a large wardrobe on the side of the room.

Lily had been so distracted by the various machines around the room—three larger, including the explosive one, one table with a few smaller appearing machines displayed, and two tables set in an L shape covered with various bits of machinery, where she assumed he did his work—she had not even noticed the wardrobe.

When he opened its doors, her body clenched as she saw the interior. The wardrobe was filled with hooks along its back and sides, even on the insides of its doors, covered with various implements of torment. Whips, a birch, a large paddle, and quite a few things she had no name for and no idea how they were used.

*This is what it means to be part of the Society of Sin.*

Although Lily was not entirely sure how she felt about the Society, a part of her was disappointed the Season was over because she was becoming curiouser and curiouser about their events. Attending one firsthand was sure to be a night of revelations.

There were several shelves set up in the wardrobe with a multitude of options of varying lengths and sizes, all distinctly phallic.

"My goodness," she said again, feeling a touch faint as Nathan picked one of them up. It looked to be made of brown leather and quite large, the stitching so tiny, she could not see it from across the room.

"This one fits rather nicely, and it's about the same size as my cock, so you should be able to handle it easily enough," Nathan said as if his words were a common day occurrence and not some of the filthiest things she'd ever heard uttered.

Wide-eyed, she watched him return to the machine and slide the base of the dildo into a slot on the machine's arm. It did indeed fit nicely, though she was not sure about the size being equitable to her husband. Perhaps because it did not come with a man attached, it suddenly seemed very foreboding.

Nathan turned to her, raising an eyebrow, and held out his hand, his other hand resting on the padded table the dildo hovered over.

"Here, Lily. I will help you up."

Gulping nervously, Lily threw all caution to the wind and put her hand in his.

# Chapter Twenty-Seven

## Nathan

For a moment, Nathan thought Lily would balk at having the machine used on her, but then she reached out with trembling fingers and touched his hand. Nathan closed his grip around them and tugged her forward, so she was pulled against him.

"Good girl," he murmured, noting the way her eyelashes fluttered at the accolade. There was not even a hint of hesitation at enjoying being praised.

Lowering his lips to hers, Nathan devoured her with a kiss, letting his passion run free. Having her here, in his private room with all his machines, was one of the most intimate things they'd done.

While he had tested out his various inventions and toys on the women in the Society, he had never shown his workshops to any of them. This particular workshop was his newest, everything moved in during the days following his father's death and before Sebastian asked him to go to London, but no woman had ever joined him in any of the previous ones, either.

Only Lily.

Only his wife.

Nathan wanted to share everything with her.

Her soft body pressed up against his as she kissed him back desperately, hands clinging to his coat. The silky material of her peignoir was soft against his hands, sliding over her skin as he caressed her. Pressing her back against the padded table, Nathan rocked his hips, and she whimpered against his lips.

The peignoir slipped off her shoulders and fell to the floor, leaving her in nothing but the nightgown.

Pulling away, Nathan looked down at her and smiled as he gripped her by the hips and lifted her onto the table. She glanced at the dildo, a hot blush suffusing her cheeks. Seeing her nipples pebbled against the lace of her gown, he took a pinch of the fabric over her stomach, twitching the gown to make it move back and forth over those tender buds.

He wanted her as aroused as possible before he used the machine. Nathan could not wait to watch the dildo pistoning between her thighs, covered in her sweet juices, recreating his sketch.

*Debauched innocence.*

That's what he was calling it in his mind.

Lily squirmed, reaching for her nightgown.

"No," he said immediately, moving her hands away. "Leave it on."

There was something about that ivory fall of silk that made her appear even more innocent. Perversely, that appealed to him even more than having her completely naked.

\* \* \*

*Lily*

Nipples throbbing and itching against the lace of the nightgown, Lily wanted nothing more than to rip the garment off and away from her, but as soon as Nathan told her he wanted it on, she let her hands fall away. There was something erotic about the way he was using her nightgown to torture her when she'd intended it to be a seductive torment for him. The tables had been turned on her, and, oddly, she liked that.

The way he tried to take control in the drawing-room, determined to keep her and her friends out of the investigations, had driven her wild. When he took control in this atmosphere... that *really* drove her wild in an entirely different manner.

"Lie back," he ordered. The heat in his eyes nearly seared her, burning away her hesitation because she did not want him to stop looking at her like that. Licking her lips nervously, Lily laid back on the table.

The padding was comfortable enough but having to bend her knees and spread her legs so the arm of the machine fit between them certainly was not. Lily's blush heated as the silky skirt of her gown slithered over her thighs, exposing her womanhood as it pooled around her hips and on the table.

"Now what?" she asked tremulously.

"That depends... would you allow me to restrain you?" His tone left no doubt of his preference, yet he did no more than ask, allowing her to choose whether or not she would be left entirely helpless to him.

Remembering how much she had enjoyed being tied to his bed, Lily found herself nodding. She trusted him. Besides which, if she could not move, it would be easier to let go and enjoy the perverseness of allowing him to fuck her with a machine. Less like she was responsible for such depravity.

Nathan's eyes lit up when she nodded, burning even hotter as he moved around the bed. Leather straps appeared as if from nowhere, and Lily quickly found her arms pinned above her head, held down by the leather restraints, while another one crossed her ribs, just under her breasts.

That one had the added effect of pulling her lacy gown tightly against her breasts, so every movement, every wobble, the scratchy lace abraded her nipples further. The tiny buds were swollen and aching in their twin torture chambers, yet the stimulation increased the hot need between her legs. Lily closed her eyes, biting on her lower lip as she wriggled against the leather, adding to her torment all on her own.

Two more straps wrapped around her thighs and ankles, restraining each ankle to its thigh so that her knees were bent, then he attached something else to each of those straps that made it impossible to close her legs. Now her knees were pointed towards the ceiling, ankles attached to her thighs, pussy wide open and vulnerable between her legs. The utter indecency of being splayed open made her squirm.

"Now, hold still, darling." The soft murmur of Nathan's voice penetrated her haze of lust, and she caught her breath as she felt the leather pressing against her pussy. "I need to make a few adjustments."

The wait seemed interminable, though it could not have been longer than a few seconds, then she felt the leather shaft slowly push inside her. Opening her eyes, she looked down the length of her body at the obscene vision she made with her knees in the air, legs splayed wide apart, a machine between them. Her maniacal husband pushed the machine forward so it could penetrate her with a thick leather dildo.

"Oh!" She squeezed her eyes shut again as it moved deeper, sliding in easily, thanks to her arousal and stretching her open.

It felt very odd. Different from Nathan's cock. Firmer in some ways, more yielding in others. Being slowly impaled as he carefully moved the machine into place was an experience in and of itself. Nathan had never thrust this slowly. She was being filled, centimeter by deliberate centimeter, with painstaking care that made her writhe against the restraints.

* * *

*Nathan*

Watching the dildo stretching open Lily's pussy, her swollen lips clasping its length, her body stretched out on the table, squirming against the restraints with her breasts straining against her nightgown, it was easy to forget everything else in the world and focus solely on this moment. So close to her cunt, the subtle perfume of her arousal filled the air, and he could see the pert nub of her clitoris peeking out from her curls.

The dildo pushed in deeper until Nathan judged it was deep enough. Once he started the machine, it would retreat, then thrust back in, the engine turning the wheel that caused the piston arm to move. It would also vibrate—the engine had deliberately been designed to be inefficient. He had found the vibrations were what the women enjoyed the most, whether it was from the smaller hand-crank machines or the larger ones, like his invention.

His cock pressed against the front of his trousers, eager and aching to be released. It was his own sweet torment to deny himself. Right now, his main pleasure would be derived from watching.

Lily looked so much like the sketch right now. The main differences appealed to him even more than the sketch had.

Instead of being completely naked, her half-clothed state made the tableau even more titillating. Her nipples jutted against the fabric, and the silky skirt of her nightgown spread over her hips, covering nothing of importance, was far more wicked in appearance than nudity would be.

The restraints on her were far more complete than what he'd originally sketched holding her totally immobile.

She was completely helpless, totally at his mercy.

Nathan relished the sight.

Reaching down, he pressed a hand against his bulging erection, rubbing it gently to give himself a bit of relief before he moved to the side of the machine. He picked up the flint and striker hanging there, and with a quick flick of his wrist, sparks started the fire. Nathan closed the door as the red and orange flames flickered to life, keeping them well contained.

It would be a few minutes before the chamber was properly heated enough for the pressure to build and the machine to start. Walking around to the side of the table, he met his wife's gaze for a moment, then, with a wicked smile, bent his head over her breast and sucked her nipple into his mouth.

\* \* \*

<u>Lily</u>
Though she wondered why the machine had not started to move yet, such questions flew out of Lily's head when Nathan bent to suckle her nipple. The scratchy lace was even more stimulating as it became

wet from his saliva, then he reached over her body to grasp her other breast, causing the fabric to shift over that sensitive skin as well.

Lily writhed for a new reason as he tormented her nipples with mouth and fingers, suckling and pinching, using the lace to his best advantage. The thick leather cock inside her added to the sensations as she clenched around it, pinned into place by its length inserted inside her and the restraints holding her arms and torso down.

Then the cock moved. It felt similar but different to Nathan. There was no heavy weight bearing down on her, no warmth atop her other than where he was playing with her breasts. The sensation between her legs was different as well. The dildo shook inside her, rubbing against her in an entirely new way she hadn't experienced before, while the sensitive nub of her clitoris was left without the direct stimulation Nathan's body atop hers provided.

The thrusts were steady and relentless, the way a human could never be, which was the largest difference.

Knowing it could go on forever, that there was no pinnacle for it to reach, no climax that would bring its thrusting to a halt, was terrifying and exciting. Lily writhed as the machine moved within her, her breasts aching in Nathan's hands. He moved his mouth from one to the other, plumping, squeezing, and sucking in a manner he would not have been able to while atop her.

"Oh, please... please..." Lily gasped out the words, stretching against her bonds, her breasts thrusting up into Nathan's mouth as the sensations began to crest.

Unlike when she begged him, there was no change in pace, no increase in intensity from the machine. The constancy of the thrusting was as maddening as it was pleasurable.

One of Nathan's hands moved away from her breast, down to her mound, and pressed against her clit, just above the leather dildo pushing between her pussy lips. The tiny nub was slick and swollen, aching to be touched, and when his fingers finally made contact, her reaction was explosive.

Ecstasy burst, spiraling from her core through her body and her limbs. She cried out, unable to contain the sensations, yet that did not release them enough. The machine kept thrusting and pumping, stimulating her sensitive walls while her body jerked and clenched, and Lily's cries continued as her pleasure was pushed higher and higher.

This was not *la petit mort*—this was mind-altering erotic bliss on a level she had not known was achievable.

Nathan's mouth, his fingers, and the machine melded together into an impossibly pleasurable cacophony, leaving her breathless, blind, and deaf to everything else around her. The restraints were all that kept her from willfully ripping herself away from the excessive amount of stimulation, the overabundance of ecstasy.

"*Please!*" She screamed the word as another wave of rapture wracked her overextended nerves. The machine could not hear her, though, and Nathan's wicked mouth and fingers were not stopping. "*Please!*"

\* \* \*

<u>Nathan</u>

Wringing three orgasms from his wife was as much as Nathan could handle, and he was sure she was coming close to her limit as well. Releasing her breasts, he moved to the machine and opened the valve, which would release the steam out the back. Pulling it away from her, the wheels creaked as the whole apparatus moved back, leaving her splayed and open on the table.

Between her creamy thighs, her pussy was dark red and glossy, and a small pool of orgasmic juices coated the table beneath her. The entrance to her body gaped now that the dildo had been removed, as though it had burrowed a hole fitted especially for him.

Lily's eyelashes fluttered as Nathan undid the front of his pants, climbing onto the table and kneeling between her thighs. His cock was rock hard, and he knew he would not last long, which was for the best, considering how worn out she was after the extreme pleasure.

"Nathan?" The whispered question skated over his skin.

"I'm here," he said, pressing his cock to her hot, wet sheath. She moaned as he thrust in, her hips automatically lifting to meet his, as much as she could within the confines of the leather strapping her down, then gasped when he slammed home, his body rubbing against her clit and lips.

"Nathan!" The different tenor of her cry was all he needed.

Two more hard thrusts, then he held himself inside her, groaning with relief as his passion poured into her. Beneath him, Lily shuddered, clenching with the aftershocks of her ecstasy as they rocked together in heated bliss.

## Chapter Twenty-Eight

*ily*

L This time, Lily did not wake up sore and alone in her bed. She woke up sore and alone in her husband's bed. It was a minor improvement. Why the change in bed made a difference, she could not quite put her finger on, seeing as she was still alone—and sorer than ever, especially between her legs.

Laying on her back, legs slightly spread apart to keep her thighs from pressing on the tender flesh between them, she stared at the ceiling, wondering why her husband had moved them to his bed, then deserted her before she woke.

*On the other hand, are you in any condition to receive his amorous attentions right now?*

Reaching between her legs, she gingerly touched her abused pussy and winced. No... no, she was not. On the other hand, her friends had talked about things they could do with their mouths, and Lily had always been the curious type.

Oh, well. Sighing, Lily stood as she accepted the necessity of sneaking back to her own room and ringing for her maid. She purloined one of Nathan's robes from his wardrobe. If he was going to leave her in his room with no clothes, he could sacrifice some of his garments for the sake of her modesty.

Properly dressed, in her most comfortable underthings to help protect her skin, which still felt exquisitely sensitive, and wearing an eminently appropriate mourning dress that made her look far more respectable than she felt, Lily left her room and hurried downstairs. She needed to find out where everyone was and what they were doing—especially her husband. There would be a great deal of things to do today as they prepared for the viewing this afternoon and the funeral tomorrow.

Reaching the top of the stairs, Lily smiled as she saw Mary and Josie coming down the opposite hall. At least she was not too far behind her friends. Pausing to wait for them, she realized being on their own likely meant all the husbands were up and about trying to do as much as possible without feminine interference.

"Look at us, the abandoned wives club," she joked as they approached. Josie scowled at her.

"You will not think it is so funny when Nathan gets in the habit of leaving you out," she warned. Lily snorted, turning to walk down the stairs with Mary between them. She was well aware of the pretty picture they made, no matter that they were all wearing dresses appropriate for a viewing and not a London ballroom.

Mary was the most petite of the three, while Lily and Josie were about the same height. With Josie's blonde ringlets, Mary's auburn locks, and Lily's darker curls, the three of them were really quite striking in their contrasts.

"Nathan has not shown any interest in involving me in his investigations, so it is nothing new," Lily replied.

"You are going to tolerate that?"

"Of course not, but I have my own duties to attend to first. If he wants to get up early and ferret out information, so be it." Lily lifted her chin, linking her arm through Mary's when they reached the bottom of the steps. "He will learn."

Sighing, Josie linked her arm through Mary's on the other side.

"I think Rex is learning bad habits from your husbands," Mary complained, frowning. "I never woke up without him in bed beside me until now."

"What do you think they could be up to?" Josie asked.

Lily shook her head. The door to the dining room was closed, but she could hear people talking within. Had they misjudged their husbands?

The thought was immediately negated when the footman opened the door, and she saw Evie seated at the end of the table with Robert Jones. His wife was not present, and it appeared Robert was flirting with Evie—and she was letting him. More intriguing, when Lily walked through the door, she could see Captain Browne at the end of the table, glaring as if he could burn a hole through Nathan's cousin with the force of his eyeballs.

Which begged the question—if Captain Browne was here, where were the other gentlemen, and why had he not joined them?

*  *  *

*Nathan*

Yawning, Nathan grumbled under his breath as he crossed another name off his list. He'd chosen to requestion the men his brother had spoken to, while Elijah and Rex went with Harker and Moore to question the rest. Anthony had volunteered to stay behind and watch over the ladies, to everyone's surprise.

Personally, Nathan had thought Rex would be the one to take that position, but Anthony had jumped at the opportunity.

It did give him some relief. While Rex was a proper Corinthian, a good shot, and adept with the sword, he was not as good as Anthony. Could not be. Anthony's skills had been honed while in enemy territory, not at Gentlemen Jim's or the dueling clubs.

Unfortunately, Nathan's morning had been a colossal waste so far. Not one of the men he'd questioned had known anything about smuggling spies, nor had his brother given them any hint why he'd been questioning them. Sebastian had been incredibly tight-lipped, even with the leaders of the gangs. Not surprising, but very frustrating.

"Dammit, Seb, you could have left me a few more clues."

He had not found the notes Harker claimed his brother had taken about the interviews despite a thorough search. He'd even thought to flip through his brother's folio this morning but had not seen anything pertinent to the investigation, so he had put it back down. Looking through Seb's folio had hurt with the reminder that his brother was gone and had ultimately yielded him nothing.

It had been a *very* early morning. Time that may have been better spent with his wife in his bed. Leaving her there had been difficult. She'd been warm, soft, and snuggly, and Nathan had fought the urge to remain there, lolling in her warmth and in sleep. Nathan yawned again as he rode Merlin back into the stable yard.

Elijah and Harker were back, getting down from the gig they'd taken to go about. Harker was still recovering from his rushed ride to London, so Nathan had not wanted to make him get on a horse again so soon unless it was necessary.

"Did you find out anything of importance?" Nathan asked, riding up and swinging down from Merlin's back. If they had, they would need to decamp to somewhere more private, but right now, Nathan felt that was an unlikely 'if.' The most likely sources of information had been on *his* list, which was why he'd taken the first names Sebastian had put on it. He had a feeling his brother had also felt those names were the most likely to know anything.

There was always the possibility someone had engaged in their own activities outside of the gangs, though.

"No." Elijah shook his head, appearing frustrated, as did Harker. "They were all happy enough to talk to me once Harker gave them the nod, but none of them knew anything. Either they were all involved and all covering for each other, which I think highly unlikely, or whoever was involved kept things quiet enough that no one else knew."

"Damn." Nathan sighed. "Let's go to my study. We can wait for Rex and Moore and regroup."

"You are also going to need to eat something before the viewing. Once your neighbors start showing up, there will not be time," Elijah reminded him, eyeing him up and down with concern.

Nathan grimaced but knew Elijah was right. Besides, right now, he did not know what their next move should be.

"I will have Cook send up a luncheon for you and your guests in your study, my lord," Harker said, turning to trot off to the back door of the manor. Only a little stiff, he was moving much better than he had been yesterday, and Nathan was glad he'd insisted on the gig rather than putting Harker back on a horse.

"We should also see how Browne is faring," Nathan said, falling into step beside Elijah. They moved slowly to give Harker some time. "I'll send a footman for him to join us."

"It should have been a quiet morning for him." Elijah chuckled. "I cannot imagine why he was so intent on staying behind."

Nathan shrugged. Browne always had his reasons and rarely deigned to explain them.

* * *

<u>Lily</u>

Breakfast was an uncomfortable though amusing affair that mostly consisted of watching Evie flirt with Robert while Captain Browne glared at both of them. With Robert at the table, their topics of conversation were limited, but at least they did not have to deal with Letitia.

According to Robert, she kept London hours even when they were not in town and would be unlikely to rise until noon. He seemed to enjoy her absence.

"Would anyone like to go for a ride this fine morning?" Robert asked as they all finished their meals, though his gaze remained fixed on Evie. Wearing a dark forest green that brought out her eyes, she smiled back demurely at him, playing the coquette to perfection.

"Oh, I would love that." Evie giggled, leaning forward on her chin and batting her long eyelashes at Robert.

Captain Browne grumbled something under his breath, gripping his fork so tightly, Lily was beginning to worry he might try to use it as a weapon.

Evie turned to look at Lily. "Do you think you will need me this morning?"

"I am sure we can manage without you if you would like to go riding," Lily said, ignoring the seething captain two seats down from her. Whatever Evie was up to, she had an agenda in mind, and Lily would not stop her.

"Then I will go change into my riding habit." Getting to her feet, Evie brushed off her skirts and gave Robert a saucy look.

"Wonderful. Shall we meet in the foyer in, say, half an hour?" Robert smiled genially as Captain Brown growled under his breath. Far from being deterred by Captain Browne's clear disapproval, Robert seemed to revel in it.

"Perfect." Evie did not wink at him—although Lily half-expected her to—but there was an extra swish in her step as she sashayed out the door. Just before she reached the threshold, she glanced back over her shoulder—not at Robert but at Lily—perfectly angled so Robert could not see her expression, which had changed completely.

Lily did not need Evie to say a word to know she wanted her friends to follow her and meet in her room. Smiling serenely, Lily waited a few minutes of awkward silence while Mary and Josie murmured back and forth to each other, Captain Browne glared at Robert, and Robert focused on finishing the last of his kedgeree, before clearing her throat.

"My goodness, there is so much to do today. I should really get started. Josie, Mary, would you mind if I drafted your assistance?" Lily kept her tone light, high. Neither Robert nor Captain Browne seemed to notice the difference, but Josie and Mary's heads jerked toward her in surprise since they had previously offered their assistance. Lily tilted her head toward the door Evie had left through only minutes ago. Mary's gaze cleared immediately while Josie took a moment longer, then a look of understanding fell over her expression.

"Yes, of course," Mary said, getting to her feet as Josie jumped to hers. "Whatever we can do."

Captain Browne blinked as if suddenly noticing they were there—and abandoning him. Robert looked a bit alarmed as he realized he was about to be left alone in the dining room with the captain.

"Ah, well." Robert got to his feet as well. "I should wait in the foyer for Miss Stuart, I expect, and send a footman to the stables to prepare some horses for us—unless there is anything I can do to assist you as well?" The offer was made out of obligation, not actual desire to help, which almost made Lily want to accept just to tweak his nose, but there were more important things going on.

Whatever Evie was up to with him, she would not appreciate Lily spiking her guns.

"No, thank you." Lily smiled at him, waving at Josie and Mary as Captain Browne watched them suspiciously, a frown forming on his handsome face. "I am sure we ladies can handle it."

## Chapter Twenty-Nine

### Lily

"What are you doing with Robert?" Lily blurted out as soon as she reached Evie's room, Josie and Mary hot on her heels.

"You mean other than driving Captain Browne absolutely wild with jealousy?" Josie asked dryly, moving past Lily to flop into the armchair beside Evie's window.

Shaking her head, Mary went to help Evie, who was struggling a little with the fawn-colored riding habit she was putting on.

"He is hardly jealous, only overbearing," Evie said irritably, twisting and fiddling with the fall of her skirt. Josie and Lily exchanged a look, Josie's eyebrows arching high on her forehead.

Neither of them missed that Evie had chosen to answer Josie's question instead of Lily's. Lily would have expected her to ignore Josie entirely, but something about the query must have gotten under her skin.

How very interesting.

Unfortunately, they did not have time to dwell on the mystery of Evie and Captain Browne, though it was clear there was far more going on than Evie had seen fit to disclose. She might claim it was all in the past, but evidently, the past had come knocking.

"I do not think Mr. Jones will know anything, but he *is* your husband's cousin. While it is unlikely Nathan's brother confided anything in Mr. Jones, he did not tell your husband, it is a possibility," Evie continued, straightening up while Mary did the buttons on her right sleeve, the ones harder for Evie to do on her own. "Besides which, it is always possible the late earl's death came at the hands of someone who wanted to move the title along."

Lily was not surprised that Evie had thought of that as well.

"You think Mr. Jones killed his cousin, and you want to go riding with him?" Mary asked, looking at Evie as though she was mad.

"Honestly, no, I do not think he did, but I think a possibility, yet the men left him here to his own devices." Evie shrugged. "I decided to grab the opportunity afforded to me."

"Captain Browne clearly riled up by the attention you were paying Mr. Jones is just icing on your cake," Josie teased, her broad smile undimmed by the dark look Evie shot her.

A knock at the door made everyone jump. Being the closest, Lily quickly turned to open it and was surprised to find Mrs. Moore on the other side. The housekeeper brightened at the sight of her, bobbing a quick curtsy.

"Good morning, my lady. I was hoping you were in here when I heard the voices. The room for the viewing this afternoon has been set up, and we've begun preparations for the dinner this evening. The Verners and Lord Warwick have both sent word they will attend."

"Warwick?" Evie appeared at Lily's shoulder, making Mrs. Moore step back in surprise. "Lord Gabriel Warwick?"

Mrs. Moore blinked at the urgency in Evie's tone.

"Yes, his estate is directly to the west of us."

"Is it now?" Evie and Lily exchanged glances, then Evie made a face. "Blast, I have to go meet Mr. Jones for our ride. Lily?"

"Yes, of course," Lily said as Mrs. Moore looked back and forth between the two of them in confusion. She was sure the poor woman did not know what was going on. After so many years of friendship, they did not always need to speak their thoughts aloud to know what the other was going to say. Lily smiled broadly at her housekeeper.

"Evie needs to be going, but please come in for a moment, Mrs. Moore. I have a few questions for you if you do not mind."

\* \* \*

*Nathan*

Frustration was riding Nathan hard with the wasted time of the morning.

Unsurprisingly, Rex and Moore had returned with no new information, either, leaving them floundering with what to do next. He had been so sure the list would have some answers, if not *the* answer, but they were no further ahead than they'd been.

"Perhaps your father was not actually a traitor," Rex suggested. He and Elijah had moved to the two chairs next to the window, turning them about so they could face the room where Nathan was pacing. Anthony was at the other window, glaring at the stable yard, with his arms crossed.

Nathan made a face. It was not that he wanted his father to be a traitor, but nothing else fit.

"Then how do you explain the money?"

"Maybe he really did win a few large bets?" There was no real assuredness in Rex's voice, so he did not believe it, either.

"Did you know your cousin Mr. Jones is going on a ride with Miss Stuart?" Anthony suddenly asked from the window. "Right there." He pointed. "See? She is joining him."

Curious, Nathan was drawn to the window.

"Why are they going riding together?" he asked, looking down at the yard. Sure enough, there was his cousin and Miss Stuart, who looked fetching in a habit and a little cap with a bobbing green feather atop it. Robert seemed to think so.

Nathan frowned as his cousin bowed and held Miss Stuart's hand as though they were in a ballroom and he was courting her. While he had sensed friction between Robert and Letitia, he would not have expected his cousin to be playing the rake at a time like this, especially not with a debutante. Though, admittedly, Miss Stuart hardly behaved like a normal debutante, even discounting that she'd been dressed as a maid the first time he'd met her.

"Because she is determined to put herself in danger." Anthony gritted the words through his teeth. "For all we know, he could have murdered your brother to put himself another step closer to the title."

"True enough, but I do not think that means Miss Stuart will come to any harm. I have my doubts if he would actually kill Sebastian, though he certainly would not weep over inheriting the title."

Going by his behavior with Miss Stuart, Robert appeared more interested in celebrating than mourning. It made Nathan sick to his stomach, and he wanted to give his cousin a facer, but it was hardly evidence of murder.

Anthony whirled around to glare at Elijah.

"Are you not going to do anything to defend your cousin's honor?"

The look Elijah returned was long-suffering. He scrubbed his hand over his face before raking it through his dark hair.

"I have learned not to insert myself into Evie's business," Elijah said tiredly. "I would prefer my cousin not disappear on me again. I do not think my father's health could handle it. Evie can take care of herself, as she has proven over and over again. Besides, he would be foolish to do her harm when he would be the only suspect."

They all sobered at the reminder of the Marquess' injuries. Anthony scowled and turned back to the window, glaring down at Miss Stuart and Robert as they mounted their horses.

"He could make it look like an accident," Anthony muttered under his breath. The same way Sebastian's death had been meant to look like an accident, but Sebastian had been out riding alone. Two horseback-riding accidents in such a short period of time? Especially with both Nathan and the lady's cousin there. Though they had kept the knowledge about Sebastian's murder close, anyone with brains would hesitate to play the same trick again so quickly, and one thing Nathan was sure of, his brother's murderer was not stupid.

Nathan was certain the only thing in danger was her virtue, and riding should be safe enough. He did not doubt Elijah's cousin could protect herself in that quarter very well.

Turning away from the window and Anthony's pouting, Nathan

had no idea what he was going to do next, but it ended up being a moot point.

The door to his study slammed open, and his wife came sailing into the room like a warship, chin high, eyes flashing, and cannons at the ready. Behind her were Mary and Josie, spreading out as soon as they came through the door, forming a phalanx.

"We need to talk," Lily announced.

\* \* \*

*Lily*

Scanning quickly around the room, it only took a moment for Lily to find her husband and pin him with her gaze.

"I am assuming you knew that Lord Gabriel Warwick is one of your neighbors?" she asked, barely keeping the sarcasm threaded through her tone under control.

"Yes, of course, but what does that have to do with anything?"

The utter bafflement on Nathan's face was satisfying in that Lily knew she was about to reveal information he had been unaware of. Trying to keep her and the other ladies out of everything... ha!

"Did you know he and his secretary visited your brother the evening before Sebastian's murder?" Lily put her hands on her hips, raising her eyebrows when none of the men reacted.

"So?" Elijah asked.

Behind her, Josie made a noise of frustration.

"Really? You have been focusing your investigations entirely on those on this estate but not the neighboring ones? Including a neighbor who visited the night before your brother's death and could have easily planted something on Sebastian's saddle?" No longer able to hold back her sarcasm, Lily let it drip from her tone.

The men looked at each other. Rex looked concerned while the others did not.

"Mitchell would have told us if Warwick was a traitor," Nathan said in the most placating manner she'd ever heard.

"Mitchell, the same Mitchell who Rex kicked out of the Society of

Sin for trying to rape a maid?" Mary asked, moving to her husband's side.

"I wish I could have done more," Rex muttered, curving his arm around Mary's waist. "The man is a reprobate, and I still do not understand why Elijah trusts him."

"He has served my father for over a decade," Elijah argued, shooting a look at Rex that indicated he did not appreciate his commentary on Mitchell's character or Elijah's decisions.

To Lily's eyes, Rex was the only man in the room showing any sense.

"Who knows what else he has been getting up to while he did?" Josie stepped up beside Lily, crossing her arms over her chest and giving her husband a significant look. "You said the reason you use him is he gets into places others cannot, that those who do not trust easily will trust him because they feel he is one of them. Have you thought about why that is?"

"Because he's not a lord, not connected to any of our families. He's a working gentleman, not part of the aristocracy," Elijah said explained.

"Or possibly, he is himself involved in unsavory activities," Lily pointed out in exasperation. "He knows *everything* you have been doing, every move you make against the traitor, all the knowledge you have gathered about him. It would explain why the traitor is always one step ahead of you—because you have involved him in his own investigation!"

"Why do you not think it is Warwick?" Captain Browne asked, joining the conversation for the first time. He was still looking out the window, but at least he was asking questions instead of rejecting the idea outright. "Why does it have to be Mitchell?"

"It is possible, but I think Mitchell is the more likely suspect unless he is reporting everything back to Warwick, who then masterminds the plans." Mary tapped her chin thoughtfully. "But honestly, from what I have seen of Warwick, I do have trouble imagining that. He is a hedonist and lazy except when it comes to sadism. That seems to be the only place he has any interest in expending his energy."

"Or it is neither of them, and you are seeing connections that do not exist," Elijah snapped, getting to his feet. "One visit versus years of service... there is no evidence."

"Well, Warwick is coming to the viewing today," Lily said, raising her chin. "If Mitchell attends with him, I think it best we ask him some questions."

"If you trust his answers," Mary added, making a face. Beside her, Rex nodded.

Elijah shot another look at the pair, glaring, before turning back to Lily and Josie.

"There is no reason not to trust the man."

"Ah, so you will have no problem if I am the one to question him, alone, with no one else in the room?" Josie asked archly.

"That is not the trust I mean, and you know it!" Elijah thundered.

Josie merely sniffed. "If a man is immoral in one way, he is likely to be immoral in others. If you cannot trust him with your wife, why would you trust him with your country?" Having laid down her point, at which Elijah floundered, Josie tipped her nose in the air. "Now, if you will excuse us, after having tracked down information you were unaware of, we still have a viewing and dinner to arrange." Turning on her heel, she swanned out of the room.

Lily could not think of a single thing to add, so she met Nathan's gaze, nodded her head firmly, and followed. Mary came out a moment later, though she had a feeling Rex had received a much more congenial goodbye than the rest of the gentlemen.

As he deserved, and her husband currently did not.

Men.

Only one out of four of them were using any sense.

## Chapter Thirty

**Nathan**

The viewing was a surprisingly crowded affair. Nathan knew the notice had gone out to all the neighbors and to London, but he had not expected the turnout. Some of them, the London guests, were mostly there due to nosiness, stopping by to pay their respects—and indulge their curiosity—on their way out of London.

The number of their neighbors who had come to pay their respects was the bigger surprise. They certainly had not appeared in such great quantity for his father.

When he thought about it, that was not as surprising as it seemed. His father had not been the neighborly sort, and it would not surprise him if Sebastian had been working to be the opposite of their father in that respect. Not to mention his brother had always been the sociable sort and had been stuck on the estates all Season. Going by the number of heartfelt condolences, he had made an impression on the local social circle.

All of which served as a distraction from the ladies. They were still miffed about how he and Elijah had dismissed their information, and he could not entirely blame them.

The more he thought about it, the more it made sense.

He just did not want it to.

The idea someone he knew, whom Elijah and his father had trusted, who was supposed to be one of *theirs*, had betrayed them... hurt even more than knowing his own father might have been involved. A double-cross—was what it would be if the ladies were correct.

It was also extremely worrisome because who knew how much classified information had gone to the enemy if Mitchell or both Mitchell and Warwick were involved.

The ideal scenario would be that Warwick was the culprit on his own, but Nathan did not see how that was possible without Mitchell knowing. He was sharp, clever, ambitious, and had a nose for ferreting out information. It was unbelievable to the point of ludicrousness to think Warwick could have been engaged in treachery without Mitchell knowing.

Which meant it was either Mitchell or both.

"If they are correct, you know we will never hear the end of it." Grim faced, Elijah appeared at Nathan's side as the foyer finally emptied. Lily had gone into the drawing-room with Lady Cavill, lending the elderly matriarch her arm and her ear. As the presiding lady on the local social scene, Lady Cavill had decided she needed to get to know his countess, and Nathan was very thankful she had.

"Is it making more sense?" Nathan asked, keeping his voice low. Elijah was more agitated than he had been earlier. No wonder, if he had been thinking the same thoughts as Nathan and coming to the same uncomfortable conclusions.

"I do not want to believe it... but yes. I would like to send one of your footmen with an urgent note to my father. He will know better how likely it is."

"Do it." Nathan nodded. Hopefully, Mitchell was not the traitor they were searching for, but if he was, the Marquess of Camden needed to know immediately. At the very least, they should not keep the suspicion from him.

If they were very lucky, he would have evidence to refute the conjecture, and they could go on with their search.

\* \* \*

*Lily*

"Excuse me, Lady Cavill, I need to tear Lady Jones away from you for a moment." Giving the old dragon her most appealing smile, Josie somehow managed to pierce the lady's scales, and her crabby expression actually softened. Lily really must get Josie to teach her how to do that.

"Thank you," she whispered under her breath as Josie pulled her away. "I do not think she intended to let me leave her side."

"Warwick just arrived with Mitchell," Josie responded grimly before pasting another smile on her face as they passed another of Lily's new neighbors. "Nathan and Elijah went upstairs for a moment. If we do not want to be cut out, you need to greet him first."

Lily picked up her pace. Out of the corner of her eye, she saw Mary and Evie moving toward the door, though more slowly, acting as though they were only walking that way. As the hostess, no one would be surprised to see her hurrying to greet a late arrival, but the other two had to be more circumspect.

Stepping into the foyer, Lily saw the two men standing in the center of it, heads bowed together as they spoke quietly. They were handsomely turned out in clothing befitting the occasion. Warwick looked up, saw her coming, and stepped forward, which neatly put Mitchell behind him. Something flashed across the secretary's expression over Warwick's shoulder, gone too quickly to be identified.

"My lord," Lily said, dipping into a very brief curtsy. As an earl, she and Warwick were social equals. "Thank you for coming."

"I am sorry we are running late. Unfortunately unavoidable," Warwick said with a sigh, stepping forward to make his bow over her hand.

"I am glad you could join us." Lily did her best to hide her distaste for his touch, though she did not allow her hand to linger in his. "You and my husband's late brother were friends, were you not?"

"Ah, not really. Neighbors, of course, but..." Warwick paused as if trying to figure out how to word his statement without sounding insulting. Lily raised her eyebrows.

"I am sorry, I misunderstood. My housekeeper told me you visited with him the night before he..." Lily's let the sentence hang, hoping Warwick would take the bait and she was not disappointed.

"Yes, I had just returned from London and knew he was in residence. Wanted to do the neighborly thing and all that." Warwick shook his head sadly. "It was a shock to hear the news the next day when I had been speaking to him the night before."

"A shock to everyone. So young and—from what everyone says—an exceptional rider." Lily paid close attention to Warwick's reaction, knowing Josie would be doing the same for Mitchell. From what she could see, there was nothing in his demeanor other than true sorrow.

"I suppose a horse can throw anyone, but I must admit, I am not much of a rider," Warwick replied. "Mitchell is an avid horse lover, though. He visited the stables while we were here. Fine specimens, you said." As he spoke, Warwick turned toward his secretary, and Lily focused on the other man.

Did she imagine it, or did Mitchell stiffen when Warwick mentioned he had visited the stables during their visit? Would such a visit have given him ample time to sabotage either Sebastian's horse or his tack?

"Mitchell. Warwick." Nathan's voice echoed through the foyer, making all of them jump. Their heads swung around as one to see Nathan looking down on them, gripping the banister overseeing the foyer. Beside him were Elijah, Captain Browne, and Rex, all appearing just as tense. "A moment of your time, if you please."

The request was snapped out like a command, nothing like the polite back-and-forth Lily and Warwick had been engaging in. She turned her head to look at him and saw nothing but confusion.

Beyond him, Mr. Mitchell had gone stiff. Grim. Staring up at Nathan. Then Nathan turned his head, and his gaze met hers, full of suspicion. Lily pressed her lips together.

"Now."

Perhaps it was the tension in Nathan's voice or that Warwick had brought up Mitchell's sojourn to the stables, but whatever it was, the man clearly realized they suspected him.

With a fluid motion, he jumped forward, his hand slamming against Warwick's side. The earl cried out, clutching the knife hilt that had suddenly appeared there, dropping to his knees. Mitchell shoved the injured earl at her and Josie, and they held out their hands to bolster him as he cried out again.

* * *

Nathan
Shock held him immobile for a moment.
*It* had *been Mitchell. It had been Mitchell all along.*
The traitor. His brother's murderer. A turncoat, double-crosser.

Fury had him springing into action, but the drawing-room was emptying into the foyer, crowding the space. The noise increased as questions were asked when one of the ladies saw Warwick lying on Lily's lap, blood slowly spreading on his coat, and the lady screamed and fainted.

Nathan was already more than halfway down the steps, Elijah and Browne beside him, Rex only a step behind, but Mitchell had a big lead on them... and all the people now whirling around the foyer were getting in their way. They pushed through—Elijah and Browne heading straight for the door and Nathan going straight to Lily.

"Are you alright?" he shouted to be heard over the cacophony.

"Yes. Go!" Lily swung her arm about, pointing to the door. "We will handle this."

Evie was already pushing through the crowd, a cloth in her hand and a fierce expression on her face. She dropped to her knees beside Lily and pressed it against Warwick's side, wrapping it around the knife's handle.

Cursing under his breath, Nathan went. It felt wrong to leave Lily there, but he had his priorities, though, and Warwick was no threat.

The ladies had been correct.

Nathan straightened and shoved his way through the crowd still milling about, ignoring the questions shouted at him.

Despite his stop, he was not far behind Elijah and the others. He could see them running headlong for the stable yard. Unfortunately, Mitchell had gotten there long before them and was already rushing pell-mell out of the yard atop his horse.

Bloody hell.

Elijah and the others scattered as Mitchell aimed a pistol at them, which allowed him to go straight through toward the road unhindered. They kept running for the yard, determined to catch him. The raised voices both in and out of the house were reaching a peak as he and the others shouted for their horses.

Confused grooms milled about before hurrying to do as ordered.

Not waiting for a saddle, Elijah swung up onto his mount with only a bit between the horse's teeth. Browne shouldered a groom out of the way, taking over saddling the black stallion in record time. By the time Nathan reached the yard, Browne was already on his way out, Rex just behind him, and Merlin was already saddled and being brought around.

Climbing on, he was barely mounted before kicking Merlin into a gallop and following the dust clouds down the road. Crouching low, he let Merlin have his head, and the stallion responded beautifully, eagerly stretching out his stride as though he was running a race. Unfortunately, Nathan was already far behind in the race.

His only comfort was that Lily was safe back at Talbot Manor, though he was sure she would be cursing his name.

Elijah was likely right.

They would never hear the end of it.

\* \* \*

*Lily*

Thanks to the combined efforts of Mary, Josie, Evie, Lily, her parents, and surprisingly, Lady Cavill, Lily finally got everything under control. She dismissed the neighbors who were still there for the viewing and settled Warwick in a room, albeit uncomfortably, while they awaited the doctor. Lily's parents retired once she had given them a very basic explanation of the events of the day. She told them about Sebastian's murder but not about Mitchell being the traitor.

It was a bit of an odd explanation without being able to explain the motive, but they accepted it, exclaimed over her, and asked if she wanted them to wait with her for Nathan's return. Lily had urged them to go to bed since her friends would be with her, and she could see how tired they were. They'd accepted her reassurances that she was fine and had gone to bed.

The doctor arrived before Nathan and the others, and she showed him to Warwick's rooms, where he set to work. Seeing Warwick was in good hands, Lily felt comfortable leaving him there with a footman to assist the doctor.

"Where is Evie?" Lily asked as soon as she entered the drawing-room. Mary and Josie were there, but Evie was gone. For that matter, so was Lady Cavill, though that was more a relief since they could speak freely in her absence.

Mary blinked.

"We thought she was with you."

Lily sighed and slumped on the couch. If she was to hazard a guess, Evie was on her way back to London. Not that she could blame her friend.

Though Evie's uncle had guards around the house since the last assassination attempt, Mr. Mitchell had been a trusted personage. She would not want to leave her uncle alone—and likely wanted to be part of the hunt. Lily had no doubt they'd be hearing from Evie sometime soon.

"What a day. What a week." Lily pressed the back of her hand to her forehead, closing her eyes and groaning.

"It has been an eventful Season," Josie agreed. Even she sounded more exhausted than cheerful.

The couch shifted as Mary moved closer and took Lily's other hand to comfort her. Lily sighed again when Mary squeezed her fingers, so glad to have had the support of her friends. She knew Evie had not abandoned them. She was just used to going her own way.

The urge to get up and do something was pounding inside her, but unfortunately, there was nothing any of them could do right now. They had to wait for someone to come back and tell them what was going on.

Letting her hand fall, Lily straightened. There *was* one thing she could do. The only thing she could think of to do.

She could do what any proper British lady did in a time of crisis—ring for tea.

## Chapter Thirty-One

### Nathan

The moon was bright, hanging in the dark sky, lighting up the country roads, but Nathan knew they were still risking the horses—and themselves—galloping down the lane.

Elijah waited at a crossroads, and Nathan pulled himself up. The moonlight was enough, he could easily see the grim set of Elijah's expression. Merlin danced beneath Nathan, wondering why they were stopping before he finally settled. Behind him, he could hear Rex coming to a halt as well, and they both finished the last bit at a walk.

"Anthony has gone ahead," Elijah said. His jaw was set. Being left out of the action always grated on all of them. "It has become clear that unless we want to ride through the night, we will not catch Mitchell... and our wives are back at Brentwood Manor." He met Nathan's gaze. "The funeral is tomorrow."

"What about your father?" Nathan asked. That was likely the largest danger.

"The footman with my note about Mitchell was dispatched hours ago, so my father will be somewhat forewarned." Elijah's jaw worked. "If Mitchell has any sense, he will go to ground or jump on a ship."

In which case, they would never find him. Nathan did not like that option. He wanted justice for his brother and reassurance the threat against all of them was over. Though now that Mitchell had been unmasked, the threat was most likely gone, wasn't it? All Mitchell's careful work had been to ensure no one would discover he was a traitor.

On the other hand, he also now had nothing left to lose.

It was possible he would be more dangerous than ever under such circumstances.

Letting him go felt wrong, but Elijah was right. Nathan had other duties he could not ignore.

"Damn!" he shouted. Merlin shifted beneath him at the outburst, and Nathan reined in his temper.

"Do we know if Mitchell had any accomplices?" Rex asked. "I think we should re-interview the men we talked to today, now that we have a name."

That was true. And it was likely that the operations had been done from Warwick's lands rather than Talbot lands, which meant they probably had a whole other crew of smugglers they would need to speak with. Under the circumstances, he doubted Warwick would resist having his tenants questioned... if the man still lived.

Nathan hoped he did. He had a lot of questions for the earl.

He nodded.

"I will understand if you want to go on," he said to Elijah. "Rex and I can return to the ladies and explain to your wife."

"No, there is nothing I can do that Anthony cannot, and as much as I want to be by my father's side, he would be furious if I did not question Warwick before I leave." Proving Elijah and Nathan were much of the same mind when it came to the earl.

He was most likely innocent, but he must know *something*... unless Mitchell had only stabbed him to create confusion for his escape, which seemed possible. They would not know until they questioned him. Elijah was right that the Marquess of Camden was already alerted to the danger. They had a witness to question, if he survived, and either way, the Marquess would want to know any information they could gather.

Though Elijah's presence at the funeral was not necessary, as an earl and a future marquess, his absence would be noted. The same with Rex.

Anthony's absence might be noted by a few, but not in the same way as the rest of them, as he was not a member of the nobility.

The best thing they could do to quell gossip was to pretend Mitchell was nothing more than a common murderer. If two earls and a marquess chased him into the night, there would be questions. Wild conjectures. If two earls and a marquess sent a captain from the army in their stead to chase down a murderer, no one would think anything of it.

On more than one front, the wise thing to do was to let Anthony go on his way while the rest of them appeared at the funeral tomorrow.

After that, Elijah and Rex would be free to do as they pleased.

Nathan, on the other hand, had to fulfill his responsibilities and sit on the sidelines. At least for a bit. The knowledge made him want to gnash his teeth, but he knew where his duty lay.

"Right, then," he said shortly, turning his horse around. "Back to the manor."

They cantered rather than galloped, giving the horses a bit of a rest. They had only gotten around the first bend when another horse came hurtling down the road. Nathan cursed, pulling Merlin to the side. The other rider did not even slow as he flew past.

In front of Nathan, Elijah swung his horse around, his dark eyes blazing in the moonlight.

"Evie!" When Elijah shouted his cousin's name his horse startled, and he barely kept his seat, thanks to the lack of saddle.

Nathan looked over his shoulder as the other rider disappeared around the bend. Yes, that was not a 'he.' Elijah's cousin had just passed them. Nathan and Rex looked at each other, then at Elijah, waiting to see what he wanted them to do. For a moment, he thought Elijah would go after her.

Elijah shook his head, then set his jaw and turned his horse around, letting his cousin go on unhindered.

"Back to the manor."

\* \* \*

*Lily*

Sitting and drinking tea was no substitute for action, yet it made Lily feel better. She did not feel completely calm until the door opened, and Nathan came in, Elijah and Rex on his heels. The moment they heard the front door, all three ladies leapt from their seats—though only Josie spilled her tea—and ran to the foyer.

The feeling of disappointment seeing the men return empty-handed was overwhelmed by her relief that they were all hale, hearty, and unharmed.

But...

"Where is Captain Browne?" she asked, rushing to Nathan to check him all over. He looked tired but did not appear to have suffered any injury.

"Following Mitchell on to London." Nathan ran his hands over her arms, checking her over in much the same manner as she was him. "Unfortunately, he had too much of a lead... we would never have caught him."

Not without riding through the night.

The words were unspoken, but Lily understood and felt for him and especially for Elijah. Looking over, she saw her old neighbor was wrapped in Josie's hug. Lily could not imagine how hard it had been for him to turn away and come back here, but she was grateful, considering all the social implications if he had not.

Quelling talk tomorrow was going to be difficult enough. If Elijah had gone on, everyone would have been wondering *why*.

Why had the Earl of Durham chased a villain into the night, leaving his wife at Brentwood Manor?

It was not a question easily answered without the truth, which was something they dared not share with anyone else. Very few people knew the Marquess of Camden was England's spymaster or that his firstborn was set to inherit both his title and his position as such, and it was best kept that way.

"Did you see Evie?"

"Yes, she rode past us as we were headed back here. You should have stopped her from leaving." A note of chiding entered Nathan's voice, then his eyes widened in surprise when she snorted in derision. Nathan did not know Evie.

"We did not know she had gone," Lily said. Elijah looked up, letting Josie go from his embrace so he could turn. "Let us go into the drawing-room so we can tell each other everything."

Seeing the sense, they decamped from the foyer. Lily rang for a fresh pot of tea as they arranged themselves around the room. This time, the gentlemen sat as well, seeing no need to stand on ceremony. Rex pulled Mary onto his lap on the couch while Elijah did the same with Josie in one of the chairs. Lily hesitated as she returned to sit down—Nathan was on the couch as well. He patted the seat beside him, between himself and the couple snuggled on the other side.

Propriety was out the window. Inwardly shrugging, Lily sat next to him, enjoying the way he gripped her hand. She leaned her head on his shoulder as Josie recounted the events from their point of view, starting from when Warwick arrived.

Though, Lily noted, she did not mention that they had deliberately intercepted him, hoping to speak with him before the men could.

About halfway through their discussion, the doctor came downstairs. Warwick had been dosed with laudanum and fallen asleep. Questioning would have to wait until morning. Thanking him, Nathan sent the doctor on his way, leaving the rest of them to finish their stories, then head to bed.

Tomorrow was going to be another busy day.

\* \* \*

*Nathan*

Feeling utterly drained, Nathan was far too exhausted for marital romps by the time he and Lily made their way back to their rooms, yet he found himself pulling her into his room. He did not want to spend the night without her.

"I... I might be too sore..." She blushed, and Nathan could not help but chuckle, despite everything. The enjoyment of seeing her blush never faded.

"Nothing tonight, but I want to hold you."

Awareness lit her eyes, and the blush did not go away, but she nodded and came into his room.

It was a different intimacy, undressing her without the intention of more. Sliding under the covers and holding each other close. Feeling the silky smoothness of her skin, the warmth of her embrace, and slowly relaxing in the haven of her arms.

Of course, his body reacted in an expected manner since she was naked. With no intention of pressing her for any kind of marital intimacies, Nathan shifted his hips away.

To his shock, Lily pressed him onto his back, her lips moving over his stomach towards his cock. At first, he did not think she could be doing what he thought she was going to do, but when she grasped his cock and moved her mouth towards the tip, he realized she *did* know.

"Where did you learn about this?" he asked hoarsely as her pink tongue flicked out to taste the tip. The soft wet heat of the lick made him shudder.

"My friends, of course." Her smile was devious.

Normally, Nathan would not approve of gossip about such delicate matters. He hoped she would not share too much of their own activities with her friends, but as she closed her lips around the tip of his cock and flicked her tongue against the spongy head, he realized, in some cases, it was not at all a bad thing. On his back in the darkness, one hand threaded through her hair, he groaned as Lily explored him with her mouth and tongue as her hands cradled the sack beneath his cock and squeezed gently.

The wet heat of her mouth moving up and down his cock was inexperienced and unpracticed, yet entirely enjoyable. Nathan had never been on the receiving end of being an experiment, but that was very much what it felt like as Lily sucked and nibbled and licked.

When his peak approached, his hand tightened in her hair, and she let him take control. His hips thrust into her mouth, his groans filling the room as she sucked, despite the increasing pace of his movements.

"Lily!" Nathan cried as he released, pressing her head down against his groin. The muscles of her throat quivered around the head of his cock as she swallowed him down, her mouth still suckling the whole time. She did not stop until his body went limp, and his cock was softening, leaving him gasping, quivering, and far more tired than he had expected to be.

Despite the events of the day, he had not thought he would actually be able to sleep, but with his body drained and his head resting on her bosom as she cradled his head, her lips against his hair, his descent into sleep was the easiest thing in the world.

## Chapter Thirty-Two

L*ily* Meeting with smugglers was not something she would have expected to do in her life, but the events of the prior day had precipitated unexpected openness into their investigation on the part of the men. Perhaps Nathan realized she had gained far more information from Warwick before Nathan had accidentally bungled things. Something she had decided not to point out. He knew.

Lily was also sure, if it were not for the funeral, Nathan and the other men would have kept her, Mary, and Josie well away from the smugglers. As it was, with everyone gathered for the service at the church, Nathan made his rounds with his questions with Lily on his arm. They kept their voices low, and Elijah, Josie, Rex, and Mary played interference for any who might try to approach them.

"Mitchell? Aye, I saw him talking to some of Warwick's men," Christopher Martin said, rubbing his chin. Lily would not have guessed he was a smuggler by the look of him—he appeared to be a perfectly ordinary man and an upright citizen. She'd also met his wife, an apple-cheeked blonde who had been called away to tend to one of their many children.

Then again, Lily did not know much about smuggling. Apparently, her husband had done some runs with the local gang when he was a youth, a rite of passage for young men along the coastline. She was learning more new things about him every day. Mr. Martin had been their leader when Nathan and Sebastian had joined them.

"Did any of ours ever join Warwick's?" Nathan asked. Mr. Martin glanced at Lily, who smiled encouragingly.

"Aye, but Jeb and Morty are both passed now. Fever took both of them a few years ago." Mr. Martin's jaw worked as the implications sank in. Likely, they had been the two who had assisted with treason... men Mr. Martin had worked with. Trusted. Of course, they could not prove it had been either of them, but it seemed the most likely as no one else had been able to turn up any proof.

Thanking the man for coming, she and Nathan moved away.

"I hope Warwick awakens soon," Nathan muttered. Lily nodded.

As they turned, she caught the eye of Robert, Nathan's cousin. Their gazes held for a moment before he turned away, cheeks slightly colored.

During breakfast, Robert had demanded an explanation for the events of the night before, and Nathan had filled him in... somewhat. The revelation that Sebastian's death had been no accident seemed to have depressed the spirits of both Robert and Letitia, and they had behaved circumspectly all day.

"There you are." Lady Cavill's voice penetrated the milling funeral attendees outside the cemetery as she stumped up, leaning heavily on her cane.

Under her gaze, Nathan straightened from an already upright posture. Lily understood the instinct. There was something terrifying about the older woman—Lily wanted to be just like her one day.

"Am I to understand the villain from last night escaped?"

"Unfortunately, yes, my lady." Nathan's tone was more clipped than normal, though he was the picture of politeness.

Lady Cavill hmphed. "Sent your friend after him, did you? Hopefully, he'll catch up. Sebastian needs justice. He would have been a good earl." Lady Cavill eyed Nathan up and down and then nodded. "You'll do, though."

With that, she swept away, her companion walking meekly behind her. Nathan stared after them while Lily put her hand up to her lips. It would not do to be seen laughing right after burying Nathan's brother, but Lady Cavill made it nearly impossible to keep a straight face.

\* \* \*

<u>Nathan</u>

After the funeral, it was time to question Warwick. He'd been awake but not very sensible that morning, so they had decided to return later. They all crowded into Warwick's room, even the women. There was no danger from Warwick, and he and Elijah were too tired to fight with them. Rex had a unique relationship with his wife, letting her run as she wished until he decided to pull on her lead.

Elijah did the questioning, though. He explained Mitchell had been involved with smuggling in spies on Warwick's lands, causing the man to blanch. Lily had not thought he could get any paler, but he proved her wrong.

"How much of Mitchell's activities were you aware of?" Elijah asked.

"I did not know." Warwick's expression was bleak, his eyes distant as he stared at the window beyond Elijah. "I know that seems unbelievable, but I truly..." He took in a shaky breath and let it out.

Chairs had been brought in, and the women were arranged on the other side of the room but with a clear view of Warwick in his bed, propped up by a pillow. He was now clear-sighted but also in pain, though it was bearable. Nathan and Rex stood on either side of the women while Elijah, the closest to Warwick's bed, led the questions.

"I did not realize at first how much of a hold he had on me," Warwick said quietly. He did not look anything like the man Nathan had met a few months ago. The news that his secretary had been a traitor, using Warwick's lands and people to bring in spies against England during wartime... It was entirely possible he would be found culpable, regardless of whether he had been involved. "My father died before his time and had done nothing to prepare me for my inheritance. It was easier to let Mitchell handle the things I did not understand or did not want to. He was eager to help, able to do everything, and he did a good job. At least, he seemed to."

"When he set his mind to it, he was very good at what he did," Elijah said. There was no emotion in his voice, yet Warwick seemed to find something comforting as if he realized Elijah understood.

Mitchell had fooled Elijah and his father as well, even though Warwick had no idea.

"He was very good. I relied on him completely after a while." For the first time, his head turned to meet Rex's gaze. "I know you did not understand why I kept him on after he was removed from the Society. The truth was, by that time, I could not have wrested control back if I tried. He has all the information I need to keep my estate and my business ventures running. Without him, I have nothing. I have become nothing more than a figurehead." The bleakness returned to his eyes.

It was a form of blackmail, and Nathan could commiserate. He was grateful to Rex, who had agreed to stay at Brentwood Manor for the next few weeks, advising Nathan and helping him learn how to run the estate. Without him, it would be very easy to fall prey to someone like Mitchell. A man who knew what he was doing and would be ambitious enough, happy enough to take it on and do it for him, would feel like a godsend.

Warwick was just incredibly unlucky who he'd trusted.

"I turned a blind eye to his faults because I needed him, and I was too proud to admit why." Warwick glanced at Rex again, then looked away.

"You spent the most time with him. Do you have any idea why he might have engaged in such... activities? He appeared to be well paid." Elijah would know since Mitchell had also received compensation for his activities as an 'operative working in an unofficial capacity for the government.' Which meant he had been earning a double income, and unlike Nathan's father, he was not a gambler, so it could not have been for the money.

It sounded as though he would have been able to get whatever else he needed from Warwick, and Warwick was flush. There had never been a whisper about debts or unpaid bills. Mitchell had done a good job for his employer in that way.

Warwick sighed.

"The only thing I can think of is he was jealous." There was a note of confusion in Warwick's voice. He was not the only one perplexed.

Nathan's brow furrowed as he considered the notion. Jealousy as a reason for *treason*?

"Jealous?" Josie's skepticism rang clear, and her husband shot her a look. She, Lily, and Mary had promised to only listen.

Warwick did not seem to notice she had asked instead of her husband. His hands smoothed out over his lap in a nervous gesture.

"Of us." He lifted one hand and waved it around, generally indicating all of them. "Our positions."

"He wanted a title?" Elijah asked.

"Yes. He wanted to run in our circles, to receive the same respect as a lord." Warwick snorted self-deprecatingly. "I know he enjoyed seeing me lowered, dancing to his tune, once he had me tied up in his string."

"Hm." Nathan had not had much interaction with the man, but he had seen nothing that would counter Warwick's claim. Mitchell had been the type to see himself as important and possibly resent those who made him feel less.

If that was true, he would have enjoyed getting one over on the Crown's spymaster.

\* \* \*

<u>Lily</u>

After exhausting Warwick with questions, they left him with another dose of laudanum to prepare themselves for supper. During the meal, there was no talk of spies or Mitchell, not with her parents and Nathan's cousins still there. It was a relief. Everything was almost normal.

Well, as normal as they could be.

Meeting Nathan's eyes across the table, Lily smiled at him. When he smiled back, a happy feeling settled around her heart.

When the ladies got up to withdraw and leave the table to the gentlemen, Robert stood as well.

"My wife and I will be making an early night of it as we need to leave early tomorrow," he announced, looking up and down the table before meeting Nathan's gaze. "We wish you well, cousin, you and your wife. I hope we can meet again soon under happier circumstances."

Letitia's pinched lips said she did not agree with her husband's sentiments. Personally, Lily would not be sorry to see the back of either of them, but they were family. One could not choose to have only pleasant relatives.

Nathan stood and shook Robert's hand while Lily came to stand by his side. They exchanged a few pleasantries before Robert and Letitia retired for the night. Sharing another warm smile with Nathan, seeing the same relief in his eyes as she felt, Lily nodded her head and led the ladies to the drawing-room.

"Well, it has been a day," Josie said, flopping down with predictable unladylike verve. Lily's mother smiled, seating herself far more decorously on the chair across from Josie. "At least we do not have to spend any more time with Letitia."

"Josie," Mary chided, settling herself on the couch next to her. "We are not supposed to say such things out loud."

That startled a laugh out of all of them, lightening the mood of the room even further. With Lily's mother there, talk of traitors would still have to wait. Lily could use an uneventful evening. They all could.

Ringing for tea, she sat in the chair next to her mother's, facing her friends.

"Well, if we are not going to talk about Robert and Letitia, what are we will talk about?" Josie asked, reaching to play with one of her curls. She turned her gaze to Lily, a slightly wicked smile curving her lips. "Should we talk about Nathan and Lily?"

"What about Nathan and Lily?" Lily asked, giving her friend a reproachful look. Her mother was in the room. If her friends brought up the Society of Sin or any of those sorts of activities with her mother there, she would be mortified.

"The stolen glances, the longing looks," Josie drawled, then giggled. "For an arranged marriage, you two appear far cozier than I would have expected."

"I will say, I am glad you and Nathan have fallen in love," Lily's mother said, turning and reaching to take Lily's hand. Staring at her mother, Lily was dumbfounded. "Your father and I were worried, but he seems like a good man, and the connection between you was there immediately. It has been wonderful watching it grow as you have supported him through this time."

*Love?*

Her mother thought she and Nathan were in love?

Lily opened her mouth, but no words came out.

"Oh, look," Josie said, a little too gleefully. "We have rendered her speechless."

## Chapter Thirty-Three

*Nathan*

Without Robert's presence, the atmosphere around the table was more relaxed. Nathan was grateful his cousin had chosen to take himself off before the after-dinner drinks. Granted, they could not speak completely freely since Lily's father was still present, but in some ways, that was a blessing.

There was nothing left at the moment but speculation, which could go on endlessly. Nathan had not had the time to sit and think through everything. He had nothing to contribute, even in the way of theories at this point. Uncovering all Mitchell's actions and his treachery would be a painstaking process.

Once everyone had a cognac, Lily's father leaned back in his chair and raised the glass in Nathan's direction.

"To you and my daughter. It has been an eventful week, and I have to say, I believe it has really shown the two of you will have a good partnership."

"Hear, hear," Rex murmured, lifting his own glass as the others did as well. Nathan found his cheeks coloring slightly.

While he felt he and Lily made a surprisingly good match—far better than he'd initially thought at the outset of their marriage—to hear it from someone else, who knew Lily so well, made him feel rather chuffed.

"The two of you have a lot in common," Elijah said, nodding after he'd taken a sip of his drink. "Fate could not have provided you with a better option, really. It is no wonder you fell in love so quickly."

Nathan choked on his drink.

The burning sensation of the alcohol in his lungs making him cough, he pounded on his chest with his fist while Rex leaned over to clap him on the back.

"Love?" he managed to gasp after a few moments, though it still felt as if the inside of his chest was on fire. "I... we... it has only been one week!" Surely, that was not enough time, not that Nathan knew the first thing about being in love. He had never been in love before.

Unless he was now.

But that was ludicrous.

Across the table, his father-in-law chuckled and shrugged.

"I fell in love with my Eliza in one day. Met her at a ball, took her driving the next morning, stayed for afternoon tea, and knew she was it for me." He rubbed his chin. "Took a bit longer to convince her, but we were married six weeks later."

"I fell in love with Mary before I realized it," Rex said agreeably and grinned. "Might have been about a week. What about you, Elijah?"

Nathan sat there dumbly, their words spinning around his head. Was it possible?

"I have known Josie my whole life," Elijah responded with a snort, shaking his head.

"All that means is you did not really see her." Rex waved his glass at Elijah, gesturing. "Once you *saw* her for the woman she is, how long before you were in love with her?"

"I..." Elijah frowned. "Two days?"

Grinning, Rex turned to look at Nathan, who stared back at him.

"See? Look at it that way, and you are behind." Rex chuckled, apparently pleased with himself. "Look, do you think you could live without her now?"

*No.*

Or not so much he could not as he did not want to. His entire being rejected the idea that he would have to give her up.

"Do you want her to be happy, especially with you?" Rex did not bother waiting for answers from Nathan, which was just as well because he did not think he had them to give.

*Yes.*

He wanted her to be happy. He wanted to be why she was happy, at least in part.

"Would you be willing to do anything for her?"

"That is love?" Nathan asked a bit hesitantly.

"They are the symptoms of love." Rex smiled. "Where there are symptoms, there is usually a cause."

He was in love with his wife.

How very odd.

\* \* \*

*Lily*

"We cannot be in love." Lily shook her head. "I barely know him."

"You have known him for weeks," Mary pointed out. "You might not know everything about him, but if I asked you to describe him, I bet you would be able to. I am sure you would defend him if someone maligned him."

"That is the proper thing to do for anyone who is maligned." Lily scowled, transferring her gaze to her mother. "Surely, you do not believe this nonsense." She would have thought her mother far too sensible.

"I believe what is obvious to others is not always known to ourselves." Lily's mother smiled serenely. "You two certainly act as if you are in love. What we can see and what you see... well, perhaps you are too close to the situation to see it clearly."

Lily took a sip of tea to hide her unsettled reaction, mustering her arguments in her mind. Truth be told, she was having trouble finding many that did not have some flaw.

They had not known each other long, but from all she knew about love, sometimes it happened that way. Mary and Rex had fallen quite quickly. In fact, she was sure it had happened before their marriage, though neither of them had realized it.

For all that Josie had sworn she was in love with Elijah's brother for years, the fact of the matter was, as soon as Joseph was no longer skewing her perception, she had fallen hard and fast for Elijah. The two of them made sense in a way Joseph and Josie never would have.

She would have argued that she and Nathan did not have anything in common, but the more she came to know him, the more she realized they had many similarities between them. They both valued their friendships, though they were not quick to make friends. They both enjoyed time for intellectual pursuits and puzzling out the solution to a problem. They both loved reading.

If she had to describe him, as Mary said, she would say he was intelligent, honorable, thoughtful, and preferred to think before acting but would act decisively in the heat of the moment if needed. She also knew she did not want to share him, and thinking of him one day engaging in activities with other women in The Society made her sick to her stomach. Not that he had said he would not be faithful, but that was hardly a subject they would discuss.

Men did not talk about their mistresses with their wives.

Thinking of Nathan having a mistress made her want to claw the woman's eyes out, then stomp on his... male appendage. Hard.

Was that what love was?

"How do I know if I am in love?" she asked aloud before realizing she was going to, but if she could not ask these women, then who could she?

Her parents were deeply in love and had been all her life. Mary and Josie had both fallen in love recently. All of them knew her well. The only person missing who knew her as well was Evie, and Lily did not know if Evie had ever been in love.

She did not know if Evie would ever allow herself to be so vulnerable.

Truthfully, she did not like the feeling.

"You will feel it, here, in your heart," her mother said, touching the center of her chest. "It will warm when he is near or when you make him happy. It will ache when you are apart or he is upset. You will want to be the one to make him smile, the one to comfort him when he is sad, but in ways so much more than as a friend. You know what friendship feels like. Love is that, amplified. That is not to say there will not be ups and downs, hills and valleys throughout your life together, but the important thing is you will face those trials together and come through them as one."

"That was beautiful," Mary said solemnly, nodding her agreement. "And very true. Rex and I do not always agree, but when we do fight, I feel closer to him after we work through it."

Josie snorted.

"To say Elijah and I do not always agree is an understatement. We get through it, though, even if I drive him batty making my point." She smiled serenely, mischief dancing in her blue eyes. "Of course, I would not have to make my point so pointedly if he did not try to run our marriage like a dictatorship."

That made them laugh. They all knew Elijah well enough to know it was true. Thank goodness he had married someone who was his match. In a similar way, Mary had needed someone who truly saw her and was wise to her tricks.

Lily supposed that was the question she was asking herself, deep down.

Was she Nathan's match?

* * *

*Nathan*

The rest of the evening passed uneventfully, though a bit awkwardly once they rejoined the women. It felt as though everyone was watching him and Lily, although whenever he looked around, they were paying attention to their own conversations. He wished Sebastian could have seen this.

Friends all gathered in their ancestral home, the way they had never been able to while their father was alive. The way they had assumed they would once everything was settled. The ache in his chest was growing stronger again, and he knew it would not be gone easily.

There were moments when he could almost forget. He and Sebastian had spent much of the past few years apart, so it felt as though it was just another time when they were living separately. With everything else going on—his wedding, the murder, the double investigations leading to one culprit—it was no wonder he kept forgetting until a moment like this.

"Are you alright?"

Cool fingers slid over his hand, jerking him out of his reverie. He lifted his eyes to his wife, who had just come over from where she'd been chatting with her parents. Beyond her, he could see her parents were on their way out the door to the hallway, likely retiring for the night.

"Yes. I was thinking how much Sebastian would have loved to be here for this." Nathan gestured at their friends. As if punctuating his statement, laughter drifted from where Mary and Josie had their heads together. Looking up at Lily's concerned expression, he felt some of the tightness in his chest ease. It was not gone, but he found comfort in her mere presence.

She looked around, then sat down next to him.

"Tell me about him," she said quietly.

He did.

Talking while the others joked and laughed, Nathan did not feel left out of the conversation on the other side of the room. He was glad they were there, but he wanted to speak with Lily and was relieved she felt the same way.

When they went back to their rooms, Nathan took her hand and drew her to his room. She went willingly, though with a hesitant look. Possibly, she was still sore, but Nathan could be gentle, or they could do something else or nothing at all, but he had a feeling his friends were right. He was in love with his wife and wanted her beside him all night and when he woke in the morning.

Drawing her into his arms, he looked into her face and felt the rush of emotion in his chest. The symptom, as it were. He certainly had not felt this way about anyone before.

"Did you know my friends think we are in love?" Lily asked as if she had read his mind.

Nathan raised an eyebrow. Interesting that the ladies' conversation had so closely followed the gentlemen's, giving more credence to the idea.

"What do you think?" he asked, noting she had not said anything about herself.

"I think... it could be possible. Although perhaps it is too soon?" Her gaze searched his, studying his reaction in much the same way he was hers.

A smile curved his lips.

In some ways, they really were so alike.

"That is exactly what I said when your father made a toast to our falling in love."

"What?" Lily's mouth dropped open, and he could not tell if she was reacting in shock or asking him to repeat what her father said or why her father had said that. Really, it did not matter because she had provided him with the perfect opening to the conversation.

"I said it was too soon. He told me he fell in love with your mother in a day. Neither Rex nor Elijah seemed to find it unusual. It made me realize, while I do not know much about love, I think I might be in love with you."

"Really?" Her face lit up from within. The ache in his chest was almost completely gone, replaced by a happy warmth. He knew Sebastian would have been happy for him, for both of them. And Sebastian would have loved Lily. "I... I think I might be in love with you, too."

Nathan had to laugh. They were a pair. He knew, deep down, their love was there. It was real. It might be new, and both of them might be hesitant to speak about something they knew so little about, but he could feel it between them as if it was a tangible thing.

Lowering his mouth, he claimed her mouth with a kiss and felt her respond. Her body pressed against his, her lips parting beneath his as Nathan's hands roved over her body.

A wedding and a funeral, all in one week. He was mourning his brother, with all of his being, and at the same time, he was celebrating his marriage, with all of his being. Both were equally true statements. Lily did not chase away his sorrow completely, but she made it far more bearable. She reminded him there was a future that was theirs for the taking.

It was not the future he had thought he would have, but with her by his side, it was a future he was happy to face.

## Chapter Thirty-Four

L*ily*
Was this what love felt like?

Wanting to be with Nathan with her whole being, wanting to know everything about him and tell him everything in return?

After all the excitement of the week, doing nothing more than talking in the drawing-room might have seemed boring to some, but not to her. Not when the person she'd been talking to had been Nathan.

Now, she wanted nothing more than to be with him tonight—except a little... differently than before.

There was something her friends had done and spoken about, she had not understood. Something she could not believe they enjoyed. Yet now, with her curiosity surging, she realized she wanted it, too. She had taken Nathan in her mouth last night, partly from curiosity, partly from wanting to comfort him.

Tonight, she wanted to give him the last part of her.

They moved toward the bed, slowly removing articles of clothing as they went. Lily was gathering her courage to tell Nathan what she wanted. Would he want it, too? From everything Josie and Mary said, there was no reason to think he would not.

When he broke their kiss to pull her chemise over her head, she took advantage of the moment.

"Nathan?" There was a quaver in her voice.

He blinked as he dropped the chemise to the floor, an expression of concern on his face. His eyes slid over her naked body as if taking note of every inch, from her breasts with the faded love bites and hard nipples down to where her thighs were pressed together in arousal.

"Yes, love?"

Lily thrilled at the new endearment. Her heart beat faster, and a hot rush of warmth flooded through her. She flushed with pleasure.

"My friends, Josie and Mary... they told me about something they do with... with their husbands... I want to try with you.... if you like." It was very difficult to get the words out. Nathan had taken charge of their lovemaking from the beginning, and she had been happy to let him.

Loved having him take the lead.

Asking for what she wanted rather than giving him what he wanted was far more difficult than it should be. Especially because what she wanted to ask for was so perversely indecent.

"What is it?" The interest in his eyes was undeniable. He was curious.

Blushing hotly, Lily stroked her finger down the center of his chest, looking at the tip as it moved through the curls adorning his muscles rather than looking him in the eyes as she finally made herself say it.

"They say they have... um, well, they have taken... they have done things with their husbands in their bottoms." Her voice dropped lower and lower until she ended in a mere whisper.

Staring directly at Nathan's chest, touching him there, she could see and feel the sudden tension that gripped his body. The press of his cock against her soft stomach became stiffer, more intent. Lily shivered as his fingers tightened on her.

"You would like to try that?" His voice was husky, and she could tell he very much wanted to. "Did they tell you it might hurt?" He did not sound put off by the idea, and the way he said it sent another flush of heat through her.

Lily liked it when things hurt a little. She had already discovered that much about herself. It made her even more curious to have him in her bottom, though it was not only curiosity driving her. It was wanting to share everything with him. The excitement of engaging in such a forbidden act, of knowing everything her friends knew, was only a bonus.

"Yes, I want to... with you. I want you to have all of me."

No sooner were the words out of her mouth than Nathan took charge again as though her permission had unfettered him. His mouth descended to claim hers anew, his hands holding her tightly against him, and her body thrilled at the domineering way he handled her.

✶ ✶ ✶

*Nathan*

Bless his wife's friends.

He had it in his mind that one day he would coax Lily into allowing him to breach her bottom hole but had hardly expected she would be the one to suggest such a thing. That she knew about it at all was a bit of a revelation, despite everything else she and her friends had discussed.

Perhaps it was truly best not to know and to just be grateful for any information shared between them.

This was an unexpected treat.

It was a demonstration of how much she trusted him, and coming on the heels of their almost-declarations of love, she was showing him how she felt when she could not yet bring herself to say the words.

Her request also neatly solved the dilemma of if her pussy was still too sore for congress tonight.

Steering her to the edge of the bed, Nathan pulled away from the kiss.

"Up on the bed, on all fours," he ordered, his voice rough with anticipation and excitement. "Here... I will help."

Piling the pillows in the manner he wanted them, so she would be supported, Nathan paused to watch as she got into position. The hot blush on her cheeks was burning brighter than ever, and she kept shyly peeking at him. The incongruity of her demeanor compared to her brazen request appealed to the primal part of his brain.

He was going to claim every part of her. He would be the only man to have her, and he would have her completely. Claimed in every manner, she could be claimed. His cock was swollen and throbbing, and he would have to practice some measured patience, so he did not hurt her.

Once she was in position, he went to his wardrobe to take down a special box from the top shelf, which contained items he had procured but never had the opportunity to use. Women at The Society tended to bring their own, had no need of them because they were used to such activities, or did not have that particular proclivity.

The hard black rubber rectal dilators were nestled in the box, waiting and ready to be used. Grinning widely, Nathan took both the box and a small vial of special oil in hand, both unopened until now. Waiting for his wife. Waiting for Lily.

\* \* \*

*Lily*

"First, I am going to use some dilators on you to prepare you and stretch you," Nathan said, getting onto the bed behind her.

The position meant she could not see a thing of what he was doing. Lily's breasts hung down beneath her, nipples brushing against the bedsheets, and she felt her insides clench in anticipation.

While she knew what dilators were in general, she had never had any problems with her bowels that would necessitate their use. Knowing this simple object was going to be used for perversion rather than medical necessity was shockingly erotic.

The hard tip pressed against her bottom hole, and she gasped at the very odd sensation of something pushing into her there.

Even stranger, even more wicked than Nathan touching her pussy because every one of her instincts told her this was forbidden territory. No one should be touching her here, not even her husband.

He was not only touching and pushing something into her but as he slid the hard rubber in deep, then pulled it back again, his fingertips brushed around her entrance.

"Oh, my," she gasped, clenching and squirming atop the pillows at the utterly filthy, exciting sensation. It did not hurt, despite what Mary and Josie had said. In fact, the sensation was highly arousing, with only a twinge of discomfort.

"That one was easy enough," Nathan said, his tone soothing. "Now for the second."

The first one had felt large and only a little uncomfortable. The second was bigger. Broader. Lily dropped her head, moaning as Nathan slowly pushed it inside her. The stretch burned where it entered, and she whimpered as he slowly twisted it back and forth, as if he was literally screwing it into her.

"Breathe, Lily."

At the reminder, she sucked in a deep breath, though it was harder to breathe as he filled her, pumping the dilator back and forth inside her, twisting it. Then his fingers stroked the wet folds below, and Lily thought she might pass out from the intimate pleasure.

* * *

*Nathan*

Watching the dark rubber dilator move in and out of Lily's taboo fundament, Nathan's breathing was becoming uneven. Seeing the way her bottom clenched and rippled, it was all too easy to imagine what it would feel like when his cock was buried inside her, and her muscles would be doing the same.

The third dilator was a little smaller in girth than his cock, but he did not think he was going to make it to the fourth. Lily liked a bit of pain with her pleasure, and from her reaction to the second dilator, he did not think she would protest moving the process along a little faster.

Her slick arousal was coating her pussy. Gently, Nathan stroked those tender folds, cognizant she might be sore from his machine two days prior. Nathan slid his fingers through her arousal, spreading it across the tiny nub of her clit.

As he pulled out the second dilator and replaced it with the third, he rubbed that tiny nub. His cock jerked at the sound she made when he began to work the third dilator into her clenching bottom.

"How does it feel, love?" he asked, pausing and pulling it out slightly, twisting it rather than pushing in deeper.

"Full," she gasped out. "So full. And it stings... but it's not bad. Mostly. Just... different."

Nathan chuckled. Different was a very good word for it. He gave her another moment, still rubbing her clit, before slowly pushing the dilator in again. Lily moaned, wriggling and shuddering as he worked it firmly back and forth in her bottom. His cock pulsed with every small thrust, anticipating what it would feel like when he replaced the dilators with himself.

"Good girl," he murmured as the dilator came to a stop at the broad flange on its base. Gasping again, she moved forward, and he put his hand on the small of her back, pinning her to the pile of pillows beneath her hips. Firmly working it back and forth, he could feel her small shudders as her moans filled the air, although he was no longer stroking her clit.

She was as ready as she could be.

Pulling the third dilator from her bottom, he placed it in the lid of the box to be cleaned later, along with the others, and picked up the vial of oil. Slicking it over his cock, he stared down at her upturned backside with the slightly gaping hole, stretched from the dilators and ready to receive him.

It still looked incredibly small, especially when he put the tip of his cock, shiny with oil, against it.

"Are you ready, Lily?" Gritting his teeth, he was holding onto his self-control with pure willpower. He was pressing against her, ready to slide into the inviting haven, but only if she was amenable.

"Yes. Do it, please, Nathan."

The please, the desperation in her voice, and the way she pushed back against his hands and cock, as if she was trying to push him into her when he was holding her in place, convinced him

Nathan let himself push forward with a groan. The tight clasp of her arse clenched around him, and he shuddered, feeling the heat of her engulf his cock, the exquisite tightness massaging his whole length as he sank into her. The ring of her entrance was so widely stretched, the little wrinkles of her star smoothed out, and she was holding him in a pleasurable grip he knew he could not resist for long.

* * *

*Lily*

The intimate invasion was similar to yet utterly unlike the dilators.

Nathan's cock was softer but with a rigid core. The dilators had prepared her well; she felt a slight, cramping pinch as he pushed deep into her body, but nothing she could not handle. The overriding sensation was of acute fullness and a sense of tasting the forbidden fruit.

Lily pressed her cheek against the bed as Nathan's body came to rest against her buttocks, and her muscles clenched around him. She felt his fingers slide over her hips and press against her clitoris again. Then he drew back his cock and thrust in again.

"Oh..." Her toes curled. Her fingers curled. Her entire body curled at the odd sensation of him moving inside her.

Unlike the hard coldness of the dilators, Nathan was hot and pulsing, foreign yet familiar.

Her hips lifted to receive him, her body rubbing against his fingers as the discomfort of having him in her bottom rather than her pussy increased. It hurt, yet it did not. The sensations were a confusing mix that superseded being taken after he had spanked her.

With every hard thrust, the stinging burn increased, and so did her pleasure. Lily writhed as he took her, his thrusts coming harder and faster. Hurting her more but in such a way, she did not want him to stop.

At her core, her ecstasy was growing in leaps and bounds as his clever fingers on her clit spurred her along.

"Nathan..." She cried out his name as the wave inside her rose. It was agony. It was ecstasy. It was both and neither, and she did not know if she could bear it. All she knew was it was inevitable the wave would crash and sweep her away.

The wave crested, taking her along with it, and she fell with a shout of pleasure, the hot bliss exploding within her. She clamped around

Nathan's cock, feeling every inch of him as he thrust, creating burning friction despite the oil that had lubricated her body for him.

"Oh God..." Behind her, Nathan pumped harder, faster, his passion spurred on by hers. The feel of him riding her through her orgasm sent her soaring. Lily screamed into the bedsheets beneath her as the erotic euphoria wrapped around them, carrying them into mutual rapture.

# Chapter Thirty-Five

*athan*
Nathan Watching his wife squirming at the breakfast table while pretending she was doing no such thing was far more amusing than Nathan would have guessed.

Last night, after he'd taken her bottom, she had been practically insensible as he cleaned both of them. They had slept in each other's arms and awoken there, which had led to a far gentler round of love-making this morning, with her pinned beneath him, legs wrapped around him.

Obviously, the aftereffects of offering her bottom hole to him lingered.

He enjoyed it even more than seeing the fading love bites on her breasts, as though he had left his mark in another, far more intimate manner. Almost as enjoyable had been her stern warning that if he tried to enjoy the pleasures of the marital bed with a woman other than herself, she would stomp on his 'appendage.' He rather liked knowing she was possessive of him.

Nathan had thoroughly enjoyed reassuring her on that matter and expressing his own similar sentiment when it came to the rakes of the *ton*, who would likely come sniffing next Season. Married ladies were considered fair game, but he was damned if he would share his Lily with another man.

Thinking about such things was distracting him from the breakfast conversation.

"Josie and I will be off as soon as we are finished eating," Elijah said. He looked as if he was sitting on the edge of his seat, ready to jump up and run. If he did not have Josie with him, Nathan thought he probably would have left the moment the funeral was over.

No word had come from his cousin or his father yet, which could mean nothing, or it could mean everything.

"I expected as much," Nathan said, nodding his understanding.

"I am sorry I cannot stay longer, but..."

"No, you need to go to your father and continue the investigation into Mitchell there. I will stay here and work with Rex and Warwick to discover what we can about Mitchell's activities along the coast."

Warwick was still too weak to join them at the table, and Nathan had a feeling the man would be his guest for a few more days. It was not a far ride to his estate, but he could hardly sit a horse at the moment, and a carriage ride would be horribly uncomfortable.

"Do not forget your wife." Elijah smiled. "I do not think she will thank you for leaving her out."

"Is that your experience?" Nathan had to ask.

Elijah answered with a snort.

"If I leave Josie out, I am liable to find her in my boot the moment I step out the door. It is better to keep her close, so I can protect her rather than finding her following a street behind me with no protector." Elijah slanted a glance his way. "Although you are not currently in London, you would do well to remember that."

Yes, he would. Nathan glanced at his wife, who was whispering with her friends at the other end of the table. They had already shown themselves to be remarkably adept at inserting themselves into situations where they did not belong. In the center of the table, Rex was chatting amiably with Lily's parents and Robert, who had also announced he and Letitia would leave shortly after the morning meal. Though, as before, Letitia had not left her room to break her fast.

"They were right about Mitchell. Do you think they are right about the Russians?"

"It would align with what Lucas has told us about the lack of enmity from France," Elijah said grimly. "On the other hand, Mitchell was initially working with the French during the war if he was smuggling spies."

"Do we know if the spies he was smuggling were French spies?" Nathan asked, and Elijah's expression grew even grimmer.

"I suppose not. Something else to investigate." He and Nathan exchanged a look.

It would be up to Nathan, with Warwick, to look into Mitchell's activities along the coast when they began questioning the smuggling gang operating on the coast where Warwick's lands lay. He was sure it would be a job keeping Lily out of that, but there would be plenty of other avenues for her to look into.

A smile curved his lips as his wife looked up, and their gazes caught. Held.

Beside him, Elijah chuckled.

"And you think you are not in love."

"Oh, no," Nathan replied softly, still holding Lily's gaze. Her dark eyes softened, the air between them thickening with emotion. "I have come to realize I most certainly am."

\* \* \*

*Lily*

"So, Mary and I will find out everything we can about Mitchell and his activities on the coast. You will have to continue the London investigation," Lily said. In Evie's absence, for the first time, they had to make their own plans.

"Trust me, Elijah has learned his lesson about keeping me both informed and involved." Josie grinned, making both Mary and Lily giggle. As impetuous as Josie was, Lily did not doubt she had made Elijah pay every time.

"You are going to get yourself spanked until you cannot sit," Mary murmured, shaking her head, though the smile did not leave her face.

"Then I shall be in good company," Josie retorted. She elbowed Lily. "This one can hardly sit still this morning, and I have a good idea why, though I do not know what you could have done to deserve it."

"It is not what you think." Lily's cheeks blushed hotly. "I decided to... well..." She lowered her voice and whispered what she had let Nathan do the prior night. Josie and Mary burst into giggles again.

"I cannot believe you *asked* him to!" Josie fanned herself, looking scandalized. She arched her eyebrow at Lily. "Are you still claiming you do not love him?"

"No." Lily shook her head. She was still blushing hotly, but it did not bother her. It was a happy blush.

Something prodded at her senses, and she looked at her husband, who was staring at her from across the table. Their gazes caught. Held. A surge of happy warmth filled her breast. The moment between them was not broken until Robert, finished with his meal, got to his feet.

* * *

After the last of their guests departed, Nathan and Lily stood on the stoop of the house, watching the dust from her parents' carriage drift along the road. Nathan reached out and took her hand in his, their fingers entwining.

Yes, this was love.

"Well, darling." Nathan turned to look down at her. She tilted her head back and smiled up at him. "Shall we get started?"

That was how they would go into the future. Together, standing side by side.

"Yes." Lily's smile widened. "Let's get started."

Turning, they went back into the house to find Mary and Rex. They were both ready to get to work.

Now that they knew who they were hunting, the chase was on.

# Epilogue

**The Night Before**
*Evie*

The ride through the night to London was not the most exhausting thing she had ever done, but fatigue was dragging at her as the night wore on. The fear driving her made it more tiring, as well as all the things running through her head, along with the cursing and absolute determination, she did not lose anyone else.

Especially not her uncle.

He had saved her from hell, and even if she did not truly feel she fit into the heaven on earth he had brought her to—compared to where she had been before—she was nonetheless grateful.

Now, he was in danger again. She had barely had the courage to leave him for a few nights, knowing she would be within a day's riding distance, then *this* happened. Whether Mitchell was headed for Camden House, either to plead his case or to finish the assassination of her uncle, Evie needed to be there.

She needed to save the man who had saved her.

Knowing he was well guarded did not matter, not now that they knew Mitchell was the traitor. He was a known entity. A trusted one. It would not be difficult for him to talk his way into the house. Which was a nightmare waiting to start. Evie did not believe Mitchell would go to Camden House to plead for mercy. No, he would go there to finish the job his assassins had started.

This late at night, her uncle might very well assume Mitchell's appearance meant an emergency. He would let him in. Even meet with him privately.

Evie set her jaw, leaning low over the horse she had borrowed from Lily's new husband. Hopefully, he would forgive her, though army captains were not always the understanding sort. He seemed a decent enough fellow, and no one had come chasing after her when she'd passed him, Rex, and her cousin on the road.

She knew Anthony was ahead of her, and she trusted he would defend her uncle with his life, but it did not matter.

She *needed* to be there.

The streets of London were mostly empty at this hour of the night, at least in this part of the city. The Season proper over, the few events had ended earlier. Those who were out and about were at the bars and taverns, not in Mayfair.

Riding up to the mews behind Camden House, Evie shouted for someone to come help but did not bother to wait, looping the exhausted horse's reins over a fence post. As she turned away, she saw the door to the mews opening, a stable boy scrubbing at his eyes as he peered out into the darkness. Hearing his exclamation of surprise at finding a horse in the yard, knowing he would take care of things there, she dashed for the house.

She would come back later with a reward for both the horse and the boy. Once she knew her uncle was unharmed.

The mews were quiet, which gave her some hope but did not stop the pounding of her heart. Why was it so quiet? Where was Anthony?

The door was locked, so she pounded on it until it opened, one of the servants staring at her in consternation.

"Miss Evie!"

Evie did not pause, dashing past the young man into the house, running up the backstairs to the family wing. Reaching her uncle's room, she pounded on the door.

"Uncle Oliver! Uncle Oliver!"

The answering shout, full of grumpy admonition, from within the room made her sink to the ground in relief, her knees literally buckling beneath her. He was safe. He was unharmed. Tears welled, but she pushed them back, one hand on her chest, the other in a fist at her mouth as she bit down on the knuckle. For a moment, her shoulders heaved.

By the time her uncle opened his bedroom door, she had gathered herself, dashed the tears from her eyes, and regained control over her emotions. Her exhaustion was the only reason she had lost it.

Evie did not cry. Had not cried for over a decade.

But the relief of knowing her uncle was safe in his room, undisturbed, had almost done her in.

"Evie?" Salt and pepper hair wild about his head, his dark eyes were wide as he stared at her like she was an apparition.

"Uncle Oliver." Her voice only cracked a little, her emotions nearly undoing her now that she knew he was unharmed. "I have some bad news."

\* \* \*

*Anthony*

Damn and blast.

He had been so close.

Though Mitchell had a hell of a head start on him, Anthony had closed the gap to see the man in the streets ahead of him—far ahead of him. Mitchell had gone into London and turned away from Mayfair, leading Anthony on a circuitous route through some of the rougher areas, then had gone to ground in the Warrens.

The twisting streets were ripe for ambushes. They were dark and lit only by the light of the moon. Those who wandered into the Warrens had best keep their eyes peeled for trouble because trouble was sure to find them.

Anthony was not afraid, knowing he could handle himself, but he also knew when a search was fruitless.

There were thousands of places Mitchell could be hiding, and Anthony might never find him. Worse would be if Mitchell had deliberately led him here to lose him, so he could go on to the Marquess of Camden's house while Anthony searched the Warrens.

After traveling a few streets, Anthony acknowledged Mitchell had managed to lose him. It was enough to make a man gnash his teeth.

So close!

So close to so many answers. So close, yet not close enough.

The feeling of failure swamped him, but Anthony pushed it away. He was used to winning but knew there would be a few battles lost before the war was ultimately won.

He hated losing.

Time to report in and warn the Marquess of Camden.

Wheeling his exhausted horse around, Anthony set off at a trot to Camden House. He would need to get the horse a treat later for carrying him through the night.

When he reached the mews, he frowned. The doors were open, and a lamp was lit within. In the center aisle, a stable boy was currying a horse, whispering gently. The youth's eyes widened when he turned and saw Anthony leading in another horse.

"Whose horse is this? Was a man riding him?" Anthony did not have time for niceties.

"No, sir, the lady."

Relief flooded Anthony but only for a moment. The boy's words registered, and Anthony groaned. There was only one lady he could think of who would be arriving on a tired horse in the middle of the night. One who would have followed him all the way from Brentwood Manor.

She must have ridden like the wind to have beaten him to Camden House, even after his detour to the Warrens.

Well, that was fine.

He and Miss Evangeline Stuart were due for a reckoning. She could not avoid him forever.

Perhaps tonight would finally be the night.

\* \* \*

*CLICK HERE for your copy of A Season for Spies, Evie and Anthony's story and the final installment in the Deception & Discipline series!*

# About the Author

Golden Angel is a USA Today best-selling author and self-described bibliophile with a "kinky" bent who loves to write stories for the characters in her head. If she didn't get them out, she's pretty sure she'd go just a little crazy.

She is happily married, old enough to know better but still too young to care, and a big fan of happily-ever-afters, strong heroes and heroines, and sizzling chemistry.

When she's not writing, she can often be found on the couch reading, in front of her sewing machine making a new cosplay, hanging out with her friends, or wandering the Maryland Renaissance Fair.

www.goldenangelromance.com

- bookbub.com/authors/golden-angel
- goodreads.com/goldeniangel
- facebook.com/GoldenAngelAuthor
- instagram.com/goldeniangel

# Other Titles by Golden Angel

## HISTORICAL SPANKING ROMANCE

**Domestic Discipline Quartet**

Birching His Bride

Dealing With Discipline

Punishing His Ward

Claiming His Wife

The Domestic Discipline Quartet Box Set

**Bridal Discipline Series**

Philip's Rules

Gabrielle's Discipline

Lydia's Penance

Benedict's Commands

Arabella's Taming

Pride and Punishment Box Set

Commands and Consequences Box Set

**Deception and Discipline**

A Season for Treason

A Season for Scandal

A Season for Smugglers

A Season for Spies

**Bridgewater Brides**

Their Harlot Bride

**Standalone**

Marriage Training

The Duke's Pursuit

Rogue Booty

# CONTEMPORARY BDSM ROMANCE

**Venus Rising Series (MFM Romance)**

The Venus School

Venus Aspiring

Venus Desiring

Venus Transcendent

Venus Wedding

Venus Rising Box Set

**Stronghold Doms Series**

The Sassy Submissive

Taming the Tease

Mastering Lexie

Pieces of Stronghold

Breaking the Chain

Bound to the Past

Stripping the Sub

Tempting the Domme

Hardcore Vanilla

Steamy Stocking Stuffers

Entering Stronghold Box Set

Nights at Stronghold Box Set

Stronghold: Closing Time Box Set

**Masters of Marquis Series**

Bondage Buddies

Master Chef

Law & Disorder

**Dungeons & Doms Series**

Dungeon Master

Dungeon Daddy

Dungeon Showdown

**Poker Loser Trilogy**

Forced Bet

Back in the Game

Winning Hand

Poker Loser Trilogy Bundle (3 books in 1!)

**Standalones - Daddy Doms**

Chef Daddy

Little Villain

# SCI-FI ROMANCE

**Tsenturion Masters Series with Lee Savino**

Alien Captive

Alien Tribute

Alien Abduction

**Standalone**
Mated on Hades

## SHIFTER ROMANCE

**Big Bad Bunnies Series**
Chasing His Bunny
Chasing His Squirrel
Chasing His Puma
Chasing His Polar Bear
Chasing His Honey Badger
Chasing Her Lion
Night of the Wild Stags

Chasing Tail Box Set
Chasing Tail... Again Box Set

CPSIA information can be obtained
at www.ICGtesting.com
Printed in the USA
LVHW080801201122
733630LV00037B/2169